The Outside Groove

The Outside Groove

A Novel by
Erik E. Esckilsen

Houghton Mifflin Company Boston 2006

Walter Lorraine Books

Walter Lorraine *wic* Books

Copyright © 2006 by Erik E. Esckilsen

www.houghtonmifflinbooks.com

Library of Congress Cataloging-in-Publication Data
Esckilsen, Erik E.
    The outside groove / by Erik E. Esckilsen.
        p. cm.
    "Walter Lorraine Books."
    Summary: Tired of having her own accomplishments ignored, high
school senior Casey, sister of the town's stock car racing champion,
becomes the local track's first female driver and discovers that there
is more to winning than crossing the finish line first.
    ISBN-13: 978-0-618-66854-0
    ISBN-10: 0-618-66854-3
    [1. Automobile racing—Fiction. 2. Brothers and sisters—Fiction.
3. Family life—Fiction.]   I. Title.
PZ7.E7447Ou 2006
[Fic]—dc22
                                                    2005030851

Printed in the United States of America
QUM 10 9 8 7 6 5 4 3 2 1

Acknowledgments

This novel was inspired by Tracie Bellerose of Gorham, New Hampshire, a track champion in the Late Model division at Thunder Road International Speedbowl in Barre, Vermont.

Telling this story would have been impossible without the racing wisdom and generous access to the Thunder Road pit provided by Tom Curley, track co-owner and president of the American Canadian Tour (ACT); track co-owner and veteran television motorsports announcer Ken Squier; and ACT staff members Tina Boutin, Marjorie Fay, Darla Hartt, and Gloria Woodard.

Several Thunder Road drivers also shared invaluable knowledge: "Wicked" Wanda Burnham, Rachel and Renee Beede, Jen Bigelow, Derrick Calkins, Melinda "Princess of the Northeast Kingdom" Gervais (and crew chief Marcel Gervais), Reno "King of the Northeast Kingdom" Gervais, Bill Hennequin, Steve Longchamp, and Ryan Nolin. Pace car driver Bob Bigelow took on a passenger to offer a unique perspective on Thunder Road's high-banked turns.

Friend, fiction writer, and former racecar driver Randy DeVita offered incisive criticism throughout the book's development; friends and fiction writers Michael Czyzniejewski and Renee Reighart (a self-sufficient automobile owner) as well as friend and poet Karen Craigo also shared generously their keen literary insights and editorial acumen.

Finally, literary agent Wendy Schmalz and editor Walter Lorraine gave this story a big push and skillful attention as post time drew near.

The Outside Groove

Chapter 1

No one had ever accused me of having a winning attitude. In fact, until I started getting interested in racecar driving one late-April Friday, no one had ever accused me of anything—good, bad, or in between. Sure, once in a while one of my teachers at Fliverton Union High School—"Flu High," as I called it—would praise my work, but as soon as I left the school building, I became invisible. Well, maybe not completely invisible. Everyone in Fliverton knew me. I was, after all, "Casey LaPlante, Wade LaPlante's little sister," as if this were a more notable achievement than being about to graduate Flu High as one of the top five students out of roughly two hundred seniors. I was especially strong in math and science. I'd run the numbers and determined that I couldn't fail out even if I stopped going to class. I'd also calculated that, even if I worked harder than ever, I wouldn't reach the very top rank. Marla Dietz, child astronaut, had that spot pegged since we were in junior high. This was actually good news to me. Not being the top student meant I wouldn't have to make a graduation speech, which I'd have enjoyed about as much as eating a load of mulch out of my father's pickup truck.

Free of that public-speaking anxiety or any reason to think about school at all, I had plenty of mental energy to focus on other things that spring, which was good because, like I said, I was starting to think about racecar driving.

Starting to. Up until that particular April Friday, just before another Demon's Run Raceway season opener, I had absolutely zero interest in racing—this despite the fact that virtually everyone else in Fliverton treated racing like a religion (an environmentally unfriendly religion, in my opinion). Therefore, people treated my brother, Wade —Demon's Run Raceway defending track champion at the young age of twenty—like a high priest, even though he was just about Fliverton's most notorious hound dog. One-Tank Wade, some girls called him, since he typically stuck with a girlfriend about as long as it took to burn through a tank of gas. Still, for every girl who trash-talked him, there was another eager to scoot on over close to him in the front seat of his pumpkin-colored vintage Nova. I'll admit, that Nova was a sweet ride.

No, aside from his lengthy record of romantic hit-and-run, Wade could do no wrong in Fliverton. Everyone was saying he could break out of local short-track racing that season and join the national racing circuit, which people referred to as, simply, "the Circuit." Whenever I wanted to annoy Wade, which was every time he'd annoyed me first, which was fairly often, I called the Circuit "the Circus."

"Like to see you out there running the high-banked oval," he'd sneer. "Longest quarter-mile on the planet, let me tell you."

Demon's Run is a quarter-mile asphalt track. That's why it's called a short track. National circuit tracks, like the kind on television, are usually anywhere from a half mile to two miles long, sometimes longer. To me, a quarter-mile, half-mile, or ten miles didn't deny the fact that a stock-car race was basically four left turns, then four more, then four more . . . The allure of the sport, if you could call it a sport—and I, a cross-country runner at the time, definitely didn't consider auto racing a sport—had escaped me. But in Fliverton, I was alone in that opinion. To everyone else there, having a driver from our home-town make it to the Circuit would've put us on the map in a way that only one other racecar driver had ever come close to doing: Wade LaPlante Sr., better known as Big Daddy. My father.

The Circuit. The big time. Way bigger than, say, gradu-ating in the top five of a high school class. People who graduate in the top five of their class go on to college and then to jobs in such pointless fields as medicine, law, gov-ernment, business, and—my dream career—environmen-tal science. Conservation. Saving the planet. Drivers who win Circuit races go on television and say, basically, "Yup. I drove around in a bunch of circles faster than the other guys" and make millions of dollars. In other words, there was no comparing Wade and me. I didn't matter. Not even a little. Like I said, my attitude was not a winning one.

This was precisely what I'd been thinking at the end of that Friday as I crossed the student parking lot and strapped into my car—not my racecar, just my regular car, the used German rig that I bought with money I'd earned baby-sitting and then tutoring the son and daugh-ter of a husband-and-wife lawyer team, the Egans, in Brogansville. (Okay, Big Daddy kicked in some cash, too.)

I was sticking my key in the ignition and starting the engine, when over the tops of my glasses I spotted Fletcher Corwin stepping to the door of his swamp-green Dodge Dart, which was parked nose-to-nose with Hilda. That's my car, a Volkswagen I named Hilda, shortened from Broom-Hilda, a purple-faced witch in a comic strip I used to love reading in the *Granite County Record* when I was a kid. My Hilda's not purple, though. She's more maroon.

Fletcher was Wade's pit crew chief, but not even that had prevented me from developing a crush on him. I know that sounds pathetic and girly, but I'm not going to deny it. Not only did Fletcher always give me a wave and a hey when our paths crossed, but he wasn't exactly the ugliest guy at Flu High. His green eyes and slightly dopey smile gave him a gentle look that seemed to match his personality. The bushy blond sideburns were a tad unkempt for my taste, but maybe that was because my father owned a landscaping company, and I tended to notice when things grew wild. Fletcher was rope-thin and tall too, an important quality in any guy I was going to have a crush on, since by my senior year I stood five feet ten inches in a pair of running shoes.

That day in the parking lot, instead of waving, Fletcher smiled and tipped the brim of his faded red WADE LAPLANTE MOTORSPORTS baseball cap, cowboylike. I waved back, threw Hilda's stick shift into reverse, and backed out before my face lit up like a stoplight.

❧

Despite my lack of a winning attitude in general, my attitude toward Fletcher Corwin specifically was very good.

And as soon as I'd left the school lot, my attitude toward the day also began to improve, thanks to a flash of midafternoon sun. As I drove through town, I wondered about Fletcher, what he was planning to do after we graduated. He was about a full year older than I was, since he'd taken a year off from school after eighth grade when his dad died and his mother developed some psychological problems. I'd heard that she was better, but I imagined that between looking after her and running the Wade LaPlante Motorsports crew, he must've been a busy guy. Maybe he wasn't making big plans for the future. I didn't know.

But I did know, as I cleared the village and crested Burnt Hill Road, that the ribbon of Willow River running across the valley below would make my heart race. It always did. Because the river never let anything stand in its way as it charged west out of Granite County. And neither would I.

At the intersection at the bottom of the hill, I did a two-tap stop and banged a left onto River Road, letting Hilda's tires whine in the turn, then punched the accelerator. I worked up to third gear in about five seconds. The roads were dry, and the frost had melted below the asphalt, smoothing out the nastier bumps. It'd been several long winter months since I'd seen what my little German friend could do. Maybe Hilda wanted to get some exercise.

Big Daddy had offered to help me pay for the car because that particular model, even the older model years, was known for safety and low maintenance. He'd said that he didn't want to have to worry about me, and I understood the second meaning of the statement: He didn't want to have to waste any precious time under

Hilda's hood that he could spend managing Wade's racing career.

Still, for a "practical" car, Hilda had very good pickup, and she liked to hug the turns. Yes, she was real affectionate that way.

I'd hit sixty miles per hour before I blew by the yellow sign with the tractor logo signaling the Dumont Farm. Knowing the Dumonts had a lot of cats, I backed Hilda off to fifty as I passed their picturesque old barn and their equally postcard-perfect house.

Just past the barn, where the cornfield started, I shifted into fourth gear and spiked the RPMs on Hilda's tachometer before upshifting. It was a lightning-quick shift, and she didn't miss a breath. In the flat, two-mile stretch ahead, Hilda sucked up blacktop like root beer. Sixty-five, seventy, seventy-five, eighty, eighty-two, eighty-five miles per hour without so much as a microshimmy. Not Hilda. I brought her back to eighty and let her enjoy it for a few moments, and she did, her engine singing a sirenlike tribute to the *performance engineering* that Big Daddy had yammered about at the dealership. I eased her back down.

Doing forty, I pinned Hilda to the right shoulder and entered Idiot's Curve—so named, by me, because that was where Wade LaPlante Motorsports crewmember Lonnie Snapp nearly ran me down on a cross-country training jog the previous summer. With even pressure on the accelerator in the turn, I pulled hard on the steering wheel to keep Hilda from yanking out toward the centerline.

As the road straightened out, my house came into view,

perched atop a hill about a mile up Meadow Ridge Road, which branched left off River. My arms tingled beneath my sweatshirt as our silver mailbox caught a glint of light, poking out from the trees off the right shoulder.

I pulled up close enough to reach the mailbox through the passenger-side window and leaned way over to yank the door open, drawing a sharp breath when I saw the white envelopes stuck in there among the magazines and catalogs. I slid the mail out, shut the mailbox door, and tossed everything into the back seat except the white envelope embossed with the Cray College logo. The envelope felt thin but not too thin. If there was only one sheet of paper inside, I estimated, it must've been thick. Tapping the letter on the gearshift knob, I tried to gauge its weight.

Holding my breath, I tore open the envelope. As I slipped the pages out—three sheets—and snapped them open, my eyes fell on one word: *Congratulations.*

Dear Casey LaPlante:
Congratulations. Your application for undergraduate admission to Cray College has been approved.

I screamed like a kid on a roller coaster and kissed the letter. Then I read it again slowly, word for word.

There was no mistake. I got in. I was going to Cray College. I was leaving Fliverton—and not just going-to-the-state-university-down-the-highway leaving. Cray College was a seven-hour drive west of where I sat idling by the roadside.

The second and third pages were from the financial aid office. There was a form to fill out before they could calculate how much assistance I'd receive. I didn't want to think about that just then, but I couldn't help remembering how, at dinner a few nights earlier, Big Daddy and Wade had argued about when the racing team could afford to overhaul the suspension on car 02 — Wade's ticket to glory. Big Daddy's company, LaPlante Landscaping, *wasn't going gangbusters,* as he said, and he was banking on sending me to State. As he and Wade bickered, and Mom just listened for her cue to tell one of them to please lower his voice, I pulled a bottle of salad dressing over to my plate and read the label, trying to see how many of the chemical ingredients I could identify by their function in the recipe. This was how I often endured Wade LaPlante Motorsports team meetings thinly disguised as family meals.

There on the shoulder of River Road, I tucked the pages of my Cray College acceptance letter back inside the envelope, kissed the envelope again, and tossed it onto the dashboard, as if to let Hilda read it through her vents.

I checked the side mirror and spotted Wade's Nova vibrating like a space capsule burning into Earth's atmosphere. He called the car the Red Snake, which made no sense, since, like I mentioned, it was more orange, and while there are snake species orange and red in color, those species have never inhabited the greater Fliverton ecosystem. Wade didn't have a name for his racecar. Maybe he couldn't come up with another one.

I hesitated to pull out, since Wade was hammering fast along the dry spring roads, just like I'd been doing. A few seconds later, he pulled up beside me.

He smiled a toothy smile and slid his sunglasses onto his

forehead, bunching up a tiny haystack of red hair, then leaned across his front seat to lower the passenger window. "Hey there, Casey," he said.

I could read his mind from his tone of voice. I shook my head.

He gunned the Red Snake's engine. "Aw, come on, Case. We never have any fun together anymore."

"Grow up."

He flipped his hair-haystack toward our house on the hill. "Wasn't that good pie Mom made last night?" he said.

"Sure was. I'm all about the raspberries, guy."

"Well, when I left the house this morning, I could've sworn I saw a piece of that pie in the refrigerator."

"I hope you took a picture."

"One piece." He revved his engine and arched his eyebrows. "Not two pieces." He revved his engine twice. "One." He revved his engine once again. "Taste pretty good with a glass of milk, don't you think?"

"Just don't drink out of the carton, Wade. It's immature, disgusting, and inconsiderate." I reached for the letter on the dashboard and stole a glance at the twenty yards of pavement between Hilda's front end and the Meadow Ridge Road turnoff. I visualized the line I'd need to follow to give Wade room when he jumped on the gas. I ran a few mental calculations—reaction time, rate of acceleration, distance. I redrew the imaginary line based on the results.

"What's that in your hand?" he said. "Love letter? Got a secret admirer, do you?"

"This—" I held the letter out the window with my left

hand—"is freedom." I waved the letter slowly, as if imitating a falling leaf. As Wade's eyes followed the envelope, I moved my right hand to the gearshift—casually, without changing the position of my body—and slid Hilda into first while depressing the clutch with my left foot.

"You sure that's not a love letter?" Wade said. "Because I know *one* guy might have a thing for you. *One*, anyway."

"Really?"

"I do believe so, yes."

"And who might that be?"

"Well, I don't know if I should tell you. How about you ask me some questions and see if you can figure it out?"

"OK." I tossed the letter onto the passenger seat and took the wheel in both hands. In gear. Clutch in. Resting my head on the steering wheel as if deep in thought, I glanced at the road again, visualizing the angle to the turnoff. I sat up straight and looked at Wade. "If this person were a piece of pie, what kind of pie would he be?"

Wade made a puzzled face. "Piece of pie?"

I punched the gas, popped the clutch, and launched over the shoulder. Jerking the wheel to the right, I shifted into second.

Wade's tires chirped on the pavement behind me.

I hugged the turn off River and onto Meadow Ridge and shifted into third gear the instant I hit the straightaway.

Wade took the outside, clinging to my bumper. He drifted in so tightly that I lifted on the gas for a split second to avoid getting rapped.

It was a trick, an intimidation tactic—and it worked.

My "lift," as Wade and his crew called a quick easing up on the gas, gave my brother the time he needed to pull up even.

Gripping the wheel and flooring the accelerator, I listened for Hilda to whine up to peak power in third gear then made a quick shift into fourth.

The Red Snake had automatic transmission, no stick shift, so Wade was all gas pedal, his big American engine roaring at Hilda like the country dogs that sometimes ran out to the roadside to chase me when I jogged by. The only place where I had a chance against the Red Snake's horsepower was in the swale about one hundred yards ahead. Whenever I pushed Hilda to the outer boundary of what her engine could handle in a particular gear, she never faltered—*performance engineering*. I might get a hiccup out of Wade's throaty engine on the incline, and that might gain me some ground.

In the last bit of flat road before the rise, I made my move: quick shift into fifth gear, losing only a nose on Wade. I honked my horn and stayed on it. Wade, startled, instinctively lifted a touch, and I floored the gas at the bottom of the dip and got full power on the rise.

Just as I expected, Wade's car needed a second to make the adjustment of the incline, and when I flew over the swale and down the other side, I had him by a car length. It was enough. As we rattled along the rutted mudpack for another hundred yards or so, Wade had to drop behind me as we both slowed to make the arcing right turn up the long, asphalt driveway. He bobbed around in my rearview mirror. I downshifted to third and got ready to shift into second in the turn. I knew I'd squeal my tires around the corner, which would earn a scolding if Mom was home from work and heard it, but I didn't care.

I glanced in my rearview mirror one more time.

Wade was gone.

And then I saw him again, off to the right. The cheater had driven off the road and across a corner of the front yard. His rear wheels slipped in the damp grass, leaving troughs, but he popped onto the driveway just ahead of me and stole the front spot.

He was out of his car and spinning his keys on his finger by the time I'd killed Hilda's engine. Mom's blue station wagon was in the garage, but she wasn't looking out the kitchen door like she sometimes did when she could tell we'd raced up to the house.

"You call that driving?" I said, approaching him.

He moved away from the car and backpedaled toward the walkway, staying a few steps ahead. "I guess I just really want that pie."

"I guess so. That's some fancy go-cart technique you've got there. That going to be your strategy this season?"

"Aw, Case, you didn't think you were going to beat the Red Snake, did you?"

Stopping in the walkway, I looked into the yard, where Wade's tracks were filling with ground water. "Red *tractor* is more like it," I said.

Down near the end of the walkway, Wade did the taunting, infantile leprechaun dance that I'd longed to capture on video for his fans. Twenty years old, living at home, working for Big Daddy but putting every penny into his cars. Dancing around like a leprechaun.

"Go on," I said. "Growing boy's got to have his pie."

Still backing toward the front door, Wade didn't see a lone patch of ice on the walkway lingering in the shade of the front step. He planted his boot heel right onto it, slipped, and lost his balance. Flailing his arms, he tossed his keys in the air.

I was just close enough to grab his arm and save him.

But I didn't.

As he landed in the yard with a delicious squish, I bounded to the door and slipped inside.

∽

"Hi, Casey," Mom said from the dining room table, where she was flipping through catalogs.

"Hey." I tossed the mail, minus the Cray College letter, onto the table on my way to the refrigerator. Mom's sweater gave off a faint piney smell, as her clothing often did when she'd been working in the plant nursery that she and Big Daddy were adding onto the landscaping office. "Where's that leftover pie?" I asked as I scanned the inside of the fridge.

"Oh, I heard your brother's car in the driveway, so I set it on the counter for him."

As if on cue, Wade entered the kitchen and zipped past me. Down at the end of the counter, he corralled the plate of pie and guarded it with his arms, like I'd seen raptors do with their wings while eating in tree branches— *mantling*, the ornithologists call it. He held the plate up to his nose. "Mmm. Pie."

I rolled my eyes.

Wade laughed, sending flakes of crust drifting to the kitchen floor.

I took an apple from the crisper.

Mom tucked a strand of jet-black hair behind her ear—she must've just had it colored—and eyed me as I crossed the kitchen. "How was your day, sweetie?" she said.

I paused to consider how my day had gone—that is, how to put it into words that Mom, on mental safari in Catalog Land, might find interesting enough to listen to.

"Great," Wade interrupted with another puff of crust flakes.

Mom laughed and shook her head. It was a gesture I wouldn't miss: the *Oh, that Wade* look. Impish jokester, man-child Wade. Our very own live-in, life-size action figure. Push a button and hear him make disgusting chewing noises.

"Dad came out to the site today around lunchtime," Wade went on, "and he said that he thinks the bank is ready to take their sponsorship to the next level. There's some equipment we could really use in the pit."

"Like new uniforms?" Mom said, holding the cover of a catalog up so Wade could see it.

"It's not a sure thing yet," Wade said, taking a last bite of pie. "But we're going to meet with Mr. Church next week—you know, a formal, sit-down type of meeting in his office—and work out the details."

"Well, that sounds pretty final." Mom bent a page corner down and resumed her skimming.

I walked over to the table and sat down next to her, trying not to be creeped out by the vacant smile on her face as she scanned the pages, no doubt imagining Wade—our fearless boy-man—in a smart-looking fireproof racing suit. "Got my chemistry test back," I said. "Aced it. Destroyed it. Ran it over, backed up, and ran it over again."

Mom didn't look up, but she did arch her eyebrows, indicating at least low-level interest. The muscles in her long neck tightened as she strained to look like she was paying attention to me without prying her eyes from the catalog. "What's that, Casey?"

"Casey's got a secret admirer," Wade said.

Mom looked up and gave me a sly, mother-daughter smile that made me want to calmly stand and throw a chair through the glass doors leading to the patio. It was a sight even more disturbing than her blissed-out, *Oh, that Wade* smile. "So, who's the mystery man?" she said.

Before I could answer, before I could inform these people that goats would fly like angels down the streets of Fliverton before I shared with them even the most trivial detail of my personal life, the front door opened.

Big Daddy blustered into the kitchen. He gave Mom, then Wade, a goofy grin, his eyes skipping over me. "You tell your mother the news?" he said to Wade, flipping the man-child a chin peppered with red-gray end-of-the-day stubble.

"Mentioned it," Wade said, a pout clouding his doughy face. "I wish they'd just give us the money now."

"Well, I'll tell you what," Big Daddy said, wagging a beefy finger at his pride and joy. "I don't know why a bank vice president would arrange a meeting right there in his own office just to tell a guy, no, he won't up his sponsorship money." He set his lunch cooler down on the

15

dining room table. "Granted, we shouldn't be counting our chickens before they hatch. I do have a feeling, though, that this time next week" — he knocked his knuckles on a chair back — "we'll be counting more than chickens."

Mom splayed the catalog on the table and slid it toward Big Daddy. "Take a look at these, hon," she said, tucking another strand of hair behind her ear.

Big Daddy took off his barn jacket and hung it on a chair, and Wade walked over so the three of them could hover together over the catalog, my father standing behind my mother, his hands resting on her shoulders as she discussed the merits of racing uniforms.

I got up from the table and walked into the kitchen, where I took my Cray College acceptance letter out of my pocket and stuck it on the refrigerator under a VALLEY SAVINGS & TRUST magnet. Standing back, I wondered how long the letter could hang there before someone noticed it. Hearing Mom say that she also found some "fun" shirts that Wade's fans could wear, asking Wade and Big Daddy if they agreed that I — she was actually, honestly, sincerely referring to *me,* Casey — would look "just darling" in . . . she flipped the pages . . . *"this,"* it hit me harder than it ever had just how little my family knew about me. I mean, I hadn't gone to Demon's Run even once over the two previous seasons, an attendance record I intended to maintain. Apparently, whether I went or not escaped their notice.

Zoning in on that one key word in the letter — *Congratulations* — my heartbeat sped up. I looked over to the dining room table, where my family huddled around a stack of catalogs like soldiers around maps—maps of a land I'd been living in, completely lost, my whole life. I slid the letter from beneath the magnet and tucked it in my back pocket.

Mom looked up as I opened the patio door and tossed my apple core onto the back lawn. "Biodegradable," I said.

"Casey, have a look," she said. "Imagine your brother and his crew in these getups."

"Maybe later." I headed for the stairs. "I've got a paper to write."

"Yeah, imagine Fletcher Corwin in one of these," Wade said, sliding the catalog away from Mom.

"Fletcher?" she said. "Fletcher's Casey's mystery man?"

I didn't even consider responding. Although it was my name being bandied about, they weren't talking about me. They hardly knew me.

∾

Up in my room, I took out my Cray College acceptance letter and reread it, just to be absolutely sure. I was absolutely sure. I'd got in.

I booted up my computer and hit the Cray website, where I spent a few minutes imagining myself wandering down tidy walkways flanked by old trees, backpack hitched over my shoulders. Or hanging out with other students on the lawns spread out before stately old buildings or on that stone fence that framed part of campus. Or collecting water samples and recording environmental data while knee-deep in the creek that ran behind the athletic fields.

I'd only visited Cray once, in ninth grade, when the college hosted the state high school cross-country meet. But I remembered the visit as if I'd gone back there every day since then, which, in a way, I had, sitting at my desk, clicking around the Cray site. When our Flu High team bus passed through that iron gate at the east end of campus, I felt something I'd never felt before: that college could be the start of a new life, a life with trajectory, with direction, without the incessant rumble of engines and stench of exhaust. A life in which I'd be known as who I was, not as whose little sister I was.

I slipped the letter into my desk drawer, covering the acceptance letter from State. Of course, I'd told my parents about the State letter, but getting into State had hardly been a surprise. State was a fine institution, no question. The guy who owned the Wimmer Granite Quarry, Mr. Wimmer, had gone to State and studied geology. A couple of senators had gone there too. My own mother had gone to State and studied travel and tourism. She'd just started working as a travel agent before marrying Big Daddy. There was nothing wrong with State. Community College? Another great option. The way I saw it, a person could study at Community College, transfer to State, get a degree, and rule the world. It happened every day.

But Community College and State didn't have one of the best environmental studies programs in the country. Cray College did.

An engine fired up in the driveway outside my window. The way the cross-country ribbons tacked to the bulletin

18

board above my desk vibrated told me that it was car 02. No mortal car ever rocked my bulletin board like Wade's ride. I pulled back the curtains and peered out, finding the late-afternoon shift at Wade LaPlante Motorsports getting under way. I expected other cars to come rumbling up to the house any minute.

I grabbed my car keys off the dresser.

Wade and Big Daddy, along with a few of Wade's crew-members, including Fletcher, were dutifully grinding more grease into our driveway as I came down the walkway. No one seemed to notice me, not even Fletcher. I looked at him as I passed, but he was up to his elbows in car 02. Wade caught me staring at Fletcher and smirked. I strapped in, fired Hilda's engine, and backed out. As I started down the hill, I glanced toward the garage but caught only Wade's eye again. When he tapped Fletcher on the shoulder, I punched the gas.

ॐ

I navigated Fishing Access Road carefully, trying to avoid potholes. When I pulled into the access lot, mine was one of only two cars there. The other was a boxy sedan backed up to the shore of the Willow River, with a boat trailer mostly submerged in the water. The car looked like an old Pontiac, white with a floral pattern of rust patches. No one appeared to be sitting inside.

I idled over to the spot at river's edge where town employees would, according to the calendar, soon run out a long, aluminum dock that also acted as a boardwalk throughout spring and summer. The blunt riverbank didn't offer much room to sit, but that was OK with me,

19

since I could sit in my car and still enjoy watching the river beating a frantic path out of Fliverton. That evening, I knew I could savor it like never before.

My world was about to get much bigger. I was going to Cray College (so long as Big Daddy could handle my recalculated college budget). I was about to meet new people, people who had no idea what short-track racing was, people who would know me as me.

The fishing access was, in my opinion, the most scenic spot in all of Granite County and, on race days at Demon's Run, the most peaceful place imaginable. I may have been the only person who *could* imagine it, since I seemed to be the only person in Fliverton who went anywhere besides the track on race days. That evening, though, as dusky light painted the river charcoal-black, I saw in the color a less cheerful reality—something neither dark nor light but, rather, absent. The access was not only scenic and peaceful but an undeniably romantic spot. I could imagine the metal dock lying atop the water, the couples strolling, hand in hand, to the end. But I'd never experienced this place that way—and never would. While it was there by the riverside that I'd fantasized about escaping Fliverton, that night the sound of the Willow River coursing by made me feel suddenly, strangely sad. I was on the threshold of freedom, but I'd soon slip away unnoticed, without having ever *been* noticed.

The sound of tires crunching gravel drew my attention, and I glanced in the rearview mirror to see a village police cruiser rolling into the lot. The way the cop took up the whole road, not hugging to one side, suggested he wanted to know who was down there, and why, and that he didn't want anyone making a break for River Road until he knew. The cruiser pulled up next to me, and I saw that it wasn't just any cop but Chief Congreve.

He got out of his cruiser and approached Hilda. The chief was no taller than average—five-eight or so—and of medium build, except for wide hips and a butt that, against the laws of nature, sank inward. A concave butt. Chief Concave, I thought of him. But he moved steadily, with a sense of ready caution, as if approaching a carload of felons along a highway shoulder. Stepping up to my window, he smiled faintly. "Hey, Casey," he said. "Enjoying the sunset?"

"Hi, Chief. Yup. That's what I'm doing."

The chief's eyes darted into Hilda's back seat and then back to me. "Planning to spend much more time here tonight?"

"No, sir. Just came to watch the sunset."

"I see. Well, I don't mean to interrupt your moment, but I thought I'd check and see who all's down here."

"I understand. I appreciate it."

Chief Congreve looked toward the river as a lone boater rowed into view from beneath a curtain of willow branches. The man drifted toward the riverbank, stepped into the shallow water, and began hauling his metal boat onto the semisubmerged trailer. He looked over, waved, and said, "Evening, Chief" in a scratchy voice that reminded me of a duck call. It was a familiar voice—my Uncle Harvey's voice.

"Harvey," the chief grumbled, the word rattling in his throat like a stick dragged across corrugated metal.

Uncle Harvey hauled his boat onto the trailer and waded ashore. He was practically swimming in thick work pants streaked with sludge where they weren't wet from the river, and he wore a forest-green windbreaker fraying at the sleeves. His Valvoline-logo baseball cap was dappled with paint, wiry gray hair sticking out on all sides like the bristles of a paintbrush left to harden on a workbench. When he was close enough to the chief to extend a hand, he finally noticed me. "Well, here's a surprise," he said with a wheezing laugh, cracking a smile that revealed at least three fewer teeth than I remembered from the last time I saw him, though I couldn't remember when that time had been. Maybe a year earlier, maybe more, probably in town somewhere. "Casey LaPlante. How've you been, old girl?"

"Hi, Uncle Harvey. I'm OK."

"Glad to hear it." He slapped a hand on Hilda's roof, and his tired-looking eyes, which bulged a little—a LaPlante male gene I didn't inherit—flickered with the day's waning light. He glanced at Chief Congreve. "So what's this all about then? Everything OK here?"

"Not really your concern, is it?" the chief said in a flat, unfriendly tone.

"Just curious, is all," Uncle Harvey said. "I see my niece parked over here. Normal to wonder why."

"Normal just to stay out of it. Don't you think?"

Uncle Harvey didn't say anything, as if startled—and understandably so—at the chief's coldness.

Despite the awkward vibe Chief Congreve had conjured

22

among us, Uncle Harvey smiled at me. "Haven't crossed your path in quite some time," he said. "Too long. You're looking fit."

As if accepting the fact that he wasn't about to make the biggest drug bust in Granite County history, or even the smallest, the chief sighed and walked back to his cruiser.

"Good seeing you, Chief," Uncle Harvey said.

The chief clicked his flashlight on Uncle Harvey's sedan. "Don't think your vehicle's going to pass inspection, Harvey."

"Fortunately I've got ten months to go on it," Uncle Harvey said, giving me a wink.

The chief grumbled something I couldn't hear and climbed into his cruiser.

"Well"—Uncle Harvey gave Hilda's roof another slap—"I should haul that boat out of here before the chief thinks of something to cite me for."

"Guy's kind of a grump."

Uncle Harvey chuckled. "He's not a bad guy, really. It can't be easy being the most unpopular man in town."

"Why's he so mean to you?"

"I'm the only one gives him any competition."

I eyed Uncle Harvey's boat sloshing in the current washing over the trailer. "Can I give you a hand?"

Uncle Harvey nodded. "Sure. I'd appreciate that."

At river's edge, I helped my uncle secure his boat for the drive home, but neither of us said much. Fact was, as relatives, we weren't close. I didn't think that I'd even mention to my parents that I'd run into him, especially not Big Daddy, Uncle Harvey's younger brother. I couldn't pinpoint a single time in my life when those two got along, though no one had ever explained to me what the problem between them was. And while I wasn't forbidden from uttering Uncle Harvey's name, over the years I'd noticed that it was sometimes avoided in conspicuous ways, like driving a conversation around a hunk of something in the road that might cause a flat tire.

While Uncle Harvey and I worked, he asked some of the questions I might've expected someone my father's age to ask if he'd known me from the time I was born but only ever saw me passing on the street or pulled up to a stoplight: "How's school going?" "Family doing OK?" "Think Wade's got a shot at his second track championship? You know, they say—"

"I know," I said, stifling a yawn. "If Wade performs well early on this season, he could get a call from a Circuit team. They've got their eye on him."

I so surely expected Uncle Harvey to launch into an analysis of how Wade could achieve that feat, the topic being a favorite among Fliverton males of all ages, that I was surprised when he didn't. "Not much interested in racing, are you?" he said and smiled that piano-keyboard smile.

"Not much."

"Don't care to spend your Sundays getting bumped and T-boned and chopped by a bunch of maniacs with more balls than brains? Oh, sorry. That was crude."

I hesitated to answer, not because Uncle Harvey had offended me but because it dawned on me that he'd just asked me if I had any interest in *driving*, not spectating. There'd never been any women drivers at Demon's Run,

24

at least not that I could remember. In racing, as in life, my hometown was generally behind the times.

"Well I can't say as I blame you." He flipped a hitch on his trailer, wiped his hands on his pants, then faced the parking lot.

It seemed an odd thing for him to say, given that, according to a story Wade had told me, Uncle Harvey had been Big Daddy's crew chief back when Wade Senior almost hit the big time. "So, you don't follow racing anymore?" I said.

Uncle Harvey looked uncomfortable as he pulled his car keys from his pocket. "Now and again," he said. "Now and again." He stared at the river, seeming to search his mind for something, as if he might've left something out on the water that he'd need to row back out and get. "What'd you say you were doing in the fall?" he said, turning back to me.

"I didn't."

"Well? What are you doing?"

"Going to college."

"State?"

I shrugged. "Depends."

"On . . .?"

"Money. I just got into Cray College. Ever hear of it?"

Uncle Harvey looked toward the river again, and as his eyes drifted along the horizon, following the river's flow, he nodded. "Oh, I've heard of it," he said quietly. "Yes I have. That's a fine institution, Cray. A top-notch institution." He turned back to me. "Your parents must be proud."

For no particular reason—maybe because I'd been raised to more or less exclude Uncle Harvey from my notion of who my family was—I didn't tell him that I hadn't broken the news to Big Daddy, Mom, and Wade yet. I shrugged again.

"You're not just going to college," Uncle Harvey said and looked downriver. The way he said it made me look away, too, and I felt like I could predict what he was going to say next: "Casey, your whole life's about to begin."

A shiver ran down my arms. "I hope so," I said. The feeling I'd had by the river's edge, that lonely feeling, welled up a little. Uncle Harvey and I sighed at the exact same time, then we looked at each other and laughed.

"Well, this was a pleasant surprise," he said and smiled, his eyes catching the last flickers of sun.

"It was good to see you too."

I wanted to hug him, but I didn't do it. We were family, but, in a way, we weren't. At least that's how I understood things.

As Uncle Harvey got into his car, I began wondering, as I hadn't done in a while, why I'd never really pressed my parents about why he'd never been involved in my or Wade's lives. Maybe it was because, from the time I was a little kid, I was never interested in those kinds of questions—*indoor* questions, dull things grownups talked about, things involving other grownups. By the time I was in fourth grade, I was more concerned with what was going on out in our back meadow among the crickets, snakes, and birds; and then about summer lightning and why the roads cracked from underneath in the wintertime. When, in junior high, Wade started racing Karts—

souped-up versions of the go-carts out at Intervale Fun Park—and my parents dragged me to Kart tracks around the state, I'd wander off in search of a swamp, creek, or field where I could pretend they'd brought me to do the things *I* liked to do. In eighth grade, I tracked a coyote for two miles through a new snowfall and didn't return home until an hour after my mother had called the police. Chief Congreve was there to greet me. I was bursting with *outdoor* questions—satisfactory answers to which I couldn't get from my parents, only from teachers, the library, and my computer. Maybe my mother and father had some of the answers, but when Wade's racing became their obsession, any enthusiasm they showed for my interests seemed fake.

As I stood back from Uncle Harvey's car, the time that'd passed since I'd last seen him swirled in the dust he kicked up in the parking lot. He was a sweet man. A person could tell that just by looking at him. And even though we'd chatted only a few minutes, I had a strong feeling that he really understood what Cray College—and getting out of Fliverton—could mean to me. It suddenly seemed ridiculously unfair that I hadn't been able to get to know him in all those years. What could've happened between him and Big Daddy to justify this wall between them—this wall between all of us?

As I was crossing the lot to my car, another car crunched down the access road: a familiar swamp-green Dodge Dart. I paused at my door, pretending to fiddle with the lock, which wasn't really locked, hoping to stall for a moment's conversation. When the car pulled up to the riverbank, though, I glanced over and saw two forms sitting in the front seat, one of them Fletcher, of course, and the other clearly female. Of course. I fired Hilda up and pulled out of there like I'd seen a tidal wave rolling in.

∾

I made it home in time for dinner, but my punctuality was pointless, since, after my mother and I put the food on the table, she still had to call Wade and Big Daddy twice more before they came in from the garage. Once we were all seated and the dishes started around the table, talk turned to racing—specifically, the season opener, sixteen days away, the ninth of May. Big Daddy and Wade got into a prickly exchange about what my father called "prioritizing equipment acquisitions" until the Valley Savings & Trust "sponsorship upgrade" was finalized. Despite Big Daddy's prior warning against counting chickens until Wade LaPlante Motorsports had a check from its primary sponsor in hand, Wade had seemingly grown more enthusiastic, not less, about spending the team's limited funds.

I read the salad dressing bottle.

During a lull in the dinner conversation when Wade put so much chicken into his mouth that we all stopped to watch him, as if getting ready to save him from choking, Mom asked me if I had any news to share. After Wade had swallowed safely, she turned and gave me that sly, woman-to-woman look that made me want to throw canned goods against the walls.

"Crush," Wade interjected in a mock cough, then repeated it, "Crush," in a mock sneeze—a stupid joke he picked up from some movie.

28

I glared at him, telepathically trying to make him chew his tongue in half.

"Wade," Mom said. "Let your sister speak for herself."

"What's this?" Big Daddy interjected in his curt, businesslike manner, like he was answering his desk phone.

"I think Casey's got her eye on Fletcher, is what I'm hearing," Mom said.

"I don't have my eye on anyone," I said, failing to keep a groan from attaching itself to the end of the statement. Like Wade, I sometimes regressed into early childhood among family.

"Well, you should go out with him," Big Daddy said, the way he might tell one of his employees where to stick a shrub. "Good kid. Fine kid. I trust him."

"I trust him, too," Wade said. "He's a good guy."

As if Wade would know what it meant to be a good guy. According to local gossip, a few months earlier the Red Snake had been spotted outside the apartment of his current girlfriend, Gail Wiggans, *weeks* before he broke up with his then most recent former girlfriend, Samantha Houle. And no one had been the least bit surprised. I, however, didn't speak to Wade for a month. I liked Samantha. We'd actually had conversations about something other than Wade's racing career. In the time they were together, almost a year—a One Tank Wade record that'd gone unchallenged—she seemed to find qualities in him that even I, living under the same roof with the guy, had missed. I'm not sure what those qualities were, but Wade acted more mature, more considerate, around her. I thought there was more to Samantha, too, than a pretty face to beam from behind the Red Snake's windshield.

"Seriously, Case," he said, every syllable like a fork jabbed into my face, "Fletcher's top shelf."

"Then why don't *you* go out with him?" I snapped.

The table fell silent.

"Don't you like him?" Mom said in a singsong voice that sounded like she was helping me pick out a swimsuit. She tapped the back of my hand.

Feeling her fingers on my flesh, with my brother and father looking on with identical expressions of amusement, I yanked my hand back and whacked my fork on the edge of the table. "For one thing," I said, "he hasn't asked me out. And for another, I believe he has a girlfriend."

"Not so sure about that, Case," Wade said. "Not what I heard from him today. No, he might ask you out. I mean, all I have to do is tell him—"

"Don't tell him anything. This is not your business."

"You know," my father chimed in, "the guys haven't exactly been busting down the door."

"Wade," Mom scolded.

"Sorry," Big Daddy said with a chuckle. "Not my field, romance. Wade and I'll stick to racing."

Although I was tempted to slide out of my chair and storm upstairs to lock myself in my room for the rest of my life—or at least until graduation day—I refused to sink to Wade's and Big Daddy's level. I simply took a bite of green beans, even though my appetite was history. When the LaPlante men stopped chuckling and spitting bits of food onto themselves, I said, as calmly as I could with my face burning like a radiator after a long drive, "As a matter of fact, I do have some news."

"What's that, dear?" Mom said with a sugary, mother-to-daughter smile.

I smiled back, matching her effort at sincerity. "I got accepted at Cray College."

Again, utter silence.

I looked at Mom first. Her expression conveyed more shock than delight, as if I'd told her I was pregnant and was planning to marry my driver's ed teacher, something that had happened to a Flu High girl who'd graduated the previous year. "Well, that's . . . ," Mom began, "that's terrific news. Congratulations, sweetheart."

"That's just super," Big Daddy said in such an awkward tone that I almost took the whole thing back, thinking that maybe we could try this all over again at breakfast. He attempted a proud smile, but I could see, in the way the lines around his eyes scrunched into a barely detectable wince, that he was calculating.

"Where's Cray College?" Wade said.

"It's west of here," I said. "Way west."

"Is it expensive?" he continued, ever the tactful conversationalist.

"I've applied for financial aid."

"Well, good." My brother took a healthy drink of milk, as if toasting my financial-aid prospects. "Because money is definitely tight around here."

"Let me worry about that," Big Daddy said. "I don't want to hear another word about money until after we meet with Church. Meantime, there's plenty of other work to do on this racing team that's got nothing to do with new equipment. Like, for starters, getting your crew to learn how to make a simple sway-bar adjustment for a car running tight."

And, suddenly, as if I'd interrupted the racing conversation to tell them how many redtailed hawks I'd seen that day, their talk shifted back to the upcoming Demon's Run season. No questions about what I was planning to study at Cray, about when school would start, about whether I'd have a dorm roommate—nothing. I looked at Mom again, but she was busy sliding another helping of string beans onto Wade's plate. I felt like I was already gone.

I thought of Uncle Harvey and how he'd gazed toward the river, like he was seeing my future materializing over the hills. My hands began to shake. "Oh, and one more thing," I interrupted, tapping Wade's shoulder, even though it was difficult to touch him without ripping his arm off for what he'd done to Samantha Houle and about a dozen other girls.

He and Big Daddy shot me an identical annoyed look, red eyebrows crinkling into arches over their bulging LaPlante-male eyes.

"I've decided to start racing," I said, the words seeming to jump into the conversation by their own power.

No one moved, let alone spoke, for about twenty seconds. "What do you mean?" Big Daddy finally said. "Like, sprinting? But cross-country's your sport. You're a distance runner."

"Not track," I said. "Stock cars. At Demon's Run. I'm going to race in the season opener. Road Warrior division."

Everyone was silent again, but I could feel the table jiggling as Wade and Big Daddy tried to suppress their laughter. Wade finally couldn't hold it in and started howling. Big Daddy cracked a huge smile, but Mom's look from across the table kept him from joining in.

When Wade had finally regained a degree of self-control, he turned to me, head cocked to one side like a dog watching something peculiar. "Race *what*, Case?"

"A car, Brake-Fluid-for-Brains," I said, my face once again heating up. "I've got some money saved up. I'm going to get a beater and run it in the Warriors." The Road Warriors were the starter division at Demon's Run—cars with more or less normal four-cylinder engines, just stripped-down street rides, really—as compared to the elite Thundermakers, Wade's division, which ran on bigger, faster, meaner eight-cylinder engines.

Wade cocked his head to the other side. "But, Case, you don't know the first thing about racing."

I was tempted to remind him of our race up Meadow Ridge Road earlier that day but decided that it wasn't worth the trouble it'd bring—for me more than him. In our household, as in the whole town of Fliverton, people turned a blind eye to whatever trouble Wade caused, never mind the feelings of the young women he tossed out of his life like fast-food bags on the highway. "How hard can it be?" I said. I forced down one last bite of string beans.

At this, Wade looked at Big Daddy with a bewildered expression. The two stared at each other for a few seconds, and the table started to jiggle again. An instant later, they both exploded with laughter.

I calmly set my napkin and utensils in the center of my plate. Out of the corner of my eye, I saw Mom watching me, her hand reaching for my arm, but I stood before she could touch me again.

Chapter 2

Uncle Harvey's place was about five miles from the village, the last right turn before the interstate, down at the end of a long dirt road. I'd only been out there a few times, as a girl accompanying Mom as she drove around town sticking Christmas cards in mailboxes, a quaint little tradition she brought to the LaPlantes from the Beech family. I edged up Uncle Harvey's driveway, a hill lined with weedy brush, but as soon as I poked Hilda's front end into the clearing of his yard, I had to yank her to the right to avoid a head-on with a tow truck lumbering toward me, its flatbed jostling over the lumpy ground. The driver, a longhaired guy who looked roughly Wade's age, didn't even flinch. I skidded to a stop on the slick grass.

A tiny box of a house painted robin's-egg blue with black trim sat back about thirty yards from the driveway. A rabbit hutch stood in the side yard, leaning to one side, looking weather-beaten and neglected. Uncle Harvey's shop, a metal building with two garage doors tall and wide enough for school buses to pass through, rose off to the left with its back to a strip of trees through which I could detect an open meadow.

I pulled up next to my uncle's white sedan and cut Hilda's engine. Uncle Harvey stepped to the threshold of the open garage door and, sliding a wrench into a loop on his work pants, waved. "Hey, stranger," he said.

"Hey." As I approached the shop, I noticed about a half-dozen cars, in various states of demolition, scattered around the yard. Way back in the yard there was another smaller metal building—a long, narrow shed—with the door closed and a motorcycle frame leaning against its side. I figured that was where Uncle Harvey kept his boat.

"What brings you out this way?" he said, yanking a rag from his back pocket and wiping his hands.

We stared at each other for a few seconds. Truth was, I shouldn't have been out there. While my parents had never said outright that I couldn't have contact with Uncle Harvey, they probably assumed they didn't need to. Served them right for assuming.

"I need some advice," I said.

"What kind of advice?"

"Driving advice."

Uncle Harvey looked at me a moment longer, then retreated into the shop. I followed him, watching as he stood at a workbench and thumbed through a manual about as thick as five Granite County phone books bound together. I took the opportunity to check the place out. Two cars filled the left half of the garage. One of them was an SUV with its front end squished in, bits of grillwork sticking out like straw from a hay bale. The other was an old Volvo station wagon with its hood open.

"Guy who drives that SUV should've come to me for driving advice," Uncle Harvey said. "I'd have told him to get off the cell phone and drive." He lifted the manual off the workbench and dropped it with a thud. "The parts on these monsters don't come cheap."

"What's the story with the Swedish job?"

"Alternator. Wear-and-tear thing. They just give up eventually, those old parts"—he flipped his chin at the SUV again—"if you don't go smashing them up first."

"So, are you doing body *and* engine work?"

Uncle Harvey smiled his gap-toothed smile. "If you've got a toaster isn't cooking your bread the way you like it, bring it on in." His smile dimmed. "But something tells me you're not here about a toaster."

"I need a car."

"What's that you're driving, a bicycle built for two?"

"I need a racecar."

His expression grew very dim, on the verge of dark. "A racecar," he said. "What's this all about then?"

"I'm racing in the season opener at Demon's."

"You are?"

"I want to."

"This year's? The one in just two weeks or so?"

"That one. I got the idea while you and I were talking last night."

"Oh, no."

"Actually, I've been thinking about it for a while. I don't want to make a career of it or anything."

"A wise choice."

"I just want to, you know, see what it feels like."

Uncle Harvey looked around the shop, his eye falling on the SUV's smashed grill. "Well then, I can get you set up and you can drive around the field out there." He gestured toward the pasture out back of the garage.

"No. I want to race. Bumper to bumper. I'm doing it."

Uncle Harvey stared me down.

I stared back. I was tempted to deliver a mini-speech

about how I was sick of living on Planet Stock Car without knowing what was so special about racing, about how racing was the only language spoken in my house or in any house within fifty miles in any direction. But I resisted. After all, Uncle Harvey had run Big Daddy's crew back in the old days. What could I tell him that he didn't already know? "I figured you might have some, you know, tips for me," I said.

"Tips. Right."

"But if you're too busy, I'll just go out to Granite Autoland. See what they've got in the way of four-cylinder—"

"Well, if you're so determined about it . . ." Uncle Harvey cut me off, eyes still locked on me and narrowed, as if telling me to spare him the game of pretending that I'd actually dare go anywhere but to him to hook up a Road Warrior ride. "I'm glad you came up. But I'll tell you something: a car's the least of your worries."

"What do you mean?"

He stepped out of the shop and surveyed the inventory, if the word *inventory* could apply to the beaters and wrecks dotting his property like a herd of sick cattle. "You don't need anything fancy, do you?" he said.

"I don't have much money to spend."

"We're not going to discuss money. We'll call this a belated birthday present for the last, oh . . ." He seemed to lose his train of thought as his eye fell on a yellowish pickup truck covered to its wheel wells in weeds. "I can get you the better part of a four-cylinder engine out of that. But the trannie's no good. Might need part of that Chevy over there." He pointed to a red sedan up on blocks. "Springs, wheel bearings . . ." He scratched at his chin stubble with his left hand while his right pointed out cars as if he were adding them up. He rested his hands on his hips and turned back to the shop. "I could get the torch and work up some kind of rollbar and cage. Pull some seatbelts for a harness. They're real picky about the harness now, I've heard." He spat.

"I don't care what kind of car it is," I said. "I just need something that runs as fast as the others. I want a fair shot."

Uncle Harvey looked at Hilda. "Well, fast is definitely important," he said. "But there's more to it than that."

"Like what?"

"Like techniques, strategies, rules, and regulations."

"What kind of rules and regulations?"

Uncle Harvey crossed his arms and looked beyond me, in the general direction of town. "So you haven't signed up for this thing yet?"

"No. Not yet."

"Did you know that you had to sign up?"

"Yes. Well, no. I figured that there had to be some kind of, you know . . ."

"Oh, there's definitely some kind of 'you know.' You need to see Don Blodgett."

"The track boss?"

"The director of racing, yes. Know where his office is?"

"Out at the track. In that cinderblock building behind Beer Belly Hill."

"That's right." Uncle Harvey snorted and shook his head. "I'd almost forgotten. The infamous Beer Belly Hill."

The few times I'd been to Demon's Run, early in Wade's career when my parents made me go, I usually sat in the grandstands. Once or twice I sat in the section at the far end, adjacent to a grassy embankment that everyone called Beer Belly Hill. That seating area got its name because it was popular with fans who went to Demon's Run as much to drink beer as to watch the races. The Beer Belly Hill crowd could get pretty rowdy, especially when there were a lot of wrecks. All that smashing and crashing got them worked up.

"What do I do, fill out a form?" I said.

"Yeah. Exactly. And you pay Blodgett the license fee."

I hesitated, and Uncle Harvey eyed me.

"You didn't know there was a license fee?"

"No."

"Well, there is. I don't know how much he's charging, Blodgett, but the license is good for the whole season. I doubt he gives scholarships. He's a businessman. Runs a tight ship."

I automatically began considering waiting for my financial-aid award letter from Cray before plunking down hard-earned baby-sitting and tutoring money on a few spins around a racetrack. "I'm doing it," I said, then repeated the statement, just to make sure I'd said it the first time. "I'm doing it."

Uncle Harvey scratched his chin again. "What do your folks think about this?"

Again I hesitated, and he seemed to pick up on something. He nodded. "I see. They don't know."

"Oh, I told them. They just don't believe me. Or if they believe me, they don't think I'll follow through. But it's not like they care one way or the other."

Uncle Harvey whistled a faint laugh through his teeth. "I had a feeling it was something like this. Don't ask me why, Casey, but when I saw you power-sliding across my lawn, I just had a feeling something was up."

"Will you still help me?"

Uncle Harvey looked at his boots. He appeared insulted. When he looked up again, he wore a serious expression. "Sure," he said. "I'll help you. You should know one thing, though."

"What?"

"If people know I'm helping you, that's not going to be such a good thing."

"Why?" I asked, though I'd sensed, the moment I left my house to come up here, that I shouldn't tell my family that I'd reunited with Uncle Harvey, not if I wanted my racing plans to be anything more than plans.

"Never mind why," Uncle Harvey said. "It's a long story, and it's got nothing to do with anything anymore. You want my help, I'm glad to give it. Just let's focus on racing." He looked into the sky above his cottage and hooted. "Two weeks. Girl wants to run the Demon in two weeks."

I resisted the urge to tell him what I was thinking, what I'd always thought: that I didn't see how there was *that* much to learn about driving a racecar around in circles. Four left turns. Then four more. And so on until the checkered flag came out. Frankly, I was surprised that no one had trained monkeys to do it yet. It seemed that simple. But instead of presenting this theory, I told Uncle Harvey, "I just want to do my best," which was true enough. It just so happened that I thought my best would be a shock to anyone who thought the idea of my racing at Demon's Run was about the funniest thing they'd ever heard. They might just notice me after all—just before I put them in my rearview mirror for good.

"Well all right then," Uncle Harvey said. "I'm not going to stand in the way of a girl trying to do her best." That light I'd seen dancing in his eyes down at the fishing access flickered.

Just seeing that light and hearing him utter an encouraging word made me feel strangely close to him, like I'd known him all my life, which I guess I had, just not well.

"So here's what we're going to do." He pointed toward his driveway. "You go and see Blodgett. Right?"

"I'll go today."

Uncle Harvey surveyed the cars again. "And I'll set up a ride. It may not be pretty, but it'll get you around the track."

"It doesn't need to be pretty."

Uncle Harvey slid the wrench out of the loop on his pants. "I'm glad to hear it," he said, "because pretty isn't worth much on a racetrack. And it sure doesn't last."

❧

Two vehicles sat parked outside the Demon's Run office, a one-story cinderblock building behind Beer Belly Hill. One of the vehicles was a new-looking, red-and-chrome tow truck with a big winch, crane, and hook. I remembered a vehicle like it from past visits to the track: People called it simply "the Hook." The other vehicle was an enormous black pickup truck that also looked brand-new. Mr. Blodgett, the director of racing, was reputed to maintain extremely high standards for his enterprise. Rumor held that he personally inspected the Demon's Run restrooms for cleanliness every race day before opening the front gates. The condition of his vehicles supported that characterization. Only a shade of dried mud painting the pickup's undercarriage and a peeling bumper sticker indicated that the vehicle had been driven anywhere but around a dealership lot. I knew the bumper sticker well. Big Daddy had one on his pickup truck, Mom had one on her station wagon, and Wade had one on the Red Snake and on his bedroom door: DEMON'S RUN RACEWAY—*CATCH IT IF YOU CAN . . .*

I knocked on the door.

A man bellowed, "It's open," and I stepped into a cramped room, where two chairs behind a coffee table faced a metal desk. The office was windowless, so my eyes needed a few seconds to adjust to the space before I spotted Mr. Blodgett rising from behind the desk. He was a large man, probably six-three and thick, which, along with his neatly trimmed beard, gave him the appearance of a tidy lumberjack. "Hello, Casey," he said, as if we were well acquainted, which we were, in a way, since he'd been with Demon's Run since before I was born.

"Hi, Mr. Blodgett."

With a wince, he shifted his weight. Mr. Blodgett had one problem leg—the result of a car accident, ironically enough, at least according to local lore. He gestured toward the chairs. "What can I do for you?"

I took a quick look around the office. It may not have been spacious, but it certainly was neat. The racing magazines on the coffee table were laid out like fan folds.

"Well," I began, "I came to sign up for the Road Warriors."

Mr. Blodgett sat down and nodded thoughtfully. "Road Warriors," he repeated, but the fact that he didn't begin opening drawers and pulling out papers suggested there was more to discuss.

"Yes. I've heard there's a season's license I have to get."

Again he nodded. "That's right." Again he didn't pull out any papers.

"How much is it?"

Mr. Blodgett drummed his knuckles on his desk. "Hold up a second." He passed one hand over his beard, smoothing it down, even though it was trimmed so neatly it looked like a patch of gray-black flannel. "It's like this," he added. "I like to ask the drivers a few questions before anyone commits to anything here."

"OK." I slipped my checkbook from my sweatshirt pocket and reached for a pen in the papier-mâché mug on his desk. The mug resembled one that I'd made in art class when I was in elementary school—same size, same shape. I could make out the word *Dad* creeping around the side of the mug. The one I'd made read *Big Daddy*.

"First off, do your folks know you're doing this?"

I nodded. "Told them last night."

"And what do they think about it?"

"They think it's pretty funny."

"Funny." Mr. Blodgett frowned, as if unfamiliar with the term. "Hmm." He straightened a couple of envelopes on his desk and clasped his big hands, then stared at the door leading out to the track. "Did they discuss with you the dangers involved?"

I shrugged. "Not exactly."

"Well, maybe they should. And once that's done—"

"My mind's made up," I said and began writing the date on a check.

Mr. Blodgett watched me for a few seconds. "You've seen your brother race," he said, "so you know those cars get banged around pretty good."

"Yes, I know."

"Now, granted, those are Thundermaker cars. In the Road Warrior division, the cars don't move as fast, but just ask Wade—he's driven in both divisions—running with the Warriors can be rough." He drummed his fingers again and tilted his head, as if hearing an odd sound off in the distance. "Come to think of it, don't ask Wade," he said. "The kid's fearless. You remember the Firecracker 50 from a few years back?"

I suppressed a sigh. "That was the year Wade made his move," I said. My eye fell upon the racing magazines as I remembered the Fourth of July Firecracker 50 Mr. Blodgett was referring to. Wade got to run in his first Thundermaker race because he'd been the Fans' Pick in the Road Warrior division heading into the holiday event. The Road Warrior Fans' Pick almost always finished dead last in the Thundermaker race. Wade won the thing—and not just won it, but won it in style. He'd started in the pole position—the inside lane at the front of the line—lost it, passed cars to reclaim the lead, got passed again, scrambled back to the front, and generally worked the

45

racecourse in a way that started people calling him the next Big Daddy.

"And what a move it was," Mr. Blodgett said with such sugary admiration that I almost laughed.

I might've let out a little squeak, because he looked at me suddenly, as if snapped out of his reverie. "That your plan, Casey? Got an eye on the Thundermakers?"

"Those rides run, what, about a zillion bucks?"

"To start."

"Nah. Four cylinders will be plenty for me. I'm not in this for the long haul."

"College in the fall?"

"That's the plan." I waved my checkbook at him. "Do I make it out to you or Demon's Run?"

"You've got a ride then, a Road Warrior ride?"

"Getting one. Nothing fancy."

"Crew?"

Feeling a blush coming on, I faked a laugh. "With a name like LaPlante? You've been to our house for a pre-race Sunday breakfast, Mr. Blodgett. People have to bring their own *forks,* we have so much crew. Now, I'm just going to write this out to . . .?"

"Make it out to Demon's Run Raceway."

"How much?"

Mr. Blodgett opened his desk drawer, removed a sheet of paper, and handed it to me. "This is the license application and release form."

"Release?" I took the sheet and read it, trying to keep my eyes from popping at the dollar figure I read in the upper right-hand corner of the form.

"How old are you?"

46

"Seventeen."

"Then I'll need your dad's signature on that. Or your mom's. Doesn't matter."

"Why? If I'm paying with my own money—"

"You're a minor. We need parental consent."

A sigh snuck out, but I filled out the rest of the check anyway.

"Racing's dangerous, Casey. Doesn't hurt to talk it over."

I wanted to remind him that my family and I *had* talked it over . . . in a way . . . and that, if the dangers of racing had been on Big Daddy's and Wade's minds at all, then they had a sick sense of humor.

"So, then, I'll just get a signature then," I said, trying to sound cheerful. I signed the check, tore it out, and handed it to him.

He inspected the check, set it in the precise center of his desk, and stared at it for a few seconds. Finally, he looked at me. "You'll be our first female driver, you know."

"Glad I can help the track keep up with the times."

"You seem very sure about this." He stroked his beard and gestured, with a flip of his head, in the general direction of the track. "You know it gets rough down there. And I'm not just talking about the racetrack."

"I've known most of those guys my whole life," I said. "I know just how they get."

After a long pause, during which Mr. Blodgett smoothed his beard a couple more times, he pulled a document the size of a biology textbook from a stack on the corner of his desk. "Here you go then," he said, handing it to me. "You've got some homework."

"What's this?"

"Your driver's manual. Rules, regulations, and vehicle specs. You want your engine guy to give it a careful read. We don't want any misunderstandings in the pits."

"Got it. I'll have my, um, team look it over." I tucked my checkbook back inside my sweatshirt and pulled out my car keys. "Well, it was good seeing you, Mr. Blodgett." I extended a hand to him.

"Good seeing you, Casey." He rose, his knees making a metallic *thwong* as they hit his desk. He shook my hand then looked down at the check on his desk blotter, as if unsure of what'd just happened, how he'd let it happen, and what it was all going to mean as the season got under way.

Chapter 3

The news that I'd bought a Road Warriors season's license, news that'd evidently beaten me home from my meeting with Mr. Blodgett, who must've called my parents as soon as I left his office, didn't please them one bit, especially not my father. As soon as I walked in the door, Big Daddy sat me down at the dining room table. Mom was in the kitchen, fixing dinner. Wade wasn't home yet. Somewhat predictably, Big Daddy began griping about the money I'd spent, and would continue to spend, on getting a ride together and keeping it running—money, of course, that I wouldn't have for college expenses come autumn. Money he'd have to come up with.

Mom, to my amazement, offered a few words in my defense as she set the plates and utensils on the table and motioned for me to begin setting. "What if she gets a sponsor or two?" she said. "I'm sure there's a few businesses in town who'd love to put their name on the car driven by the track's first woman racer. You know people will be watching her closely."

Big Daddy groaned and turned toward the dim living room. "Right, watching her bite wall," he said.

Mom frowned sharply at the sink.

"I'll be fine," I said.

Big Daddy turned back to me. "And who's going to crew for you? And where are you going to garage this thing? I just don't think you know what all's involved, Casey."

"How could I not know what's involved, Dad, living above a racecar garage my whole life?"

Big Daddy furrowed his eyebrows at me.

Mom also watched me as I stood and began setting the table. "Where *are* you going to keep this car?" she said.

"At school." I kept my eyes on my task. "In the lab lot outside the industrial arts wing."

"And crew?" Big Daddy repeated.

I took a moment to line up the silverware perfectly next to the plate I set before him. "Still working on that."

Big Daddy sighed. "I just don't know, Casey. I need to think about this. *You* need to think about this —"

The Red Snake pulled into the driveway, its growling engine interrupting Big Daddy in midsentence. He got up and started for the door leading out to the garage.

"Wade, we're eating in five minutes," Mom said with a slight edge in her voice.

Big Daddy just grunted, "Yup."

When we were alone, Mom gave me a long, serious look. "Is there anything you want to tell me?" she said.

"About what?"

"About this racing business?"

I stared at her, trying to read in her eyes how much she might already know about my racing plans. She'd defended me a few moments earlier, keeping negotiations open with Big Daddy. I was grateful for that. But did that mean she sincerely supported my decision—and how fully? "What about this racing business?" I said.

Mom's look hardened, her eyes narrowed, her jaw

muscles taut—an expression I rarely saw, since I'd never done anything to suggest to her that I was even capable of irresponsible behavior, at least not compared to Wade, whose romantic irresponsibility was the stuff of Fliverton legend. I didn't crack, though, and a few moments later, Mom's expression softened to one conveying simple worry. "I'm going to sign the release form," she said. "I don't like this idea of yours, but I'll sign it."

"Thanks."

"But you're going to indulge me a lecture on the dangers of auto racing."

"But, Mom, Wade—"

"You're not Wade." She squinted once, quickly, a flickering reminder of that stern face I'd seen a moment or so earlier. "And you're going to listen. It's not open for debate. I'm your mother."

❧

Cresting the hill of Uncle Harvey's driveway, on the watch for maniacal tow-truck drivers, I spotted my uncle and the longhaired guy standing next to the wrecker that'd almost wrecked me about a week earlier. On the truck's driver's-side door, in obviously hand-painted black letters against the rust-colored truck body, were the words J.B.'s TOWING. In the right bay of the shop sat a car that made my stomach clench. If it could've even been called a car. It was more like a mistake of geometry. The front and rear ends were perfectly rectangular, with the boxlike roof sitting directly in the center like the pilothouse on a tugboat. That's what the car reminded me of—a tugboat. A

51

tugboat that had been painted with what looked like vast amounts of pea soup.

As I pulled up to the shop, Uncle Harvey gave me a wave with one hand while holding a crowbar with the other. When I got out of the car, he handed the crowbar to the longhaired guy and they both started circling the car.

"What do you think?" Uncle Harvey said as I stepped into the shop.

"It has a certain retro appeal."

The longhaired guy smirked.

"This is Jim Biggins," Uncle Harvey said.

"How you doing, Jim?"

"No complaints," he said with a nod, then set his jaw as if contemplating something.

Standing next to him, I noted that Jim was stockier than he'd seemed cranking across my uncle's yard in his truck, and he looked older than Wade by a couple of years at least. Sandy blond hair hung to about his shoulders, and when he turned, brown whiskers caught sunlight. I thought his eyes were blue, but I didn't want to stare, and, anyway, what I noticed first about his eyes were the dark circles underneath them.

"Jim here's your pit crew," Uncle Harvey added. "And your car's an old Chevy, mostly. Chevy, a little Ford, and four other cars. Six in all. Blodgett likes his drivers to run the same equipment, and his preference is for Fords— Mustangs in particular. You'll see some Tempos too, and some cars, like this one, that are harder to classify. But I read his manual cover to cover, and I'm pretty sure this ride'll do." He chuckled. "Chassis comes from an old cop car, if you can believe it."

"I've always wanted to ride in a cop car," I said.

Jim tapped the driver's-side door with the crowbar. "It's not as much fun as it looks."

Uncle Harvey smiled at Jim, the corners of his eyes drawn down.

"You know a lot about racecars, Jim?" I said.

He shook his head. "Not much. But I've got a tow truck, so you can at least get this thing to the track."

I turned to Uncle Harvey. "What about you?"

"What about me?"

"You're in my pit crew, right?"

Uncle Harvey laughed, but as he stuffed his hands in his pockets, I caught an anxious flash in his eyes. "Ah, I'm afraid not, Casey," he said. "Got more than I can handle just staying on top of my work here."

"You found time to build me a racecar."

Uncle Harvey clenched his jaw. "That I did. And that's going to be the extent of my involvement in all this."

I shot Jim a curious look.

His gaze revealed nothing.

"You don't even want to come and watch?" I said.

Uncle Harvey looked at the ground. "Wish I could. Really, I do."

"Why can't you?"

"Look, time's a wasting." Uncle Harvey whirled around, pulled his hands from his pockets, and clapped them together. "You've got eight days to learn how to drive. Helmet's on the seat there. We can get you another if it doesn't fit. Now get in and fire it up. See how she feels."

I didn't say this to Uncle Harvey, but I'd already decided that the car was a *he*—Theo, after a tugboat character named Theodore in a video that Blaine and Maddy Egan used to watch, when I baby-sat them, before they got so studious and I became their tutor. I shortened the name to Theo, which was also the name of artist Vincent van Gogh's less-famous brother, the one of the two that actually had some common sense—a quality I felt dwindling within me.

ॐ

If Theo looked like a tugboat on the outside, on the inside he was more like the storage hold on a tuna trawler. There was nothing in this car. Nothing. Everything had been stripped out. There was just a seat sunk way down low, a harness to strap myself in, and a wide rearview mirror. Not exactly riding in style.

But what Theo lacked in style he made up for in nimbleness. This was a quick car. He felt a bit loose in the clutch and steering—he didn't respond immediately to turns of the wheel—but as I rolled into the pasture behind the shop and gave him some gas, he lurched at the tap of my foot, like a dog eager to run off-leash.

I circled Uncle Harvey's pasture a few times, not opening Theo up too much, since the ground was bumpy in spots. I was afraid that, if I went too fast, I might bounce through the roof, even with the harness holding me like a fly in a spider web.

After about a dozen laps or so, I started to get a feel for this guy. I put him tight in the turns and accelerated. That was going to be the cornerstone of my racing strategy:

Take the inside corners, geometrically speaking the shortest distance around the track. Maybe Bean St. Onge, the Demon's Run track announcer who'd coined the nickname Wade "the Blade" LaPlante, would give me a nickname like Casey the Insider.

The pasture turned to asphalt in my mind, the trees framing the field becoming grandstands. I could see the fans on Beer Belly Hill cheering and clanging beer cans as I came screaming around turn three. I could see Big Daddy and Mom smiling as I whiplashed through traffic like a huge metal eel. Maybe even Wade, standing in his pit, would look out onto the track as I ripped the racecourse apart. Maybe Fletcher, too.

Chapter 4

In the week before the Demon's Run season opener, no one said much to me at home. Big Daddy and Wade were consumed with preparations for his first race as defending track champion. Mom seemed almost as frantic as they were, and I don't suppose that my decision to race did her nerves any good. Ever since I'd got my license and started driving Hilda to work at the Egans, she'd let me come and go without asking too many questions. She trusted me—both my parents did. Still, every so often that week before the season opener, Mom would give me a fretful look as I passed through the kitchen, car keys twirling on my finger, as if I were heading out on a date with a dangerous man. Her suspicion was correct.

At the dinner table, Big Daddy would occasionally shoot me a concerned look and ask me how my race prep was going ("OK, I guess"), if I needed any driving tips ("No, thanks"), and where I was practicing ("A big pasture on public land out near the interstate"—not a lie but not the whole truth either). I could tell that he didn't like the idea of me behind the wheel of a Road Warrior car, but I could also tell, from the way he'd glance at my mother after I answered his questions, that he considered my racing plans more her responsibility than his.

When Sunday, the day of the season opener, finally arrived, I got up at dawn but skipped my morning jog. I stretched out, though, and pulled on some cargo pants and my cross-country team sweatshirt. I tied my hair back in a ponytail and slid into my old black Chuck Taylors, knowing their rubber soles would grip the accelerator, clutch, and brake while allowing some bottom-of-the-foot sensitivity.

I crept downstairs as quietly as I could, grabbed a couple of energy bars from the cupboard, and headed out the kitchen door leading to the garage. As I crossed the garage, I heard the kitchen door open behind me. Getting into Hilda, I looked back to see Mom passing through the garage and stepping into the driveway in her bathrobe. I started the engine but rolled down my window as she approached.

She bent over to peer in. "Be careful, Casey," she said. "Promise me you'll be careful."

"I promise."

Mom started to say something else but hesitated, looked toward the house, then turned back to me. She wore a strange expression. It was one of her woman-to-woman expressions, and yet somehow different. The early-morning lines in her face scrawled an anxious message that I couldn't read. "You OK, Mom?" I said, even though I was running behind schedule and she and I really didn't talk much anymore.

"No. But you're going to do this anyway, aren't you?"

I revved Hilda's engine in response.

Mom stood and folded her arms. She gazed toward the river, tight-lipped in the gauzy morning light. I might've expected her to be concerned for my safety, but she seemed unhappy about my decision for other reasons, reasons she wasn't disclosing. After a few moments, she sighed. "Remember, Casey," she said, "you promised to be careful." And with that, she turned and walked back to the house.

❧

Uncle Harvey had driven Theo out of the shop and into his front yard by the time I arrived. He appeared to be checking the tires. I got out of Hilda just as he stood and disappeared into his house. I walk up to Theo and touched the black numbers on the driver's-side door— 06—then inspected my fingertips for wet paint. A few days earlier, Uncle Harvey and I had decided that 06 was the only logical choice, given that six cars went into making one Theo. The number adorned the doors, roof, and hood.

"I considered champagne," Uncle Harvey said, returning with two glasses of orange juice. "But you're underage, and Blodgett would smell it on your breath." He handed me a glass.

"I don't drink and drive," I said. "Don't even drink."

"Smart." Uncle Harvey held up his glass. "Here's to the Road Warrior division, which is as close to pro wrestling as you can get without putting on a pair of tights."

We clinked glasses.

"Oh, speaking of which . . ." Uncle Harvey reached into Theo and pulled out a mint-green firesuit thankfully not as drab-looking as the car's paint job. He tossed it to me.

"Thanks," I said. "How much?"

"It's your birthday present for the last, oh, few years."

"That's what you said about the car."

"We needn't debate this, I don't think. Got a buddy downstate sells the stuff. We did a little bartering."

I held the firesuit up to my body. It looked more or less my size, although it must've been cut for a man slightly larger than me, because I could tell it'd be baggy.

"So," Uncle Harvey said, rapping his knuckles on Theo's roof, "any words to mark this momentous occasion?"

I'd never been much of a speechmaker, so I just raised my glass and said the first thing that came to mind: "To family."

As I moved to clink Uncle Harvey's glass again, he pulled his hand back, a glower falling over his face. He caught himself, though, smiled, and touched his glass to mine.

A couple of seconds later, Jim's truck cranked up the hill. He angled the front end toward the shop and backed the flatbed toward us. "Morning," he said with a wave out the cab window.

"Hey, Jim," I said.

He climbed out of the truck. "That rig ready to load?"

I looked at Uncle Harvey.

"It's not going to be the homecoming parade, you know," he said.

"I know."

"You're going to get hit—maybe hard and maybe often."

"I'm prepared for that."

He scratched at his chin and chuckled. "No, you aren't. But you're going to get hit anyway. Did I tell you that you could die?"

"Yes, you told me. But I won't."

"No, probably you won't. But you know that you could?"

"Yes."

Uncle Harvey took a couple of steps back, a distant look in his eyes as he stared toward the pasture I'd used as my practice track. "Figure out what your limits are, and figure them out early," he said.

"What do you mean?"

"Take your car around the course as fast as you can, but build up your cornering speed gradually. Push yourself a little harder each lap until you know where that threshold is where you'll lose control. Don't be shy about cornering in the outside groove just because it's outside and not right tight inside."

"Makes sense," I said but secretly disagreed with him. While I didn't know my uncle well enough to assess his geometry skills, I was exceedingly confident in my own, so I held to my plan to run on the inside track—the shortest distance around. A mathematical truth.

"And if a driver bumps you from behind, hold on tight and keep your rig straight. He's looking to move you this way or that and slip around you. Bump-and-run, they call it."

"Bump-and-run."

"Yeah, just a nuisance, really, if you're ready for it."

"I'll be ready."

"This is dangerous, Casey. That's all I'm saying. What kind of uncle would I be if I didn't give you fair warning?"

"You've warned me."

Uncle Harvey spat. "Well, just remember this last thing then," he said.

"Shoot."

"You can't win a race in just one lap, but you sure can lose one."

I looked at Jim, but he just shrugged. "I'm not sure I understand," I said.

Uncle Harvey held out his arms, palms skyward, like a preacher reciting a prayer. "Take what the race brings you. Patience," he said. "That's what it means."

I didn't see what patience had to do with being the first car to pass underneath a checkered flag, but I nodded anyway. I gave Uncle Harvey a thumbs-up, and Jim and I loaded Theo onto the wrecker.

❧

As Jim and I plunged down Uncle Harvey's road, I reached to stop a booklet from sliding off the seat and onto the floor. Resting it on my lap, I read the cover: *GED Mathematics: The Most Comprehensive and Reliable Study Program for the GED Math Test.*

"You studying for this now?" I said.

Jim glanced at the book. "Right. Took the test once already. Failed."

I flipped through the booklet, stopping here and there before finding the most advanced exercises. They looked pretty basic to me. I set the booklet in a more secure spot on the dashboard. "You taking it again?"

Jim grabbed the booklet and stuck it behind his seat. "That's my business," he said. "I'll take it when I'm ready."

The guy was obviously comfortable not making a lot of small talk as we rumbled through town. I'd never been the most talkative person, either, but I might've at least tried to get to know him a little, find out where he was from, that sort of thing. The way he sat behind the wheel, though—stone-faced, checking his mirrors like a pilot checking instruments—told me that this errand was more like work to him than a social outing. I didn't know why he'd agreed to haul me to Demon's, since he owed me no favors, but it seemed like he and Uncle Harvey had some kind of agreement about it. Given that I hadn't had another plan in mind for transporting my ride to the track when I decided to start racing—didn't even have a car—I didn't try to coerce Jim into conversation. His silence unnerved me, but the drive to the racetrack wasn't that long.

Chapter 5

Jim and I were one of the first race teams, if you could call us that, at Demon's Run. Mr. Blodgett stood inside the back entrance to the pit area, wearing a navy blue windbreaker with DEMON'S RUN TRACK OFFICIAL on the back and white racing stripes down each sleeve. He had a clipboard tucked under one arm, and he was talking to some guy in a navy blue DEMON'S RUN baseball cap, red earphones encircling his neck like a scarf, and a fire engine red DEMON'S RUN TRACK OFFICIAL jumpsuit. I thought he might be the pace-car driver or one of the Hook men. It'd been a couple seasons since I'd been there.

When Mr. Blodgett saw Jim's tow truck, he gestured for him to pull in and drive to a vacant space near the end of a row of spaces, each roughly twice the width of a regular parking space, maybe twice as deep. As Jim and I passed Mr. Blodgett and the other guy, they both stared at me. "Take a picture, it'll last longer," I muttered.

"Wicked mature," Jim said.

I'd almost forgotten he could talk.

As Jim and I offloaded Theo, I tried to ignore the drivers and crewmembers watching me. Since Jim and I collectively knew exactly zero useful things about racecar preparations — "setup," Wade and Big Daddy called it — we didn't have anything to do once Theo was in his slot. Jim went to the concession area for coffee. I climbed inside my car and waited, peeling old stickers and tape off my helmet. The thing had enough scrapes and gouges in it to make me think that the previous owner hadn't been a racecar driver but maybe a parachutist with a tendency to miss his mark. Or a guy in a circus who got shot out of a cannon—and onto a pile of rocks.

Another trailer, one hitched to an aggressively loud white pickup truck, backed into the adjacent bay. The racecar on the trailer was a pickup too, an old Chevy painted rust red with a yellow number 49 on the door, roof, and hood and FRENCHIE'S FIREWORKS NOOK in yellow across the front panel. A man climbed out of the driver's side, and out the passenger side slid a kid I recognized from school, Kirby Mungeon, a wild-eyed junior with a shaved head. Kirby looked at me and smiled—and I wouldn't have called it a friendly smile. I fought the impulse to slink down below my dashboard but, instead, nodded to Kirby and pretended to be adjusting my safety-harness straps.

When Jim returned, I got out and sat next to him on the wrecker's tailgate while he studied for the GED. I was anxious and bored enough to consider inviting Jim to let me know if he had any questions about the exercises in the book, but I held back. He and I still weren't exactly best friends.

As the pits filled up with cars, the area transformed from a sunken, fan-shaped asphalt tarmac roughly the size of four football fields into something more closely resembling a Civil War battle encampment. It'd been a few years since I'd been back there, so I'd forgotten that Blodgett, in keeping with his general meticulousness, arranged the cars in a particular order: The Thundermaker Sportsmen formed an arc across the outside of the fan, their fancy enclosed car trailers aimed toward the woods surrounding the pit area. The Road Warriors arced across the middle of the fan. The tire compound and tech area, two adjacent bays of activity, were situated roughly where the handle of the fan would be—between Road Warrior pit row and the track itself. The turn-one/turn-two bank rose behind the tire compound and tech area on the other side of a chainlink fence, fifty yards of grass, and a big grassy berm. One-way signs kept cars moving in a clockwise direction through the pits.

As much as I admired the orderly results of Blodgett's pit design, I also cursed the fact that, once the Thundermakers started checking in at the tire compound and tech area, they began a relentless circular parade of eight-cylinder engine roar around Road Warrior pit row. I also could've done without some of the looks I got from Thundermaker drivers as they rolled past.

Looking beyond the pits and into the grandstands didn't calm me down any, though, so I pretty much focused on the patch of asphalt right in front of me. A few minutes later, I was startled by Jim noisily closing his GED book and sliding off the tailgate. I looked up as he walked quickly down to Theo, where Big Daddy was circling the car. "It's OK, Jim," I said, not sure what he was about to do. I still knew almost nothing about the guy.

I didn't catch what Jim said to my father, but when he waved Big Daddy away from the car, Big Daddy laughed. "Who's this, your crew chief or your bodyguard?" my father said as I caught up to them.

"This is Jim Biggins. Jim, this is my dad."

Jim and Big Daddy shook hands awkwardly. "Sir, you're not supposed to be in this pit," Jim said.

Big Daddy smiled. "I know that, Jim. I know the rules. I just thought I'd drop by to wish my daughter luck. That all right with you?"

With his eyes still on my father, Jim tilted his head toward me. "It's up to her."

"It's fine," I said.

Jim turned to me, back to Big Daddy, then back to me again. Then he walked back to the wrecker.

"Guy takes his job pretty seriously," Big Daddy said.

"Yeah, well, he's the only crew I got."

"So . . ." Big Daddy turned his attention back to Theo, and I could see him holding back a smile. "This is your car."

"No, it's a bicycle built for two."

Big Daddy winced and faced me. "Look," he said, "I just came down to see if you're absolutely sure you want to do this."

"I'm sure—"

"Because I sure would rather you didn't."

I didn't say anything.

"It's dangerous," Big Daddy said, "and it's going to cost you."

I nodded and thought about how, for so long, our family income had gone up in smoke from Wade's tailpipe. As a cross-country runner, I'd been a real bargain of a daughter. I guess with my Cray College announcement, Big Daddy could see my price going up. It made sense that he'd want me to spend as little of my money as possible before I left for school. Too bad for him I didn't care.

"I'm worried you're going to get hurt," he added, not sounding all that worried, really.

"Don't be. But thanks."

"Take it slow."

"Now, what kind of strategy would that be? A stupid strategy, right?"

Big Daddy scowled fiercely and crossed his arms, a stance I'd seen him take many times in the garage while locked in debate with Wade. I didn't want to debate with my father just then, not that I ever wanted to. All I wanted was some scrap of calm to hold onto as I plunged into whatever chaos I'd signed on for back in Mr. Blodgett's office. The longer Big Daddy stood there, frowning, the jumpier I felt.

The track loudspeakers clicked on, and Bean St. Onge called the Road Warriors onto the track for our practice laps. I kind of brushed my father aside as I reached into the car for my helmet. Big Daddy said nothing as I put it on. Jim walked down, leaned inside Theo, and yanked the steering wheel off its post. I climbed in through the window and strapped in.

"Wish me luck," I said as Jim handed me the wheel.

"It's just practice," he said.

I jammed the steering wheel onto the post and flicked the electric ignition switch.

Big Daddy turned and walked away, shaking his head.

As I put Theo in gear and rolled out to the end of the line of cars filing toward the pit gate, I was glad that I hadn't eaten a big breakfast.

Just as I was about to pull onto the racecourse, Kirby's

FRENCHIE'S FIREWORKS pickup flew in front of me, nearly clipping my right front end. I cranked the wheel to the left and punched the gas to avoid getting tagged. I wondered if someone had forgotten to tell Kirby we were only running practice laps or if maybe he was just a freak. Either way, it struck me that, despite the confidence I had in my racing strategy—tight cornering, good geometry—I'd also have other drivers to contend with. And not one of them did I consider a friend.

It also suddenly hit me that I'd have the track to contend with—an experience for which, I could tell as I ran my first lap, driving around a grassy meadow hadn't prepared me at all. I ran slowly to start, following the outside of the track, discovering that the highest part of each banked turn was on the same elevation as the outside lane. This meant that running on the outside in the straightaways brought me into the high part of the corners, looking down the bank to the inside track. Running the inside in the straightaways led into the corners at the bottom of the banked turns. I wasn't exactly sure what to do with this knowledge, but for the time being I just tried to get used to it. Running slowly, the incline of the banked turns felt like the slope of a huge asphalt wave. As I gained speed, though, trying to build up my cornering speed gradually toward that "threshold" Uncle Harvey had mentioned, the track seemed to flatten out.

Still, the experience was very disorienting. The fact that I was looking out at traffic through a Plexiglas windshield, a plastic helmet facemask, and my glasses didn't help. With no side mirrors, just a rectangular rearview mirror in the car, I felt partially blind. I'd grown accustomed to the rumble of Theo's engine, but being surrounded by other rumbling engines was like being trapped in a car wash, except that, unlike in a car wash, cars leaped out of nowhere and up to my doors, sometimes one on each side of me in the same instant. My seat rode so low that I couldn't see Theo's front end, meaning I was never one hundred percent certain where the front end *was*. Add in the vibrations that seemed to travel from the asphalt, directly up my forearms, and into my neck and head, spreading across my chest along the way, and I found it impossible to hold a single, coherent thought.

Maybe I wasn't supposed to think.

That prospect made my heart race even faster. Thinking was something I was good at. In fact, outsmarting those guys was the cornerstone of my racing strategy.

Coming into the final straightaway after an indeterminate number of laps, I noticed the lap clock, a large board standing roughly ten yards back from turn three. The clock indicated less than a minute left in practice, so I hammered into the turn-three/turn-four bank to get one last sense of where that threshold of control was. I straightened out in the main straightaway, which ran along the infamous "Widowmaker" wall separating the track from the grandstands, and slowed way down to slide into the line of cars filing into the pits ahead of me. "Thundermaker Sportsmen," Bean announced over the more-subdued din of our idling four-cylinder engines, "please take to the racecourse for practice." I was drenched with sweat. I felt like I'd just run ten miles.

As I pulled into my slot, Jim walked to my door, crowbar resting on one shoulder like some British gentleman's umbrella. I yanked the steering wheel off its post and handed it to him. "How's it feel?" he said.

I pulled off my helmet and set it aside, unhitched my harness, and climbed out the window. "Pretty good," I said. "Good pickup in the straightaways. Handles well in the turns." I paused, struck by an image, viewed out my bedroom window, of Wade and Big Daddy having the same kind of post-race conversation in our driveway. I kicked one of Theo's front tires. "What would we do if my rig wasn't driving well?"

Jim shrugged. "I'm just the crowbar guy."

While the Thundermakers were running their practice laps, I tried to calm my nerves by flipping through Jim's GED booklet. I let my eye drift to the little ovals on a practice quiz and imagined myself zipping around and around. I also tried to ignore Bean as he welcomed spectators to the season opener and yammered about the Thundermaker drivers. Naturally, he didn't say a word about the Road Warriors.

Bean's disdain for our division was pretty much reflected in a race day's program. There was only one Road Warrior race but an entire *series* of Thundermaker races—qualifying heats leading up to the main event, known as the "feature." The Road Warrior "feature"—with no preceding qualifying heats—was usually wedged in between the last Thundermaker heat and the intermission event, which was whatever goofy halftime-type show Blodgett's staff had concocted for that day. In one popular intermission show I remembered from back when Wade started racing, the local Shriners Club—old men who organized charity events—staged a mock race in miniature cars that they also drove in town parades. They wore fezzes on their heads, the Shriners. I never figured out why. Or sometimes the intermission event found the winning Thundermaker drivers from the previous week's race crammed onto tricycles and running a sprint against kids picked from the grandstands. The intermission show was always followed by the ticket-stub raffle, in which a few thousand bucks went to whoever held the other half of the ticket Bean had some local celebrity pick out of a bucket down on the infield. Junior Miss Fliverton, whoever she was that year, picked the ticket once or twice over the course of a season, and a big-league baseball player from Fliverton named Kip Rochford made an appearance every so often.

I'd almost tuned Bean out completely, but when the words "Wade 'the Blade' LaPlante" pierced the high-pitched roar of the eight-cylinder cars, I reflexively looked up. Car 02 drifted off the track and slithered into the pits, a line of Thundermaker cars forming behind him. I watched Wade pass. His rig looked brand-new, his sponsors' names—VALLEY SAVINGS & TRUST and GRANITE AUTOLAND—popping out in gold letters against the royal blue.

"And with the Thundermakers back in the pits," Bean said, "all drivers are to report directly to the turn-one bleachers for a drivers' meeting."

Down the row of pits, drivers started walking toward the set of bleachers inside the pit area roughly behind turn one and the gate leading onto the racecourse. I handed Jim the GED booklet and, pretending to know what I was doing, followed the other drivers.

When I approached the bleachers, Mr. Blodgett saw me and checked something on his clipboard. I came around to the front of the bleachers and, seeing the stands two-thirds full of drivers, some of them sneering at me, some laughing openly, took a seat in the front row, my back to them.

Wade must've been one of the last drivers to arrive, because Mr. Blodgett glowered at him as he checked his clipboard. "Nice of you to join us, Wade," he said.

Wade wagged his thumb at me. "I figured I'd get the notes from my sister."

Everybody laughed.

Blood scorched my face.

If Mr. Blodgett was at all excited to get the season under way, he contained it well. Speaking in a gruff voice laced with exasperated inflections, he basically repeated some of the rules encoded in his ten-pound driver's manual. He issued a litany of threats to would-be cheaters, placing emphasis on two vehicle-related infractions—something called "boring out your cam lobes" and "clipped or heated springs"—and two driving-related infractions, the "bump-and-run," and "chopping." Uncle Harvey had told me about the bump-and-run, and Blodgett's discourse on chopping I remembered from the manual:

If the trailing car's front end is at least equal to your rear tire, you may not turn toward the trailing car. That is "chopping," and it will send you to the back of the line. If an accident results, you may be disqualified. Frequent choppers will face points deductions and monetary penalties or be barred from racing at Demon's Run Raceway.

In general, the scolding tone of Blodgett's speech seemed unfair, more like something one might expect to hear *after* a cheating-filled race day. But, then, he was known for running a tight ship, and that apparently started on day one of the season. I just tried to look like I understood what he was talking about.

Mr. Blodgett looked right at me at one point, toward the end of his talk, and said, "If you can't run a clean, fast race, then you can't run here. Stay home."

The other drivers ignored me as we walked back to our cars, which was a relief. They clearly spoke their own language back there, one that I'd never learned.

Bean's voice crackled over the scattered noise of engines and clanging metal tools. "I've just received word that the drivers' meeting is over," he said. "So, what do you say we get the season officially under way? And that means, Road Warriors, it's time to run what you brung. To the course for our first feature—twenty-five laps. Road Warriors. Folks, let's welcome the Crunch Bunch."

Scattered clapping and cheering kicked up in the stands.

"Show time," I said and eyed the GED booklet in Jim's hands. I was tempted to bring it into my car for good luck. Maybe I could sit on it and actually see where I was going. The booklet contained questions I could answer. The racetrack—it was a mathematical problem I was still working out.

Jim tossed the booklet onto the flatbed and handed me my helmet.

I followed him to Theo, conscious of being watched by other drivers, crewmembers, drivers' buddies, drivers' dads, drivers' girlfriends in T-shirts bearing their racecar-driving boyfriends' names. I tried to ignore them, focusing on my Chuck Taylors crossing the pits until I reached my door. I climbed in, strapped into my harness, jammed the steering wheel on the post, and fired up. The engine rumble freed a bead of sweat that trickled down my temple.

Jim banged his fist on the roof and stepped back, giving me a thumbs-up. We still weren't best friends, but I was grateful for even the small show of support.

Entering the track, I steered high onto the outside of the first banked turn, letting cars drift by on the inside as I waited to slide into my position. Being a brand-new driver, I was thirteenth in line out of fourteen cars. Kirby Mungeon must've registered after me, because he was dead last. Thus it was written in Blodgett's racing bible: *Newcomers start at the back. Learning to reach the front of the field through skillful driving is fundamental to the competitive racing practiced at Demon's Run.* This was fine with me, since starting near the back would, I figured, only make my performance more impressive—and expose this whole racing "sport" for what it was: testosterone-crazed idiots driving around and around in circles.

After we'd driven a couple of laps behind the pace car— a gleaming red station wagon with a flashing yellow light on the roof—a headphone-wearing track official standing in the backstretch made an X sign with what looked like two relay batons, signaling that we were to "cross over," or pair up, for the start. I took a few deep breaths as I rounded turn one and saw Kirby slide up beside me on the outside. I was already burning up inside my firesuit. I gripped and regripped the wheel, hands swelling inside my gloves. I just caught a very small bit of glare off my glasses as the sun peeked through the clouds.

We rolled around the track one more time, becoming a long column of pairs. Coming out of turn two and heading into the backstretch again, the pace car suddenly veered to the left and off the track, darting down a single asphalt lane cutting into the infield. The column of cars automatically compressed, like a squeezed accordion. We were running bumper-to-bumper into turn three. I looked across the infield and saw the flagman leaning over the track from his roost above the Widowmaker midway down the main straightaway. I turned back to the bumper of the car ahead of me, a white Mustang with a light-blue hood and number 25, his rear end bearing the words MAMA MIA'S PIZZA & DELI. I glanced at the flagman again, and he was already flapping the green. A clean start. An explosion of sound rocked my car and I instinctively punched the gas. Theo lurched.

As the column of cars started flying around the oval, I felt like someone had reached inside and was shaking me. I bit down and focused on the rear wheels of MAMA MIA 25. I ran a lap in line before the field began to shift, the pack loosening as racers made their first moves, sometimes stretching up the banked turns two or three cars across. I stayed as close as I could to car 25.

By lap three, Kirby was coming up hard on my right. I chased him down the length of the Widowmaker, keeping him from overtaking me in one blast. When he was only half a car length ahead, though, he cut hard in front of me—a clear chop. I had to lift to keep from getting clipped.

I was running dead last.

But I wasn't worried. I clung to Kirby's bumper as I entered turn one on lap four. Theo strained toward the outside, but I held him tight to the corner and sped up, slowly but steadily, right up to the point that I sensed the rear tires starting to skid. Lifting a touch, I stayed tight in the turn. Pulling into the straightaway, I hadn't lost an inch on Kirby.

Theo wanted to drift out in the straightaway, but I held him to the inside. I'd get Kirby on the next corner, I thought. Coming out of turn four, I floored the gas. Theo leaped, as if showing off for the Beer Belly Hill crowd.

As I reached turn one again, I backed off the gas. I held the inside track with two car widths between Kirby and me. Again, Theo pulled outside, but I pulled back, pushing him to the brink of control—finding my threshold.

In the second half of the turn, Kirby's truck flew down from the bank so fast that it seemed like he was about to drive across the track apron and into the infield. He chopped me again at precisely the spot where the turn opened into the straightaway. Somehow, he was now more than a car length ahead.

Sweat trickled into my eyes. I blinked, shook my head, and accelerated.

The inside lane belonged to Kirby, but I pushed Theo right up to the truck's rear, close enough to make out the row of Martian-looking men painted on the back end, each little Martian laughing and pointing at me. Maybe Kirby got anxious having me so close, because he drifted outside. When he'd given me almost one car width on the inside, I gunned for the space. It was a tight fit, and I accidentally tapped him. It was just a tap, though, and it didn't push him out much farther.

I lifted going into the turn and held the car as tight to the inside as I could while accelerating again. Theo's rear wheels slid a tiny bit, but I recovered. In the second half of the turn, my forearms stinging from wrestling Theo into our lane, it happened again: Kirby chopped me from the outside, plunging into the stretch. Only now he had a car on his outside and another one close behind him.

Behind him?

I glanced at the lap clock: I was only going into lap nine, but I was on the verge of being lapped.

My whole body was on fire, my head spinning. The numbers didn't lie: The inside lane was the shortest distance around the track. I was driving as fast as I could, in a car presumably as quick as the next guy's. I asked myself a question: *Why am I getting smoked?*

In the time it took me to get angry, I had another car on my right and another one on my tail. The car on my right, a midnight-blue Mustang adorned with silver 07s and INTERVALE FUN PARK AND DRIVING RANGE decals, was simply faster. At least it seemed that way. In one run down the backstretch, FUN PARK 07 edged up half a car length. He held his edge in the turn and overtook me in the next straightaway. One more corner, and he dropped in front of me. *Lapped.*

For the next few laps, I tailed car 07. I knew this driver, Dale Scott. He was the only member of Wade's crew who raced, and he got a fair amount of ridicule for running in the lowly Road Warrior division. Despite Dale's obvious speed, he seemed to be all over the track, moving outside and inside, outside and inside. Midway down the stretches, he drifted way out to the wall. At the start of the turn, he began crossing to the inside, shooting down the bank on a line leading to the start of the next straightaway.

Aha.

I tried driving Dale's line for a lap. *Yes.* It suddenly made sense: While hugging to the inside, I strained to keep Theo from going where he wanted to go—outside. Centrifugal force. I'd learned about it in physics class. Meanwhile, drivers like Dale and Kirby let their cars move to the outside in the corners so they could begin accelerating as they *approached* the straightaways. They were making a small sacrifice in the fight against centrifugal-force resistance in exchange for being able to accelerate even *before* they'd reached the stretches. Driving on the inside, I was cranking the wheel hard right up to the moment the track straightened out, delaying the moment when I could get my speed back up.

Though it privately shamed me, I had to acknowledge my error: A Demon's Run race wasn't about traveling the shortest distance around the track. There was a more complicated equation at work, one combining geometry *and* physics. How could I have been so stupid?

Fifteen laps into the twenty-five lap race, and I'd been lapped so many times I'd lost count. On lap sixteen, when the yellow caution flag came out, signaling a wreck somewhere on the track, the field slowed to about twenty miles per hour and stayed in position—a track rule. I tried to cobble together a revised strategy, but with the race volume diminished a bit, I could unfortunately hear Bean's voice over the speaker system: "And bringing up the rear is car six, Casey LaPlante, evidently sponsored anonymously by the high school Driver's Ed Department. That's some good, cautious driving, Casey." So much for my focus.

As I rounded turn two on the caution lap, I saw the reason for the yellow flag. Kirby's aggressive driving had apparently earned the FRENCHIE'S FIREWORKS truck a trip down the turn-three embankment. The Hook zipped along the shoulder of the track, three guys in jumpsuits riding on the bumpers.

Kirby must not have gone down that hard. As I rounded turn three, I saw that his truck was still upright. "And Kirby Mungeon makes Demon's Run history, folks," Bean said with a chuckle. "He's the first one of the season to get the Hook. Congratulations, Kirby."

As the line of thirteen remaining cars—twelve of them ahead of me—crossed over in the backstretch and then passed Beer Belly Hill, I glanced at the crowd. I regretted it an instant later. Unless I was hallucinating from body heat, people up there were having a blast, many of them laughing and pointing. At me. I was the life of the party.

That's it, I said to myself. *No more "cautious driving."* After the Hook had hauled Kirby's truck back to the pits, I set a new goal: Pass someone.

When the pace car darted off the track and the green flag dropped, I yanked Theo to the outside and gunned it.

Running alone far outside, I technically passed a few cars, but dropping down to the inside lane on the straightaways, I never seemed to get ahead of anyone.

I kept trying. Evidently, FUN PARK Dale Scott didn't care

for my strategy, especially after I nearly tagged him as I flew into the backstretch out of turn two, lifting but not soon enough to avoid tapping his rear bumper. His rear tires spun to the inside, he overcompensated by turning them back out, and in the process he lost a position to the white Mustang, MAMA MIA 25, which took him on the inside.

I went back to running the inside track, but that didn't work any better than it had initially. By lap twenty, I was physically and mentally drained. I'd pushed Theo as fast as . . . I could go. I'd found my threshold, and it wasn't good enough.

During a moment of self-pity, as I stewed in my firesuit, I lost focus long enough to get pinned to the Widowmaker by Dale coming out of turn four. Expecting him to drop down into the middle of the lane, I turned into him. I gave his car a smack—door to door. He must've smacked back with a strong pull on the wheel, because Theo scraped the last piece of Widowmaker before turn one, sailed off the top of the turn, and plunged toward the berm and fence fronting the pit.

I instinctively threw my car in neutral and took my foot off the gas, slamming on the brake and gripping the wheel with what strength I had left. I fishtailed in the grass, spun three hundred and sixty degrees, and slid to a stop facing the tire compound. Fortunately, thanks to the high-banked turn, I was invisible to the spectators. Unfortunately, I was perfectly visible to Wade and half his crew, including Fletcher, who were standing around car 02 on the other side of the fence. Wade smiled and waved.

As I stepped out of the car, I heard Bean say, ". . . car

six, newcomer Casey LaPlante. Spotters say she's fine, folks. Sugar and spice, but she may be thinking twice."

What I was thinking about, in fact, was going up to the announcer's booth and feeding Bean his microphone for lunch. Until I saw Theo's right side. My ride along the Widowmaker had peeled back the front panel like the lid on a tin of cat food.

The Hook crew ran around my car, unspooling cables and cranking winches. A lanky guy with a black buzzcut and wraparound sunglasses asked if I was OK.

"I'm fine," I said.

I looked at Theo again. He wasn't fine. The crew was already hooking him up. "Find a spot for yourself on the bumper," the guy said. "There's four laps left to go. Looks like you're done for today."

"Looks that way," I said.

As I approached the truck, a short, beefy guy with a goatee offered me a lift up. I ignored him at first but, realizing I could barely lift my arms, took his hand.

∞

Back in the pits, Jim watched me jump off the back of the Hook. "You all right?" he said.

"Fine. Don't know about the car, though."

The Hook crew lowered Theo into my slip and then jetted back to their position inside the pit gate at turn one.

Jim tossed his crowbar onto the flatbed, got a hammer and some work gloves from inside the cab, and walked over to the car. As he started banging away, trying to make the front end look like a car again, not a piece of modern art, I heard my mother call my name from over by the pit gate. She was standing on the spectators' side of the fence because each driver is only allowed so many pit passes, and Wade LaPlante Motorsports was carrying the maximum crew, and I hadn't signed her in as my crew. "Are you OK?" she said, and I felt the blood rush to my face as the drivers around me witnessed the spectacle. I gave her a silent thumbs-up, since I couldn't imagine saying anything that wouldn't make me sound like a bratty kid who simply wanted to be left alone. It didn't seem like a good way to act if I wanted the other drivers to take me seriously. She looked toward Wade's pit, and I turned too, seeing Big Daddy standing there, watching me. His expression was a little harder to read, but it looked more like annoyance than anything. I didn't bother to give him the thumbs-up. I figured Mom could do it for me.

The family reunion kept growing. When I turned back to my ride, Wade sauntered by, flanked by Fletcher and Lonnie Snapp.

"Where'd you get that tin can, Case?" Wade said. "You raid somebody's recycling bin?"

Lonnie laughed.

"Just kidding," Wade said. "Welcome to the world of short-track racing. Short track and a short *race* for you."

Lonnie laughed again, and as they walked away, he added, "Your sister's ride looks like my grandmother's car on the day they made her give up her license. She kept running over shopping carts in the parking lot at Wal-Mart."

I looked away, watched the other Road Warriors—the survivors—file off the track and back into the pit. "And car seven, Dale Scott, takes the checkered flag in this, our first Road Warrior feature of the season," Bean said over the loudspeakers. "Congratulations, Dale." A track official took the flag from the flagman and ran it over to Dale's window, and Dale began driving it around for his victory lap.

When I turned back around, I was startled to find Fletcher still standing in my pit. Jim flipped his chin at me from over by the wrecker, but I waved him off.

"How'd it feel out there?" Fletcher said.

Wade and Lonnie cast glances back, and Wade pointedly cleared his throat, but Fletcher ignored them.

"Things move a lot faster than I expected," I said.

Fletcher nodded. "Everybody says that, first time out."

"And you sit so low you can't see the front end. Weird."

Fletcher eyed Theo's front end as Jim ran a winch line from the wrecker. "Know why you bit the wall?" Fletcher said.

"Because it was there?"

"No. Well, yes and no." He pointed toward the main straightaway, where Dale was "returning the colors," as Bean said—in other words, bringing the checkered flag back to the flagman. "Coming out of four, Dale pinned you up high," Fletcher went on.

"I rapped him before that. I deserved it."

"Saw that. Point is, you didn't have to keep pushing with him. You could've lifted, dropped in behind."

I looked toward turn one, reliving the moment when Theo snacked on the Widowmaker. "Should I have? Lifted?"

Fletcher shook his head. "You said you were surprised at how fast the field moves. Seemed to me you were trying to keep your speed up. Thing is, you're not going to beat a racer like Dale by slamming at him for a lap or two. Guy is not new here, no offense, and he's a tough competitor."

"I learned that the hard way."

"Sometimes you need to just drive a good line for the better part of a race, improve your lap speed, and seize an opportunity if you see one. If."

"And if you don't?"

Fletcher shrugged. "There'll be other days."

"Patience, is what you're saying." I was reminded of Uncle Harvey's advice: *Take what the race brings you.*

Fletcher nodded. "TRS—a total race strategy, we call it back at Wade LaPlante Motorsports World Head-quarters." He smirked. "Still, at least you pushed yourself. You gave the fans something to watch."

"They're not my fans."

Fletcher turned to the grandstands and then back. "Not likely, no." He looked toward the ring of Thundermakers and trailers along the backside of the pits. The rest of Wade's team was circling car 02, gesturing, discussing, debating. "But still," Fletcher said, "now you've got your first race out of the way. That counts for something. Congratulations."

The strains of a horrific pop tune simpering out of the track loudspeakers diverted my attention to the main straightaway again, where a dozen or so girls in leotards were falling into formation, batons at their sides. "And now for a little intermission entertainment," Bean called out over the crowd. "Let's give a big Demon's Run welcome to the Brogansville Baton Brigade."

I turned back to Fletcher, but he was jogging away. I

shouted, "Thanks!" forgetting that human voices didn't travel well in that environment. I watched him, hoping he'd turn. He didn't. I felt stupid that I hadn't thanked him for the compliment. He didn't exactly say that I had any racing skills, but what he did say was sweet in its own way—if that word, *sweet*, had any place at Demon's Run.

Chapter 6

The Demon's Run season opener was historically followed by what I'd termed the Days of Shrieking. These were the days in May when Flu High females were asked to attend the prom. Tradition dictated that the prom be held over Memorial Day weekend late in the month. So, for the few weeks prior, the corridors echoed with the shrill sounds of young women announcing, at brain-cleaving frequencies, that they'd snagged a date. I did my best to stay sane during the Days of Shrieking, but it was never easy. I found myself continually on the brink of death-by-embarrassment for the way others of my gender behaved. Had I been more outgoing, I might've pleaded with the guys in my school to understand that not all women behaved that way. I'd have handed out ear protection.

Crossing the student parking lot and entering the school building the morning after my Demon's Run debut, such as it was, I was greeted by shrieks of romantic achievement piercing the lobby chatter. I navigated a pod of popular, curvy girls with button noses, smooth skin, and lips perpetually parted in glossy pouts—the Dolphins, I called them—who were jumping up and down, shrieking and clicking, and wagging their noses. I headed for my locker in the foreign languages hall.

Rounding the corner, I found myself stuck behind a wall of three guys—Bo something and the Gravelle twins,

Jesse and Jud—moving at a slow rate of speed. As I nearly collided with Bo, he glanced over his shoulder. Then he stepped out of the way, dragging the Gravelles with him. "Watch out, guys," he said. "It's Casey."

The Gravelles laughed and stepped aside. "Rookie of the Year," one of them said. I wasn't sure which one, since I'd never learned how to tell them apart.

"Yeah, in, like, fifty years maybe," the other Gravelle said.

It actually wasn't a bad joke—for a Gravelle.

"Look at her go," Bo said. "Just look."

I ignored them. I also ignored the I BRAKE FOR MOOSE bumper sticker stuck to my locker and the yellow caution flag someone had managed to stuff through the vents in my locker door. As I collected my books for my first-period class—English—I ignored the various automotive sounds guys made as they passed, especially the imitations of tires screeching and cars smashing.

I took out the book I'd been reading in English class, the library's hardcover edition of *The Great Gatsby,* and slid off the dust jacket. I pulled from my backpack *Racing for Keeps*, by famous autoracing guru Francis "Flip" Brackey, which I'd received in the mail the previous Saturday. I slid *The Great Gatsby* dust jacket over *Racing for Keeps* and closed my locker.

I read as I walked to class, avoiding eye contact with the dolts in my school who were deriving far more amusement out of my racing failure than it merited. I focused intently on every shred of advice that Flip Brackey had to offer so that I'd soon be able to shut everyone up.

I looked up as someone crossed my path so

closely that I almost tagged him: Fletcher.

He smiled and stopped.

I closed my book and smiled back but not too much.

"Must be a good book," he said.

"Oh, sure. Full of twists and turns."

"Speaking of which," he said, "I wanted to tell you again, you gave it a good run yesterday. You know, for a first timer."

"For a girl."

"That's not what I said."

Fletcher looked at his boots, and I felt mean.

"Anyway," he went on, seeming to regain his composure. "That's not what I wanted to talk to you about."

"What's up?"

He hesitated, but I knew what he was about to say. It was in the air.

"What about the prom?"

"The prom?" The words caught in my throat.

"Yeah. The prom. We go. Together. In the Dart. I'll wash it. It won't be that bad."

Fletcher smiled again, and I was struck by his confidence. He was known for being on the shy side, but right then he was standing tall, looking me in the eye.

I turned to suppress a blush. Fletcher had given me credit in the pits when no one else would, not even my own brother. Adding in the fact that it was one of the earlier Days of Shrieking, not those tense final days before the prom weekend, when dateless girls wandered the halls looking frantic and sleep-deprived, I felt safe in assuming that Fletcher sincerely wanted to take me to the prom. It was only those last-minute proposals that carried the stigma of being a second or third choice.

When I looked at him again, I thought I detected a twinge of nervousness in his eyes. His green eyes. That was OK, the nervousness. I didn't need another cocky guy in my life. Wade was worth a hundred of them. "Sure," I said.

"Great." Fletcher released a breath. "Well, we can talk details later—you know, dinner, parties, and whatnot."

"Right. We have some time."

"OK, so . . ." He started backing away, as if eager to escape. "I guess I'll see you around."

"I'm sure you will."

He laughed, and I laughed, even though neither of us had said anything particularly funny. He walked away, and as I rounded the corner by the guidance counselors' offices, I let out a shriek so faint that only I could hear it.

Chapter 7

Uncle Harvey was in a strange mood. While he must've expected that I'd want to race again, something about it seemed to bug him. His grouchiness flared up every time he looked at Theo's scarred front end. As I leaned against the shop workbench, he paced, disappeared behind a copper-colored sports car with its hood open, whacked on something, then reappeared. He yanked the rag from his pocket, cleaned off his hands, and shook his head at me.

"What?" I said for about the tenth time.

He disappeared again, invisible except for random clangs.

Jim rolled in with a mangled racecar on the flatbed. It looked bigger than a Road Warrior car, but it wasn't as tricked out as a Thundermaker. It was somewhere in between. I'd never seen one like it before. He drove around back.

"I told you it'd be dangerous," Uncle Harvey shouted from the sports car's front seat. He waved his wrench at me.

I hadn't complained about wrecking in the first place, so I didn't say anything.

He scrambled out of the car and crossed the shop, tossing the wrench onto the workbench. "What was I thinking?" He stopped in front of me, yanked out that rag, and shook his head again. "What in the world was I think-ing."

"I'm fine," I said.

"Oh, you think so, do you? You think taking a run down into the turn-one pokey is just fine?"

I honestly didn't know what to say. Drivers, especially Road Warriors, wrecked all the time. And it wasn't like I'd been driving carelessly when I crashed. I'd just got swept up in the competition, pushed myself a little too hard. Uncle Harvey's reaction was confusing. Confusing and unsettling. I feared he was going to tell me I couldn't race again, something he actually had the power to keep me from doing, since he did all the work on my car. Arguing with him didn't seem like a wise strategy.

Jim stepped into the shop doorway.

"What do you got?" Uncle Harvey said.

"Flying Tiger."

"Repairs?"

"Nah." Jim took off his baseball cap and wiped his fore-head with the back of his hand. "Parts. Kid over in Byam says he's done with it. He'll take three hundred. Struts are bent, but the battery's new. New pistons. Relatively new exhaust. According to him."

"Well, I'll take a look, and then we'll see what he'll take." Uncle Harvey fixed me with a stare. "Tell you what, Casey. Kid who cracked this car up is probably wearing stitches somewhere, maybe a cast."

"You don't know that for sure," I said, the words slip-ping out before I could stop them.

Uncle Harvey clenched his jaw and stormed out of the shop, around back, then back in again. "Did you get a *look* at that rig Jim hauled in?" he said, his eyes bulging as he gestured with his thumb out the door.

"From a distance."

He took a few steps toward me and, before I could react, started dragging me out of the shop by my sweat-shirt sleeve. I yanked the sleeve back but followed.

"Get in," he said when I reach the twisted hulk. The car's front panels, both of them, were peeled back like tin-foil from a casserole dish, and it looked like someone had dropped a load of boulders onto the roof. The body was black with rust-colored number 07s and the words CORKUM COUNTY ANIMAL HOSPITAL stenciled across the hood and panels. "Where'd this come from?" I asked because it couldn't have been Dale Scott's car 07. The FUN PARK car 07 was blue.

Uncle Harvey pointed at the driver's-side window. "In you go," he said.

I slid into the front seat, which was hard to do with the steering column almost pressing against my chest. The seat back was bent at a weird angle.

"Comfortable?" Uncle Harvey said. He pulled down a flap of metal on the front end and let it spring back. "Looks to me like this car was hit on both sides and maybe . . ." He scooted around to the rear. "Yup. And from behind. I don't think I need to tell you, from the look of the roof here, how this ride was sitting when it stopped moving."

"Upside down," I said, just to make sure he knew I was paying attention. What I really wanted to ask him was where the car had come from.

Uncle Harvey approached the driver's side and leaned

on the window. "But still, you aren't impressed. Don't think this could be you."

"I know it could," I said, trying not to whine or sound snotty. "I understand there are risks. I just . . ."

"What? You just what?"

"I just want to try again. I think I can do better."

Uncle Harvey slapped the door and stepped away. "No, it's personal, Casey. Just be straight about that. You don't like being laughed at. No one does. But, I'm telling you, racing to prove yourself to others, that's just the kind of . . . of objective . . ." He held me with a very stern look. "That's going to get you hurt."

I gazed across the bent surface of the hood. "So, OK, it's partly personal," I said. "So what?"

Uncle Harvey circled the car. "So, I don't like it, that's what. If it's *too* personal, it's more dangerous than it needs to be."

"It must be dangerous," I said. "It scared you off."

Uncle Harvey halted and squinted through the rear window frame.

Jim tapped him on the shoulder, but Uncle Harvey kept standing there, squinting. "I told the kid to call you tomorrow, Harvey," Jim said. "Three hundred he's asking."

"Fine," Uncle Harvey said. "I'll talk to him."

Jim walked to the tow truck.

"Hey, Jim," I said as he climbed up into the cab.

He flipped his chin at me.

"Where'd you get this car?"

"Byam," he said.

"Where's Byam?"

"Just east of Gale Falls. About a hundred miles south, give or take."

"Oh, right. Little place."

He nodded. "Maybe a couple thousand people. Used to be a granite town. Now there's a paper mill. Not much else." He gestured at the car I was sitting in. "Except a racetrack."

"Racetrack." I gripped the steering wheel.

Jim climbed into the truck and, a few moments later, bounced across the yard and out. When I turned back to Uncle Harvey, he was still giving me the stink-eye. "What?" I said.

"Just what did you mean by that?"

"By what?"

"By my being scared away."

I shrugged.

He stepped up to lean against the driver's-side window frame. "You want to know why I don't go to Demon's Run?" His voice was low and rough.

I nodded.

"Because I'm not welcome."

"Why?"

He stepped away. "That's my business. Understand?"

I didn't nod or say anything. I didn't understand anything but the fact that my uncle was in a foul mood.

He stared at the ground, arms crossed, one hand scratching at his chin stubble.

I tried shifting the gears but only got the stick into first. I tried ramming the stick into second. It wouldn't go. I pumped the clutch to make sure I was pressing it all the way down but got only a metal knocking sound when I tried to upshift.

"Still not convinced, are you?" Uncle Harvey said.

I rested my arm on the open window. "I'm racing again."

"You don't have the skills, Case. I'm telling you."

"Can I get them?"

"Not without seat time."

"What do you mean?"

"Seat time. The time it takes for you to feel like you're actually a racer, not a human roadblock getting in everyone's way. Most drivers need a whole season for that."

"I don't want to wait that long."

Uncle Harvey chuckled. "No. I can see that. I'm telling you, though, you're not speeding the process along if you've got a lot of other nonsense on your mind."

"Like what kind of nonsense?"

"You know what kind of nonsense, Casey. Demon's Run. You get rattled there, with your brother and everyone around. You'll never learn there."

I looked over the mashed front end of dead car 07. "What about Byam?" I said. "They race Road Warriors?"

"They call them street stocks down there, the four-cylinder division. The Flying Tiger, there, is an eight-cylinder car. But, yeah, your ride would probably be up to street-stock specs."

"You welcome at that track?"

"The Corkum County Speedbowl? As a matter of fact, I am welcome there. Slide on out now. You're making me nervous."

I climbed out, banging my right knee on the steering column.

"Speedbowl's just a touch longer than a quarter-mile," Uncle Harvey said, "but I doubt you'll notice the difference. I guess it's all new to you anyway. They're running a street-stock enduro a week from Saturday. I believe it's two hundred laps."

An enduro, I knew from past dinner-table conversations at Wade LaPlante Motorsports, is just what it sounds like: a long race under "green flag conditions," meaning there's no yellow caution flag for crackups. If there's a wreck, the other cars are supposed to drive around it while one special car tries to bump the breakdown out of the way. If there's a bad wreck, a red flag comes out and everyone stops where they are. When the green flag drops, the drivers jump on the gas. At least that was how they ran the enduros at Demon's Run. They held one or two over the course of each season, but they weren't prestige events. Wade called them "slamjams," also the local slang for a demolition derby.

"An enduro," I said. "There. That'll be some seat time. Can I get in?"

"I'll check and see, make a phone call." Uncle Harvey started for the shop.

"What about a few driving lessons in the meantime?" I said as I followed him.

"OK, *now* we're getting somewhere. Now we're talking." He spat into the grass. "Take your ride out into the field, there, and I'll give you some pointers." He spat again.

I spat, too.

Chapter 8

With the Corkum County Speedbowl enduro awaiting us at the end of our drive, Uncle Harvey became very involved in helping me formulate a racing strategy. Success, he said, would depend on "exit speed." And, as if I might not be able to remember those two little words, he kept repeating them—"exit speed, exit speed, exit speed." I didn't mind him repeating the words, but each time he said them, he'd remove his right hand from his steering wheel and draw a quick half-circle in the air. I had to lean back a few times to avoid getting smacked, and the sedan always jerked toward the shoulder. "You want to exit that corner with your foot punching that accelerator. Matting it."

"Matting it?"

"Mat it. Floor it. You want to be already accelerating when you hit the straightaway."

"Got it," I said. "I want to carry speed *away*, into the straightaways, not just take the shortest route around the turns. I'll add some distance to my path around the corner, but I'll be driving a line that'll give me optimal exit speed." I didn't disclose this to Uncle Harvey, but I'd already read all about exit speed in *Racing for Keeps* by Flip Brackey:

When you drive on "the line," you drive farther than

you would on the inside, but the added distance allows you proportionately greater speed coming out of the turn.

"That's right," Uncle Harvey said. "It's about how your car settles in the turns and how you come out."

"Radius."

"What?"

"The radius of the turn." I drew an imaginary oval in the dust on his dashboard. "The larger the radius, the least resistance."

The equation combines cornering force, the force of gravity, and turn radius measured in feet. Do the math (see table 4.1): Your line leads to better lap times.

Uncle Harvey looked at me like I was spouting gibberish. I'd have told him about studying Flip Brackey's book, but I didn't want to insult him. And I didn't want to be reminded of what, in my gut, I knew to be true: the notion of *studying* my way into winning stock-car races was foolish. Still, I clung to the idea. Studying was not only something I was good at, it was something I understood to be good behavior. This last point helped offset the anxious feeling that, by racing, I was doing something I wasn't supposed to be doing and that, sooner or later, someone would force me to quit.

Of course, that feeling had little to do with racing and everything to do with spending time with Uncle Harvey. We hadn't talked about that, not even on the long drive to Byam, but every time two seconds of silence fell between us, the fact that I'd crossed into forbidden territory to be with him surrounded us. Surrounded me, at least. Fortunately, racing put Uncle Harvey in a chatty mood. We experienced no more than two periods of two-second silence in the first fifty or sixty miles out of Fliverton. My drawing in the dashboard dust had brought about another.

Uncle Harvey squinted at the dust oval. "Radius," he said. "Hmm. Maybe so. Never thought of it like that. To keep it simple, remember that you're basically trying to make a circle out of an oval."

"Same thing. The *turn-in* point on the corner starts outside, not tight to the inside."

"You definitely want to avoid a lot of cornering on the inside. You're pinching your car driving that way, basically making a square out of the oval. Hard turn, straighten. Hard turn, straighten. That won't get you anywhere but the back of the pack."

"But with the wide arc going into the corner, I'm coming *down* from the top of the turn, *down* to the inside, picking up speed as I hit the inside of the second part of the turn, the *apex*. And then I 'mat it' into the straightaway toward the outside again, the *track-out*." I drew a couple of routes around the corners of my dashboard-dust racetrack.

Uncle Harvey reached over and erased the imaginary racecourse with his shirtsleeve, and, again, the car lurched toward the shoulder. "I need to clean this car," he said. "Anyway, well, sure, that's all great in theory, Casey, but you've still got to race a bunch of other drivers."

Thirty-two, to be exact, at least according to Uncle

Harvey's latest update from the Corkum County Speedbowl's director of racing, a man named Doug Ladd. Apparently, the Speedbowl didn't have a Thundermaker division, just four-cylinder street stocks and eight-cylinder Flying Tigers. Uncle Harvey said that this was because Thundermaker-type cars cost too much to buy and maintain, and the Corkum County economy was hurting. Not that Fliverton was a wealthy community, but we did have industries there. Our granite quarry was still operating, and we also had a printing plant and a pretty big furniture factory. And Wal-Mart, of course.

I gazed out the window, watching the robust farm country of Granite County yield to brown fields dotted with mobile homes. I glanced back at Jim, who was driving the wrecker alone with Theo on the flatbed. I considered waving but didn't. Jim was kind of grumpy in the morning.

About an hour later, we crossed the Byam town line, passed a cruddy strip mall, cruised down what seemed like a Main Street lined with stores—every fourth one with its windows boarded up—and turned down Speedbowl Road. About a half-mile farther, pulling into the Speedbowl lot, I understood what Uncle Harvey had been talking about with regards to the Corkum County economy. Uncle Harvey's beater sedan was a popular car there, at least among race fans. The grassy lot was full of them.

∾

Rolling into the pit area, I noticed three girls who looked roughly my age walking in a pack. The way they swaggered along, laughing and waving to people, led me to speculate they were popular—maybe Byam's equivalent of the Dolphins. Two of them wore tight-fitting T-shirts, and one girl was wearing a tube top. They all had on what looked like men's work pants cinched at the waist with wide leather belts and rolled up to the shin. They scuffed the dirt path leading into the pits in high-top sneakers with no socks. Their key accessory seemed to be sunglasses—the old-fashioned, square kind that made me think of the 1950s. All in all, it was a bizarre look they had going on—a look with an edge. They seemed more like Sharks than Dolphins. One girl, a redhead with a long braid, looked at me as Uncle Harvey and I passed. I looked away, but I'm sure she caught me staring.

A tall man with silver, slicked-back hair and roundish, pilot-style sunglasses stood outside a trailer, clipboard in hand, talking to a teenager in a black-and-neon-green fire-suit and black baseball cap and a man who looked like the kid's father. The guy with the clipboard said something that made all three of them laugh, then he whapped the kid on the butt with the clipboard. The kid and his dad walked away.

Seeing Uncle Harvey's car, the silver-haired man motioned for him to pull around behind the trailer, and then he checked something on his clipboard. Jim found a pit midway down the row and started maneuvering the flatbed into position.

"That the racing director?" I said as I got out of Uncle Harvey's car and walked around to the front of the trailer.

"Yeah. That's Ladd. Mr. Ladd, you call him. A good guy. He's an old friend, but he's still doing you a huge favor, letting me swap some repair work for your license fee."

"I'll pay you back."

"We're thinking about racing, Casey. That's all we're thinking about today. So listen to what Ladd says."

Uncle Harvey shook Ladd's hand while I hung back. Then I walked up and extended a hand. "Hello, Mr. Ladd."

"Casey," he said. "Welcome to the Speedbowl." He shook my hand. "Glad you came out. We always need new drivers, new blood—uh, I mean, not blood, but, well, you know what I mean." Mr. Ladd rested a hand on my shoulder—a gesture I wouldn't ordinarily have welcomed but one that seemed natural here. At least it wasn't a whap on the butt with a clipboard. "You ready to raise a little hell out there?" he said.

I wasn't sure what the correct answer was, since what I'd been hoping to do was run a full race without eating too much wall or getting knocked off the track. "Raising hell" wasn't on my to-do list. "I suppose I am," I said. Mr. Ladd and Uncle Harvey laughed. I guessed I'd given the right answer.

❧

My practice laps felt pretty good. Sure, I got plenty of cold looks from the other drivers, but that didn't bother me. Fletcher had been right: Getting that first race out of the way made me sit differently behind the wheel. I couldn't see Theo's front end, but it didn't unnerve me that much anymore. Also, being away from Demon's Run, out there in Byam, where no one knew me, I could focus better. Theo's mood also seemed to have improved. He handled great in the corners, even when I pushed him. This might've had something to do with what I'd heard Uncle Harvey saying to Jim back at the shop, something about making tire-pressure adjustments to account for the weather, which was supposed to be on the cool side.

Pulling into the pits after practice, I noticed the three mean-looking Speedbowl girls—the Sharks—flirting with the driver and crew two pits down from mine. They tracked me with their square shades as I climbed out the window and hovered around my ride, pretending to be inspecting it.

Uncle Harvey came over and nudged me in the arm. "Handles a lot better, doesn't she?" he said.

He, I mentally corrected him. "Definitely. I noticed it right away, especially in the turns." The redheaded Shark drifted toward Jim, who was sitting on the wrecker tailgate, thumbing through his GED booklet.

"Feel free to push it," Uncle Harvey said, gazing into the sky. "If the track warms up a little, we should still be OK. You're running two hundred laps, though, so expect your car not to respond as well in the later laps."

"Why's that?" I asked, thinking it'd be a triumph if I could stay in the race until these fabled "later laps."

"You're going to lose tread," Uncle Harvey said. "Track'll heat up, your tires will expand, and the car will start pushing across the asphalt instead of gripping as you turn. That's what we call 'pushing.'"

"What should I do then?"

"Save your tires by lifting on the gas going into the turns, but not braking. Drift your line in the corners, giving just a tap on the gas here and there, and then really mat it when you're ready to exit."

"Lift and tap."

"It's called feathering the throttle. You'll figure it out." He turned to the track. "Seat time," he said. "That's what today's all about, Casey. Seat time."

I looked over at Jim, who was surrounded by the Sharks and didn't seem happy about it. Catching my eye, he practically leaped off the tailgate. Halfway to me, he pulled a slip of paper from his back pocket and waved it. "We drew numbers," he said, handing me the slip. "Me and the other crew chiefs."

I read the slip: 19.

The track loudspeakers clicked on: "Drivers, please report for the drivers' meeting," the announcer said. "Drivers, all drivers, to the pit bleachers, please."

As the other drivers filed past, I looked around for the pit bleachers. I must've looked lost because the redhead Shark caught my eye and waved me over. "Which way are the pit bleachers?" I asked her.

"We'll get you there," she said. "Name's Bernadette. Bernie." She cocked her arm back, giving me one of those swooping handshakes the guys at Flu High gave each other.

"I'm Casey."

"This is Tammy," Bernie said, gesturing to the girl in the tube top, who nodded and adjusted her top.

"And she's Tammy too," Tube Top said, pointing at the girl in the pink T-shirt, who had most of her tar-black hair crammed inside a gray knit cap better suited to winter than to spring.

"We call her T.T.," Bernie said. "Tammy Too, get it?" She held up two fingers. "Or Two."

"Got it."

A few drivers walking ahead of us glanced back and snickered, laughed, said things I couldn't quite hear.

"Dogs," T.T. muttered. "Pig-dogs. This here is a pig-dog race."

I'd never heard of a pig-dog before but figured, judging by how T.T. used the term, that maybe pig and dog were words she attached to things she didn't like.

"You been driving long, Casey?" Bernie said.

"Nah, I was just in one race."

"One?" all three of them said.

"Yeah." I shrugged. "Wrecked with five laps to go."

"Drag," T.T. said.

"I was in last place anyway. Over in Fliverton."

"You wreck it good?" Bernie said.

"Good enough to need the Hook."

"Fricking stone," T.T. said.

I looked at her. "Stone?"

"A saying we have around here," Bernie said. "It means, like, rugged. Courageous."

"So, why are you running down here in Byam?" Tammy said, adjusting her tube top again. "It's kind of a hike from Fliverton, isn't it?"

"I guess it is. But I want to run this enduro. It's a long race. Maybe I can learn something . . . if I can stay in the thing."

"Aren't you, like, freaking?" Tammy added.

Two drivers passed us, each kind of sneering at me. I waited for them to walk out of earshot. "I'm wicked nervous," I said, "but not as bad as last race."

"Stone," T.T. repeated.

"That is pretty stone," Bernie said. "You're the only girl driver we've ever seen here. We were surprised to see you strap in for practice."

"I'm still a little surprised just to be here."

Bernie nodded in a definitive way, as if she'd made some sort of judgment. "Well all right then," she said.

T.T. jabbed a finger at the crowd of drivers gathering on the pit bleachers just ahead. "Run these skunk-pig-dogs," she said, smacking me on the back. "Run 'em hard."

"No guarantees," I said. "I'm not very good at this."

The Sharks slowed down, and as I drifted away from them, Bernie said, "Maybe not yet."

∞

The Corkum County Speedbowl drivers' meeting was almost identical to the Demon's Run meeting in content but completely opposite in tone. Mr. Ladd said he wanted his drivers to know that there would be teardowns if he suspected illegal car modifications but that he wasn't going to assume anyone was cheating. "You're a winner until we tear you down and discover otherwise," was how he put it. He gave a spiel similar to Mr. Blodgett's about the bump-and-run and chopping, but he presented it more as a clarification of the rules. "And remember," he added, "there are kids over there who look up to you as role models." He pointed toward the grandstands. "As ridiculous as that sounds." He smiled and a bunch of drivers laughed.

I turned around to look at some of the other drivers, but

most seemed to look right through me. A couple dropped their smiles when our eyes met.

"Now get out there and raise some hell," Mr. Ladd said and clapped his hands.

The bleachers shook as the drivers climbed down. I hung back, out of the stampede.

∾

The Sharks were waiting for me after the drivers' meeting, and we walked back to my pit together. Every ten steps or so, a couple of other drivers passed by and smirked. Each time, the Sharks provided a name and a couple of tips on how I might race such a "pig-dog," to use T.T.'s term.

The grandstand loudspeakers clicked as I reached Theo. "Drivers and race fans, we're ten minutes away from the start of the Corkum County Speedbowl spring street-stock enduro," the announcer said. "Street-stock drivers, return to your pits at this time, please."

Jim reached inside Theo and pulled out my helmet and the steering wheel. He handed me the helmet.

Uncle Harvey gestured for the Sharks to step back. "We're talking about an hour behind the wheel," he said, "probably a little more."

"Any last-minute strategies I should keep in mind?"

Uncle Harvey shook his head and looked toward the track. "Take what the race brings you. Patience." He clapped me on the back. "And keep turning left."

The field rolled around the track a few times behind the pace car, engine noise blocking out all other sound. We crossed over into pairs, and on the next lap, pulling up onto the high bank in turn two, the pace car accelerated and knifed its front end for the infield lane. Rounding turn three, I spotted the flagman down the front stretch leaning out, a green flag tucked under his arm. The announcer shouted something indecipherable. I took a few deep breaths and swallowed, my mouth salty with saliva the way it sometimes got after a grueling cross-country run just before I puked in the grass. A film of sweat coated my face. In the next instant, the lead cars rounded turn four, the green flag unfurled, and seemingly every driver out there matted the gas. Theo lunged into the main straightaway.

The field of racers seemed satisfied to run two laps in position, maybe to settle into the race, but the column of cars had loosened by the third lap. Coming into the main straightaway, I saw space open up on the outside, so I cut over and edged up on two cars heading into turn one. Coming out of turn two, I'd passed one cleanly, probably on engine and tires alone: Theo was feeling downright spry. In the backstretch, I slid to the inside barely far ahead enough of car 12—a lemon yellow ride with black numbers and lettering for BYAM CENTRAL BEVERAGE—to be innocent of chopping. I glanced in my rearview mirror and saw fifteen cars where, five seconds earlier, there'd been thirteen.

In turn one on the next lap, I drifted out and stayed high on the bank. I focused on getting to that line I'd driven during my practice run—the wide radius, the boundary between the shortest distance around and minimal resistance, the line that made the asphalt oval into the closest thing to a circle I could drive without flying off the race course. I had the line mapped out like this: In turn one, straddle the jellyfish-shaped oil spot. In turn two, run my right wheel over the tar blotch. Floor it. In turn three, run my left tire over the crack in the asphalt where a tuft of grass grew through. In turn four, trace with my right tire the smile of a skid mark midway up the bank. Stomp the gas. Exit speed.

I drove my line for a few laps. It was a good line, good enough, at least, to keep me from being passed. So I started thinking about being a passer.

Noticing the condition of car 03 ahead of me, a red metal box almost as stupid looking as Theo, with a banner in white paint for YANDOW PLUMBING & SEPTIC across the back end—but with few major dents—I considered the driver might've had some skills to keep his car looking so fresh. I got my right-front end up to his left-rear bumper and dogged him.

Car 03 didn't move much in the field, but in the turns I could tell he had a good line. I drove it with him for a couple of laps. Then I started to experiment. Drifting out from car 03, I took a wider arc midway through the turns, searching for a spot where the line around the corner straightened out sooner, allowing me to pick up speed a nanosecond earlier. I remembered something I'd read in *Racing for Keeps* by Flip Brackey about how, when two cars are running at the same speed, one leading and one trailing, the trailing car that pulls outside won't pass the lead car unless the driver can improve overall lap speed. And faster lap speed, I'd learned, began with corner exit speed—those gains in time that multiplied down the straightaways by entering the straightaways a mile or two per hour faster.

I started trying to nail a more precise spot in the turns that'd shoot me into the straightaway sooner. I stayed just to the outside of car 03 coming into the straightaways. I picked up a little distance on him on every lap—not enough to take him, but enough to let him know I was there. I worked him, wore him down, haunted him like a green ghost.

And I remained patient. Five, six laps later, PLUMBING & SEPTIC car 03 and I were dead even. He wobbled slightly on the inside, as if nervous running door-to-door. Maybe this driver got tweaked by collisions, I considered—hence his relatively dent-free ride. But I tried not to race *him* so much as the course for the next few laps, hugging my line, my better line. I just drove it and drove it and drove it.

Five more laps, gaining a foot or so every trip around the oval, and I had this kid. We came out of turn four on lap thirty-two and into the straightaway, and I just glided on over across car 03's front end, feeling him lift as I ripped the inside up the front stretch.

In turn one again, now running with no one beside me, I pushed Theo to see how he was holding up. His tires still gripped tightly, and he was still responsive to the steering. Then I thought about how *I* was holding up. Although I was soaked with sweat, the adrenaline rushing through my body wasn't messing with my stomach the way it had at the start of the race. I felt pretty good. No, better than good. I was genuinely having fun.

So I drove my line—jellyfish, tar blotch, tuft of grass,

smiley skid—watched my mirror, and felt for the slightest push in my tires settling in the corners. Car 03 stayed close, and a black Mustang with a number 88 painted in neon yellow pulled up even with him, but no one was blowing my doors off. No, one thing was obvious: I could maintain speed. I wasn't in anyone's way. I could race these guys.

The sun came out another ten laps or so later, throwing a glare across Theo's hood, stinging my eyes. I almost wanted to shut them and go to sleep. That's when I understood, in a way that I never had as a Demon's Run spectator, the nature of an enduro. The race was about half over, and, never mind Theo's tires or engine, I wondered if *I'd* endure to the end.

I was startled by a cloud of dust and smoke swirling in the turn ahead. Three cars tangled and spun down the banked corner, tumbling to the inside lane. One of them rolled backward into the infield. I looked in my mirror and found room on the outside, but not much. I slid over. Car 03 slid with me but not car 88, coming up on car 03's outside. He must've seen what I was trying to do because he chopped car 03 out of the way and kept moving down the track until he tapped me with his door. I mashed back against him as we went into turn one together. He slapped me back, trying to nudge me into the carnage clogging the inside lane, but I didn't let him. I slammed back even harder, accelerating in the turn. I felt my tires sliding across asphalt but car 88 holding me in place. As I passed the wreck, I yanked the steering wheel to the left and plunged into the straightaway. Exit speed.

I flew down the stretch and looked in my rearview mirror. A couple of cars that'd been ahead of me, but running on the inside lane where the three-car wreck settled, were now part of the mess. Car 88 was trying to take me on the inside, and I gave him some room there, knowing my best line was in the outside groove. When car 88 rapped me, I absorbed the blow and pushed back. Lifted in the turns. Feathered the throttle. Exiting the turns, I worked Theo for all he had. I lost track of time. Felt faint. Raced on.

Another rap on the driver's-side door from car 88 heading into turn one and I was through playing tag with this guy. I drifted out high on the banked turn heading to turn two and accelerated a second earlier than usual toward the straightaway. Car 88 tracked me with his front end on my tail. I looked in the mirror and assessed his position, concluding that he hadn't come up far enough on me to be technically passing. Car 88 was sticking his nose where it didn't belong. I told him so in the only way I could: I cranked the wheel left and forced him to lift—not a chop, more like rolling up a huge metal newspaper and threatening to slap him on the nose with it.

A swell of cheers from the grandstands and the announcer's manic shouting drew my attention to the flagman leaning out over the track. He waved the checkered flag as a column of cars—fifteen in all—sailed underneath it. The sixteenth car was mine. I'd done it. I'd endured.

ご

As I pulled into the pits, Uncle Harvey gave me a gap-toothed smile and a thumbs-up. I rolled into my slot and killed the engine. Even with the engine off, I felt like I was vibrating, the adrenaline still surging. Jim walked over to my window, and I took off my gloves and helmet and handed them to him. Then I yanked off the steering wheel and set it aside. I got out of the car and hopped down onto the grass, grabbing Jim's shoulder as my knees buckled.

"You OK?" he said.

"I feel like I just ran a marathon."

Uncle Harvey clapped his hands, then gestured with a thumb over his shoulder in the direction of the track. "Now that was a good, clean race. I notice you picked up a few positions by staying out of that wreck. There's a trick to file away for future reference."

I looked at Jim, detecting the trace of a smile. "Shoot," he grumbled a second later, glancing down the pits.

The Sharks approached, ignoring the eyes watching them pass. I had to admit, the sight of them walking together was hard not to give a second glance—something about the cool attitude they affected in their strange uniform, a uniform that announced to the world that they didn't care how they looked to others. Sure, they wanted people to look at them, and they seemed to gain power by ignoring the attention.

I felt honored, in a crazy sort of way, that they seemed to be heading for my pit.

Bernie gave me one of her swoop handshakes with a complicated tangle of fingers at the end. "You did all right out there, Casey," she said. "Not half-bad."

"I took that one driver, at least," I said. "Number three. The plumbing and septic car."

"Septic about describes him," T.T. said, tucking loose black hair into her cap. "That was Scooter Walsh."

The girls laughed—not the lilting laugh of the Flu High Dolphins. There was some bite in the Sharks' laugh.

At the sound of the tow truck door opening and shutting, they all quieted down. Jim came around the rear of the wrecker and pulled out a tire ramp. "Sorry to break this up," he said, "but I've got to get back to work."

"No problem," T.T. said, thumbs hooked in her pockets as she twisted back and forth at the waist.

Jim didn't look up.

When he was finished rolling Theo onto the flatbed, he gave me a light punch in the shoulder. "Good run, Casey," he said. "I'll catch up with you in a couple of days."

"Thanks, Jim. I appreciate your help."

The Sharks said nothing as they watched Jim drive away.

Uncle Harvey was talking to Mr. Ladd up in front of the racing director's trailer. He gestured for me to join them.

"I've got to go, too," I said. "Good meeting you."

"Jim, was it?" Bernie said.

The Sharks all looked at me, as if hanging on my words. "Yeah," I said. "Jim's my crew chief. He's my whole crew, actually, except my uncle."

"Well, he's plenty, that Jim," Tammy said, fixing her tube top again. "He's not your man?" Her cell phone rang. She pulled it from her pocket, examined the display, and silenced the ringer.

"Jim's just a friend," I said, "and my crew."

"Big Jim," T.T. said, tugging her pockets with her thumbs.

"What about you?" Bernie said, her sunglasses passing over me like an airport metal detector. "Got a boyfriend? Girlfriend?"

I looked at the ground for a second, not sure how to respond. "I've got a date to the prom. Does that count?"

"The prom," T.T. laughed. "Hey, Bernie, you get asked to the prom yet?"

Bernie turned toward the track. A tall driver in a brown firesuit, maybe thinking that she was watching him, waved. She didn't wave back. Another driver a couple of pits down, a guy roughly Wade's age, leaned against the front panel of his car, drinking a cup of coffee. With his shades on, I couldn't tell what he was looking at, but it seemed to be Bernie, me, or one of the other Sharks.

Bernie turned in his direction.

He raised his coffee cup to her.

"This here is my prom," she said and waved back. She didn't walk over, though. She slid her shades onto her forehead, and when she smiled at me, her blue eyes made it easy to see why she was so popular around there. "You coming back next week?"

I looked at Uncle Harvey, who waved me over more ani-matedly. "I'm up for it," I said. "Definitely."

"We're going to need your number," Tammy said, pointing her phone at me.

"Yeah, and I've got to show you something." Bernie took a step closer and extended her right hand. "Shake," she said. She gripped my hand and shook it. As I was pulling my hand away, she hooked her fingers in mine. "Hook them," she said. "That's one. Then it's two, the thumbs." She tapped her thumbprint against mine. "Now flex out your fingers so that the backs of your fingers flick against mine." I did it. "That's three. Now hit palms." I smacked palms with her. "Four," she said. "Now do it fast. Shake, hook, thumb, flick, palms."

I did the handshake again, and then a second time, and by the third time, I had it down.

"It's the Byam grip," Bernie said. "It's just for the three of us—well, four now." She slid her shades back down and looked toward the driver drinking coffee down pit row. "Come back anytime you want, Casey. We'll be right here."

Chapter 9

When I came downstairs the next morning, Wade LaPlante Motorsports World Headquarters was in full-on pre-race preparation mode. The driveway and garage were a frenzy of males arguing and drills shrieking, an engine grumbling periodically as if to punctuate the noise. As I passed through the dining room on my way to the back patio door, I saw Fletcher through the door leading from the kitchen to the garage. We exchanged a quick wave.

I stepped outside and gauged the weather—just a tad breezy. I zipped my cross-country sweatshirt and started out on a long, slow loop—long enough so that, by the time I returned, the entire Wade LaPlante Motorsports team would be up at Demon's Run.

I ran about five miles out, three back, and then walked the last two miles home so that I could pass through the village, which I knew would be quiet as people drove home from breakfast or church and headed up to the race-track. A few people waved from inside their stores as I strolled by. As I reached the corner by the Coffee Pot Café, an elderly man and woman across the street turned around. "Hi, Casey," the man said. I recognized them: Mr. and Mrs. Prout. Mr. Prout had been the superintend-ent of schools when I began at Fliverton Elementary. Mrs.

Prout had been my mother's piano teacher when Mom was a kid.

As I waved to the Prouts and passed through an invisible cloud of coffee vapors, I felt swaddled in a cocoon of safety—unlike the jittery feeling I got driving past the abandoned buildings and boarded-up storefronts of Byam. I felt like I'd just stepped out of the Willow River, and a few good neighbors were wrapping me in a towel just because they'd watched me grow up, they knew my family, and this mattered to them, when all that mattered to me was that I get far, far away. I wondered if they'd care about me when I was gone.

I walked all the way home, skirting the river for the last mile or so, eager to hear the steady hum of the spring thaw coursing through the valley. The morning had grown overcast, the water turning pencil-lead gray, but the damp soil smelled of spring, and the willow trees, recently stiff in the winter air, now leaned over the flow.

Standing at the water's edge, I remembered how, when I was very young, I used to imagine the river leading to the ocean, and the ocean leading to some exotic destination, like the places I wrote essays about in school: Spain, Egypt, Australia. Some days, if Mom and I decided to sit on the dock and read (which we never did after Wade started racing Karts), I'd pretend that boats passing by had come from those places and that the people aboard were not familiar at all. They weren't the same people I saw every day in town. They didn't even speak English.

I gazed downriver and wondered if I'd miss this

spot when I was finally kicking through the fallen leaves scattered along the cobblestone walkways of the Cray College campus. I knew I would.

∾

Jim and Uncle Harvey didn't even look up from their work in the shop as Hilda and I crested the hill and crossed the yard.

Uncle Harvey had a gauge in one hand and a rag in the other. Jim rested one boot on Theo's front end. As I stepped into the garage, I spotted the GED booklet on the workbench.

"How's it going?" I said.

"Not too bad," Uncle Harvey said. "You got out of Saturday's race in pretty good shape, all things considered."

"Felt pretty good."

"Speaking of which," Uncle Harvey said, "I'm parched. You two want anything?"

"I'm set," Jim said, chatty as ever.

"Nothing for me, thanks," I said.

Uncle Harvey stepped into the yard.

Jim took a rag from his back pocket and wiped his hands, then tossed the rag onto the workbench.

I picked up his GED booklet. "Want me to quiz you?"

Instead of his usual grousing, Jim said, "Go ahead," and he slid his boot off Theo and crossed his arms.

I flipped to the section on geometry. "So, you've got a right triangle."

"Yup."

"You've got the two smaller sides—"

"The sum of the squares of both of the short sides equals the third side squared. The hypotenuse. The long side. That one."

"Nicely done."

"Pythagorean theorem."

"You've been studying."

Jim leaned back on his boots and looked across the yard.

"Do you mind me asking you a personal question?" I said.

Jim walked to the edge of the garage. For a second, I thought he was going to leave, but he stopped and looked into the sky. "Probably going to get some weather," he said.

I walked over and stood next to him. "Maybe a little."

After a minute or so, during which thunder pounded dully off in the distance, probably still a couple of towns away, Jim said, "You want to know why I didn't finish high school?"

"Yeah. I mean, I don't blame you. School can be pretty boring."

"I ran away from home some years ago."

I didn't know what to say to that.

"Had to," Jim added. "Got into some trouble, most of it my fault, but not all of it."

"Where was this?"

Jim set his jaw and narrowed his eyes, as if he'd spotted a snake in the yard. "I don't like talking about it," he said.

I held my words, not wanting to find myself standing there with grumpy Jim Biggins, the sullen John Henry of the pits, instead of the guy who, a couple of minutes earlier, seemed to be having the tiniest bit of fun with a GED quiz.

"Point is, I'm getting settled here," he said and nodded at the booklet in my hands. "One step at a time."

"Seems like you might be ready to pass this thing."

He took the booklet from me and flipped through the pages. "I didn't even know about this until I came here," he said. "Didn't even know taking this test was an option. No one had told me." He shook his head. "Didn't know about anything. Just kind of flailed around. It's funny, the things you have to learn if you don't have someone to show you. Simple, little things. But I'm getting it."

"How'd you find out about the GED?"

Still flipping through the pages, he gestured toward the cottage. "Towed a car up here one day and got to talking to Harvey."

I looked at the house, where I spotted Uncle Harvey passing by the living room window. For the first time, I noticed the flowers in the flower box under the window—white flowers. I also noted that he'd planted some others in a pot on the front steps. There was something very inviting about the cottage, despite the side and back lawns being a junkyard—car and truck bodies in various states of demolition, his fishing boat leaning against the shop, the narrow tin shed listing a bit to one side under the weight of a motorcycle frame.

"He ever talk to you about racing?" I said.

Jim laughed softly. "Lately it's all we ever talk about. You keep us pretty busy."

"I know," I said, my eye resting on the tin shed. "And I'm grateful, believe me."

Jim closed his book. "Harvey's helped me out a lot. I was a lost puppy when I hit town. Like I said, he's the one who told me about the GED. And when I took it and flunked it, he said I just had to study harder, but if I needed a quiet place to study, I could use the shop or the cottage if he was working. That was, oh, two or three months ago." Jim laughed again. "I've got to tell you, Casey, I've never seen him this happy. Now, I don't know the man well, but he seems twenty years younger than he was before you got him all hooked back into racing. Talk about racing? Try to get him *not* to talk about racing."

"I meant, like, *his* racing. When he and my dad had their team. He ever talk about that?"

"Strange, isn't it?" Jim said, looking toward the house. "You'd think he would. But, then, he doesn't seem to care much for people around here."

"That's not so strange."

Uncle Harvey emerged from the cottage.

Thunder crackled again, closer, seeming to creep up from the south.

Jim left in the wrecker, and Uncle Harvey started tinkering with Theo.

"Well, I should be going," I said. "I've got to work."

Uncle Harvey, crouched down next to Theo's left front tire and looking up into the wheel well, just waved a wrench at me.

Halfway to Hilda, I stopped in my tracks at the sight of my mother's blue station wagon turning up Uncle Harvey's driveway. I reflexively turned to my uncle, who, maybe sensing something strange in the air, stood, leaving the wrench on the shop floor. He shot me a puzzled look, maybe because of the expression on my own face: horror.

Uncle Harvey walked no farther than the threshold of the shop as my mother pulled into the yard and got out of her car. "Hi, Harvey," she said, sounding relatively cheerful considering the rather menacing glint in her eyes as she approached me.

"Hello, Carol," Uncle Harvey said and stuffed his hands in his pockets.

"Hi, Mom," I said, just to say something.

She walked up close enough to hug me. But she didn't hug me. "I'm very disappointed," she said in a low voice, as if to keep this conversation between the two of us.

"I didn't think you'd let me — "

"You didn't think, that's what you didn't do," she said. "You didn't think how I'd feel to be lied to." She scanned the wreck-strewn yard. " 'Behind the industrial arts wing,' did you say?" She let out a huff. "Why, that looks like your car right over there."

"You never told me I couldn't come up here," I said.

Mom narrowed her eyes. "And you never said that you *were* coming up here."

"Would you have let me?"

Mom hesitated.

"What about Big Daddy?"

A look of panic flashed in her eyes.

"See? No one cares about what I do until I do something they don't like — "

"I signed your release form," Mom said. "I trusted you."

123

I didn't have a response, so I looked away, reflexively turning to Uncle Harvey, who was still standing on the threshold of the shop, looking very uncomfortable.

"Can I get anybody anything?" he said, stepping into the yard.

I shook my head.

"No, thanks," Mom said.

"Well, suit yourselves." As he passed us, Uncle Harvey pasted on a smile so fake it looked painful, and nodded at Mom. "Carol. Good to see you."

"You too, Harvey." Mom's smile also looked fake, but she seemed to wear it more easily.

Uncle Harvey retreated into his little house.

The break in my exchange with Mom had evidently bolstered my confidence, because as soon as Uncle Harvey's front door closed behind him, I asked her, "What happened between him and Big Daddy?"

Mom winced as if I'd just pinched her. "That," she said, "is a very private matter, one I doubt you'd find interesting —"

"So, why do you think I just asked you about it? I'm interested."

Mom looked at me, seemingly exploring my eyes for evidence that I could be trusted. A couple of seconds later, she turned away again, letting a vacant stare fall on her car. "I can't tell you," she said.

"Can't or won't?"

"Now is not the time," she said, still not looking at me.

Neither of us said anything for a minute or so, during which I sensed, from the set of Mom's jaw and the distance in her gaze, that now really wasn't the time. She seemed a long way away, and I worried that bringing her back to be hammered with questions might produce undesirable results for me and my budding racing career. No, if she wanted to keep this secret, I'd let her . . . for now.

"How'd you find out that I was coming here?" I said delicately.

Mom turned toward Uncle Harvey's house, a strangely sad look tugging at the corners of her eyes and mouth. "I had a feeling from the very beginning," she said. "And then I followed that tow-truck driver." She regarded me, still wearing that sad expression, but smiled faintly. Her smile didn't last but a couple of seconds, though, before she looked away again in the general direction of town. "We're not going to discuss this meeting," she said. "Up here. Understand?"

I nodded and crossed my arms, turning my attention to Theo in the shop. "But I've got to keep racing."

Mom waited a few seconds before letting out a sigh. "Fine," she said. "Be careful."

As she got into her car and drove off, a tingle rippled through my arms and legs with the realization that Mom hadn't come up to Uncle Harvey's to shut down my racing career. No, she'd come to see what I knew about what had come between my father and my uncle. She'd come to see if I knew their secret—the secret that, I suddenly understood, might've been even more dangerous than racecar driving.

My limbs were still tingling as I listened to Mom's car engine fading on down the road. My cell phone rang, and, right away, my heart slipped into my stomach. I didn't have to look at the number to know who it was. "Hello, Ms. Egan," I said.

"Hello, Casey?" She spoke in the la-di-da voice that she sometimes used to create the impression that something was no big deal when, obviously, it was.

"Ms. Egan, I'm so sorry. I'm on my way, but . . ."

Ms. Egan gave me a moment to offer an excuse, but I couldn't come up with one. "That's fine," she said—*la di da, la di da*. "I was just concerned that you might have forgotten."

"No, I just . . . I've been running a little behind schedule today."

"Not to worry. We'll see you soon then?"

The way she phrased this as a question made my face light up, as if she didn't quite believe that I'd show up, even though I'd never *not* shown up in the five years I'd been baby-sitting and tutoring Blaine and Maddy. "I'm five minutes away," I said, shortening the actual time by about ten minutes to give the impression that I'd been booking it toward their place for fifteen minutes already.

"OK," she said. "The kids will be eager to see you."

"I'll be right there."

I crammed the phone in my pocket. "Got to run," I said to Uncle Harvey as he stepped back out of his house. "See you tomorrow afternoon?"

"I'll be here," he said and waved.

I sprinted across the lawn.

ॐ

Fortunately, there were few cars on the roads, since every one was up at Demon's Run, so I let Hilda gallop a little, let her drift toward the centerline on the wide turns, trying to find that invisible line, that wide radius where power and resistance made their peace. She settled in the corners pretty well, responding to the steering like she did the day I drove her home. Good girl.

I slowed down for a tighter left turn with about two miles to go before the Egans' road and eased around, eyeing the road for that spot where the curve met the straightaway. I lifted but didn't brake, and when Hilda's nose seemed to straighten out, I punched the gas, feeling her lunge into the stretch as if shoved from behind. Exit speed.

I blew through gears like snapping my fingers, and in a few seconds, I was splitting the difference between my "five minute" white lie to Ms. Egan and the truth. The sun flashed in my mirrors suddenly, flickering as if through a stand of trees. I reached for the visor and, while glancing up, discovered that it wasn't the sun but flashing lights behind me. Chief Concave was right on my tail.

I pulled over. Although I was tempted to make a quick call to Ms. Egan, I decided that this might only make the Chief angrier than he probably was. I had no idea how fast I'd been going, but it was likely pretty fast. I got my registration out of the glove compartment, hoping that maybe saving the chief from having to ask for it would improve his mood. I rolled down my window.

"Casey," the chief said, resting a hand on Hilda's roof.

"Hello, Chief Congreve."

"You in a hurry?"

"Yessir. I'm late for work."

"And now you're going to be even more late."

"Appears that way."

"Tell me something." He shifted his weight but didn't reach for his ticket book—a good sign. "You make a lot of money at this job of yours?"

"No, not a lot. I'm saving for college."

"College. I see. Got a bright future ahead of you, don't you?"

"I'd like to think so, sir."

"Sure, you do. You're a smart girl. There's just one problem."

"What's that, sir?"

"You hit a tree going as fast as you were going back there and you're not going to college. You're not even going to the emergency room. We even get you out of that car alive . . ." He put his hands on his hips and stared at the ground for a moment, as if to calm himself. With a snort, he shook his head then looked at me again. "You understand what I'm saying?"

"Yessir."

"And you're saving for college, you said. Saving your money?"

"That's right."

"If I write you a ticket, well, that's going to put a little crimp in your savings, isn't it?"

"Yessir."

"Yes indeed."

"I'm very sorry, Chief Congreve. I just . . . I was paying attention to the road, watching for cars."

"You didn't see me, though, did you?"

"No. I didn't."

"Thought I might be up at the races."

I didn't say anything. I was getting the distinct impression that the chief would rather have been at the races than dealing with me. This was something we had in common.

"Problem is, Casey, I've got a job to do. Got to make sure the roads are safe for the people who aren't at the races."

"I understand. I'm very sorry—"

"Rumor has it you tried your hand at racing up at Demon's."

"Yessir. Two weeks ago." If there was a bright spot in this exchange, it was that any rumors of my Corkum County Speedbowl debut that were circulating in Fliverton hadn't reached the chief, which meant that maybe no rumors were circulating at all.

"Well, how'd that go?"

"It didn't."

"How's that?"

"I didn't do well at all. Wrecked. Didn't even finish."

"Ah. I see. Well, your brother's doing pretty good."

"Yes, he is."

"He might put Fliverton on the Circuit map yet."

"Let's hope so."

At this, Chief Congreve leaned to rest his hands on my window and look me in the eye. "Do you really hope so?"

"I do."

"That's interesting."

"Sir?"

"Oh, just that, well, the last time I saw you, you were talking to your Uncle Harvey, down at the fishing access."

Again I said nothing.

"I sometimes feel like he doesn't hope so," the chief said. "Don't ask me why, but I just get that sense. He certainly didn't hope so for your daddy."

"But he was my father's crew chief."

"And a good one too. Circuit-level all around—and a genius about tires, people said. But I guess family matters are personal matters." Chief Congreve straightened up and his gaze traveled up and down the road. A truck rumbled over the hill to the south, and as it blew past, the driver and the chief exchanged a wave. "Casey, I'm going to give you a warning," he finally said.

"Thanks. I really can't afford a ticket."

"But I've got to tell you, it most genuinely upset me to see you hammering along the way you were."

"I understand. I'll slow down, Chief."

"Yes, you will. Now get to work safely." He turned and walked back to his cruiser. As I tracked him in my rearview mirror, my heart started racing. And it wasn't out of fear that I might be about to lose my job. I realized, as Chief Congreve got into his car, that somewhere in that block head of his lingered a detail of our local history that no one had ever told me, something about Big Daddy and Uncle Harvey's racing days—*family matters are personal matters*. I could've got out of my car, walked back there, and asked the chief about it. I was that close to the answer. But I didn't want to press my luck. And I didn't want to be any tardier than I already was. And, deep down, I was a little afraid of what the chief might tell me.

Chapter 10

As I came downstairs early that following Saturday, I was puzzled by the sound of the television coming from the living room. Neither my mother nor Big Daddy was a regular television watcher, and while I might've called Wade's sense of humor about as sophisticated as the average cartoon, he never watched much television either. Stepping into the dining room, I glanced into the living room to find Wade and Big Daddy both sitting there, Big Daddy in his chair and Wade on the couch, watching what must've been a DVD of a Demon's Run race.

"See, Savard was pushing you out in turn four," Big Daddy said.

"I remember."

"And you let him. He pushed you off your line."

"I didn't lift, though—"

"Watch." Big Daddy snapped his fingers and pointed at the screen. "You're right. You didn't lift. And look at your back end coming down along the Widowmaker. You're out of control there, Wade. Out. Of. Control—"

"I got it back—"

"You want me to rewind that thing so you can see it again? You were out of control. I'm telling you, if you don't get your head on straight—"

"I won the race, didn't I?" Wade grumbled and turned to Big Daddy. In the process, he spotted me watching them. A cheesy grin broke across his face. "Good morning, prom queen."

"Prom's tonight, Wade," I said.

"It's tonight?" Big Daddy asked Wade, which didn't make sense, since I was the one going to the prom.

"Where you off to now?" Wade added. "Going to get your hair done? Maybe get a manicure?"

"That's right," I said and walked into the kitchen. I opened the refrigerator door, which blocked Wade's view of me. I stood there for a few moments, rooting around in the crisper for an apple, letting the blood drain from my face.

"Going to get . . . a pedicure?" Wade sang as I shut the door.

"Yup, the whole deal." I bit into the apple. "Enjoy your cartoons," I said and turned my back on them.

∾

By the time Uncle Harvey and I pulled into the Corkum County Speedbowl pits, the Sharks had already staked out a slot, the three of them hovering there in identical mint-green T-shirts. Bernie had her sleeves rolled up and the shirt knotted above her bellybutton. When Jim swung the wrecker around behind them, they turned, and I read the words printed on their shirts:

GO CASEY GO RACING

As Uncle Harvey and I got out of the car, T.T. approached with some shirts slung over her shoulder. She tossed one to each of us and veered toward Jim, who was wearing his just-let-me-work face. T.T. tossed him a shirt anyway. He caught it, held it up, then looked at Bernie and Tammy, who stood with their hands in their back pockets, staring at him from behind their sunglasses. "Thanks," he said with the enthusiasm of a bucket of driveway sealant.

Uncle Harvey pulled his T-shirt over his windbreaker and summoned the Sharks to gather round. He yanked a notebook from his pocket and handed it to T.T. Jim lowered Theo into the pit just as the announcer gave the ten-minute warning for practice. I walked over to help him.

"They got you a T-shirt, guy," I said and bumped my shoulder against his.

"This'll go over real well down at the diner—"

"Oh, you can't wear it in town, Jim."

He smirked. "I wouldn't wear this in front of a firing squad."

"Well, will you at least wear it here?"

With a deep sigh, he wrestled the T-shirt over his work shirt, taking care to pull the collars so they flapped out from beneath the T-shirt. "If it'll keep them out of my face, I'll try anything."

"Oh, you love it."

"Whatever you say, Casey," he muttered, pointing to the letters on his chest. "You're the boss."

∾

As I pulled off the track after my practice run, Jim was sitting on the wrecker tailgate, thumbing through his GED booklet while Tammy, T.T., and Bernie huddled around Uncle Harvey. Uncle Harvey held a tire upright on the flatbed while Bernie fiddled with the valve and a tire gauge. I cut the engine, climbed out the window, and walked over to the wrecker, where I set my helmet and gloves down next to a white metal tank about the size of a scuba tank.

"Well?" Uncle Harvey said. "How's the car handling?"

"Pretty good," I said, "but it's cornering weirdly. More like, it's *not* cornering." I leaned against the flatbed.

Uncle Harvey looked at Bernie, T.T., and Tammy as if he'd been expecting me to say this.

"Tight," Bernie said with a definitive nod. She turned to Uncle Harvey. "Her car's tight. Pushes instead of turns."

He nodded and scratched at his stubble. "Sounds that way." He looked at the track. "So, ladies, let's see if we can put this all together." He stuck out his thumb. "Car's tight, and we've got a track that's still a little wet. Now, the weather report says the clouds will burn off in about an hour, just about the time the track's dry. What does that mean to you gals?"

"It's going to get warmer," T.T. said. "Air temperature and the asphalt both."

"That's going to bring the tire pressure up," Tammy added. "The air inside will expand."

Uncle Harvey extended his index and middle fingers. "Tight. Warmer. Increased tire pressure." He looked at Bernie and let his hand drop to his side. "Who's making the call?"

"Where's the tire pressure at now?" she said.

Uncle Harvey smiled. "That's the right question. We're

134

at maximum pressure or close to it."

"Well . . ." Bernie bounced the tire gauge on the tire. "We could probably lose a few pounds all the way around, let the tires spread out and grip a little better."

"Now remember what I said before," Uncle Harvey interjected. "It's your right front tire that's bearing the greatest load in the corners. You feel that, Case?"

I nodded. "Feels like the whole rig wants to dig into the track on the right."

"So," Uncle Harvey continued. "We can let out some air. I like that idea. But let's make sure we keep the pressures higher on the right than on the left, to account for the load shifting from the rear of the car to the front, on the right side in particular, as Casey slows in the corner and pulls the steering wheel left."

"Stagger," T.T. said.

We looked at her as if she'd just sworn at us for no reason.

"Stagger," she repeated. "The difference between the pressures on the right and left sides. Pressure makes the tires bigger, and you can measure it, the size of a tire, and compare it to the tire on the other side. The difference is called the stagger. I read up on it. We can figure out stagger to get the car settling in the corners better."

Uncle Harvey scratched his stubble, a gesture I'd come to know meant that he was either worried or impressed. This time he was clearly impressed. "Stagger," he said. "Yes. I know something about this. Nice work, Tee." He reached onto the flatbed and picked up a U-shaped metal bar about a foot wide at the tips. "And what we've got here is a gauge to measure that very thing. This device is, in fact, known as a stagger gauge." He handed the gauge to T. T. and smiled at me. "Casey, unless I've never set foot in a short-track pit before, I'd say you've got yourself quite a crew here."

As the Sharks went around with the air tank adjusting the tire pressures to the stagger ratios Uncle Harvey gave them, he and I sat on the wrecker tailgate together, watching the Flying Tigers run their practice laps. "You seem to be getting the hang of racing, Casey," he said. "And you seem to be enjoying it. That surprise you at all?"

I nodded. It was a strange thing to admit, but since my ill-fated debut at Demon's Run, I'd come to crave the adrenaline rush of racing. As a cross-country runner, I'd experienced those rushes before, but more out of nervousness, and they only lasted until I settled into my running pace. Strapped in behind the wheel, there was no such thing as pace, not really—just a hunger for speed, an almost animal instinct to pounce on a choice piece of asphalt. We drivers literally roared at each other, racing side by side. We nipped at tails, shoved each other out of the way hard enough to send each other slamming into walls. Cross-country running was never like that.

I could've said all this to Uncle Harvey, but I sensed he knew it already. He seemed to know me well. In the time we'd spent together up in his shop and driving over here to Byam, he seemed to have got to know me better than anyone ever had.

"You think hard about what you're doing, I can tell," he said. He tapped his temple with a grease black fingertip. "You're tracksmart. I expected you would be. You've got racing in your blood."

For the first time in my life, my family ties to racing cheered me the slightest bit. As I watched Uncle Harvey gaze down pit row, as if being transported back to his glory days, I couldn't hold the question back: "Was Big Daddy tracksmart?"

Uncle Harvey's lips drew into a taut line, his jaw muscles working, his eyes narrowing on a spot about ten feet ahead of him. I'd seen this reaction before: from Big Daddy on those rare occasions over the years when Uncle Harvey's name had come up at the dinner table. Unlike Big Daddy, however, Uncle Harvey didn't just scowl off into space for a few moments. He walked away.

◦◦◦

When I got back to the pit after the driver's meeting, the morning clouds had burned off. The crew and I—minus Jim, who was reading his GED booklet on the wrecker tailgate—sat on Theo's hood and went over the day's competitors, a rundown drawn from the Sharks' knowledge of the local drivers and information gathered cruising pit row. T.T. seemed particularly into this part of my race preparations. "Remember, you're racing drivers, not just cars," she said in a serious tone that didn't really match her ski cap and goofy sunglasses.

"Good point," I said as Bernie and Tammy both swallowed a laugh.

"I'm going to give you a few names and numbers," T.T. said.

"Look at *you*," Tammy said. "All schoolteachery."

T.T. frowned, then, noticing the way she was holding

the notebook in front of her, like a book from which she'd been reciting poetry, started laughing. "These are the cars you don't want to be stuck behind," she said, once again serious. "Today, these guys won't be the movers. And if you *do* find yourself with the wrong crowd, start thinking about a lane change. If you see the caution flag come out for a wreck, try to move quickly so you don't get behind these guys on the restart."

"Got it," I said.

As T.T. was finishing our pre-race briefing, the track loudspeakers clicked on, and the announcer ran down the starting positions. I'd learned that, unlike in an enduro, in which starting positions were often determined by a lottery, most regular races used a statistical formula to assign track position. Handicapping, Uncle Harvey had called the formula, and he said that it was usually an average of a racer's previous finishes. For my twenty-five lapper at the Speedbowl, track officials had me lining up fifteenth out of twenty-two, starting inside of car 55.

Bernie punched me in the shoulder. "These guys want a piece of you. You're in for some bump-and-run, guaranteed."

"If they want to push you off the track," Tammy added, "make them work for it."

"But most of all," T.T. said, "just try to run your race."

I slid off the hood. Tammy ran around behind me and leaned inside the car before I got there, yanking out my gloves, helmet, and steering wheel. I was struck by the realization that, about a week earlier, I'd have crossed the street to avoid passing these girls, but suddenly they were treating me like a queen. No, better: like one of them.

I felt like a different person driving a completely different car. Theo's tires seemed custom-fitted to the track. As I ran a couple of laps behind the pace car, I tried to get a fix on who was positioned where. The Farnham brothers, Buck in CHIMNEY CORNERS MAXI-MART car 04 and Chuck in MAXI-MART car 05, were in the front half of the pack — mine for the taking, according to T.T. Ty Baxter's BAXTER BROS. HEATING & VENTILATION car 21 — " a moving road-block," T.T.'d called him — was directly ahead of me, in the thirteen slot. That made getting out of his lane my first priority. I squeezed the steering wheel: It was good to have a goal.

As I took turn three on my second pre-start lap, the pace car darted for the infield, and I spotted the flagman holding the green flag at his side. As I came out of turn four, an earthquake of engine power rolled back from the front of the pack. In the most remote corner of my peripheral vision, with my eyes focused on Ty Baxter's rear bumper, I saw a green flag flapping — a clean start. I jammed the accelerator to the floor.

We ran two settle-in laps more or less in position. In the third lap, rounding turn four, I gunned to the outside, forcing car 55 to lift, nearly scraping his sponsor's name — TESSIER'S GARDEN CENTER — from his door. I pulled up even with Ty's car 21. I ran him down the front in the outside groove and into the first turn. When he didn't drift to bump me farther out, I looked for the first mark I'd chosen while finding my line during practice, a skid mark with treads still visible. I rolled over it with my right tire and looked for my turn-two mark, a cauliflower-shaped grease splotch. I hit it. Accelerated in the turn.

Already, going into the backstretch, I could tell that I had a better line than Ty. I'd picked up at least a wheel's worth of track on him. He drifted out closer to me and gave me a tap. I pulled down close to him—and did it sharply. I felt him lift. Reflex action.

In turns three and four, I drove over my marks: a circular tar blotch about the size of a cow patty and an X-shaped crack in the asphalt. I accelerated going into the straightaway.

I opened Theo up and dogged Buck Farnham's car 04 on the outside going into the next turn. He stayed far enough away for me to drive my line. It was a good line. I could feel it. I was making a nice little circle out of this oval. Exit speed.

I took Buck's car 04 on the outside and ran right up to brother Chuck's car 05 bumper. Chuck swayed to the inside, clearly aware of my presence. I followed him to the inside and lifted in the turns, feathering the throttle. Going into the straightaway, I ran up to car 05's bumper again. Chuck swayed to the outside. I followed him, noticing, as I headed into the next turn, that if I trimmed my line closer to the inside, I could almost drive the line perfectly and still have the inside track on him. That was my next move. I dropped down the bank and gunned the gas, sticking my front end as far into the gap between the inside of car 05 and the inside of the track apron as it'd fit. I kept it there, holding the wheel steady and running this line, inching as close to my marks as I could in the turns. Two laps of this, and I'd coaxed car 05 a bit farther to the outside. Good. I could drive my line and push Chuck out, where he'd have more distance to cover. Bad geometry—for him.

Two laps later, the Farnham brothers' car 04 and car 05 were in my rearview mirror. I was in the tenth position. I drove my line but increased the acceleration in the corners right up to the point at which Theo's rear tires started to slide. I tried to record in my bones and muscles how the speed felt when I hit that threshold, so I'd know I was at that breaking point just before I felt it next time. I drove on. Hit my marks. Drove my line. Drove.

Another two laps later, heading into the main straightaway, I spotted car 01, a severely dented Tempo with red numbers on a gray body and sponsorship lettering for GLUCK'S PUB, dancing in my rearview. The car reminded me of a water rat, and Bernie had called the driver, a kid named Perry something, "totally off his chain." Water Rat wanted the inside lane. It was a gamble that, this late in the race, I was willing to take. He'd pinch his car cornering tight to the apron while I stuck to my line. I ran a lap and looked back. Water Rat had gained a little on me, but his right front tire must've still been short of my left rear. Maybe Water Rat wanted his rat nose slapped. I considered the option.

Rolling into turn one again, I glanced across the infield to see car 88 and the car right on his tail, car 25, starting to skid sideways toward the inside lane just around turn two. Car 25 almost regained control, but he must've overcompensated. He and car 88 spun down the bank. I lifted and let Water Rat come up on the inside, then I accelerated to keep him from passing. Around the corner,

141

I guided him right into car 25 and car 88, both of which had just stopped dead, car 88's dented hood spewing smoke. Water Rat had to brake. I rolled up to turn three and spotted the flagman waving the yellow caution. We all eased off for the restart.

As I moved slowly around the track while the caution flag was still out, I surveyed the field. Water Rat had fallen back two track positions for getting hung up in the wreck, and two other cars originally ahead of me had met the same fate. I was in seventh place. Scooter Walsh in his red box PLUMBING & SEPTIC car 03 was right behind me.

I rolled with the column of cars behind the pace car, and when the pace car darted to the infield, I scrunched up with the pack. Coming around turn four for the start, Scooter roared to my outside, cheating me a little, but the flagman was focused on the leaders, so the green flag dropped. I matted the gas but lifted a second later as the car in front of me, a yellow Mustang with a blue number 11, hesitated long enough for me to read the words MR. MUSIC D.J., a Web address, and phone number stretched across his rear end.

Scooter's slight gain, combined with the slow car in front of me, gave car 03 a half-car-length lead heading into turn three. If he was driving his line, though, it was farther out than mine. I got my right tires just to the inside of my mark. My exit speed was not optimal, but I kept up with Scooter, losing only a wheel's worth of track in another lap.

Heading into the backstretch, I drifted to the outside, not far enough to tap Scooter but far enough to budge him. In the next turns, I came closer to hitting my marks.

My exit speed improved. I was racing Scooter dead even in another lap, and Buck Farnham's car 04 seemed to want a piece of Scooter's rear end. I ran with those guys as close as I could to my line, watching for nonsense in my rearview mirror.

Sure enough, heading into turn one, Buck decided to play bump-and-run. He tapped Scooter, whose rear tires slid to the outside. I accelerated and dropped to the inside track to avoid Scooter's spinning front end. I got knocked on the right rear, but I was ready for it. I lifted and rolled around turn two, and then lead-footed to make up exit speed.

As soon as I was in the straightaway, I glanced across the infield, where two other cars were now spinning like square dancers in the front stretch. The two cars ahead of me were running to the outside. In the next turn, I plunged down to the inside before they could react. Around the next corner, I hugged the inside but moved at top speed while the drivers on the outside slowed for the wreck. I blew by them.

Welcome to second place. Problem was, I realized, as the field followed the pace car around the track, the flag-man had the white flag under his arm while he waved the yellow caution flag. White flag: On the restart, it was going to be the lead car's last lap.

The leader, an orange Tempo with a blue number 76, shimmied as I pulled up alongside him, crossing over in the backstretch. I didn't know the driver, but I did know that he'd held the lead the whole race. He'd started out in the lead, in fact. I knew I could safely assume that he was running a good car, but I also thought I could assume one more thing—and hang my final-lap strategy on that notion.

On the drive over to Byam, Uncle Harvey had told me that sometimes the driver in first place will push his car too hard, trying to drive his line, maintain maximum speed, and keep an eye out for people coming up on either side all at the same time. Unless the driver in car 76 were some kind of racecar-driving Albert Einstein, fighting off the entire field for twenty-four laps must've been a rigorous mental workout. If his car was still running strong, I figured, then maybe *he* was at the breaking point.

The pace car darted for the infield, and we rolled into turn three. Rounding turn four, I saw the flagman leaning out with the green. Car 76 accelerated a split second sooner than I'd expected and pulled ahead almost a full car length. I must've been thinking too much. I gunned Theo's engine and made my decision.

Knowing Theo was running fast and cornering well, I favored the inside on car 76 as we blew down the main straightaway. Instead of drifting out to run my line in turn one, I held the inside track, watching to see if car 76's white-knuckle driving would lead him wide in the turn. I stuck right to his bumper as he drifted outside—way out—at the top of the turn one–turn two bank. I drifted with him, eyeing a spot pretty close to my optimal turn-two mark, the cauliflower grease splotch, and made a quick move to exit as I passed it.

In the backstretch, I owned the inside track, so I matted the gas and stayed as close to car 76 as I could, keeping the pressure on. Again, Car 76 left a lot of room for me down the center of turn three, so I went a little farther outside than on the previous corner. I felt the difference in my line. Car 76 fought me, hugged close, but we both must've felt Theo pulling ahead on the good line. I hit my turn-four mark—X-shaped asphalt crack—and matted the gas for home.

I pushed the pedal to the floor until my ankle hurt. I locked my arms and held my breath. I flew under that checkered flag. Before anyone else.

∾

I ran a victory lap with the checkered flag, probably driving a little faster than winners usually do, since I was pressed for time. At the pit gate, the Sharks waved me in like they were landing a jet that'd just flown through a violent storm—which, I guess, I had. Jim and Uncle Harvey stood back, Jim with the crowbar resting on his shoulder, Uncle Harvey with his arms folded but wearing a huge jack-o'-lantern smile. I smacked Theo's dashboard with my right hand and let out a whoop. My ears popped.

I pulled into my pit, killed the engine, yanked off my steering wheel, and hurled it out the window as far as I could. The Sharks rushed over and practically dragged me out of the car. We tumbled onto the ground, shrieking and rolling and acting like little girls. But we didn't care.

After the Sharks and I picked ourselves back up, Uncle Harvey walked over. "Just plain good short-track racing," he said. "You see?" He rested his hands on the shoulders of my firesuit. "You run a clean race, you run *your* race, and it pays off."

Jim stepped up and pulled me to his beefy side. "Good run," he said, then strode over to Theo.

A few moments later, my name was announced over the loudspeakers. "Go on and get your trophy," Uncle Harvey said, gesturing toward the pit gate.

The moment I stepped onto the track, I felt dizzy, the high-banked corners and rubber-rutted grooves playing tricks with my sense of up and down. Then the adrenaline spike of triumph yielded to the anxiety of public speaking. When I reached the announcer—a thin, middle-aged man in khaki pants, a gray windbreaker, and thick glasses—he said, "And here she is, folks, your street-stock winner, Fliverton's Casey LaPlante." I felt the urge to vomit. "Casey, we haven't had but a couple of women racers since I can remember. How'd it feel running out there with the Corkum County boys?"

"Pretty good," I said. "I definitely ran the best race I could, I got a couple lucky breaks, and I guess that's what it took to get to Victory Lane today."

"You ran real strong in those last laps. What made the difference, do you think?"

"Tires. Getting a good tire setup and also getting a sense of who was moving around the track and who wasn't. Got to thank my crew for that."

"Well, congratulations, Casey. Great run. Folks, let's hear it for your street-stock winner, Casey LaPlante."

A smattering of applause.

The announcer gave me my trophy and I turned and jogged back to the pits.

As soon as I passed through the gate, the Sharks handed me a bag of dresses, like relay racers passing a baton. I flipped them a speedy Byam grip and sprinted for Uncle

Harvey's car, which was idling up next to Mr. Ladd's trailer. "Thanks, Jim," I called to him as he winched Theo onto the flatbed.

He smiled—a smile that I'd never seen before. "Have a great time at the prom," he said.

❧

The whole way back to Uncle Harvey's, I prayed that we didn't get pulled over, not that we were tearing up the country roads in his junker. Still, he knew I was running late if I intended to go out on one decent date in my high school career. We passed through light rain showers about thirty miles from the Fliverton town line, but by the time I was scrambling across Uncle Harvey's slick lawn toward Hilda, the rain had let up.

I fought the urge to floor it all the way home. With one warning from Chief Congreve already, I took it easy down roads where he might be hiding, cornered more cautiously.

Pulling into the driveway, I could see, through the open garage and kitchen side doors, Fletcher sitting at the dining room table. I walked in the front door, dashed up the stairs, and dove into my room.

I tossed the bag of dresses onto my bed, got undressed, and sprinted to the bathroom to take a shower. I stepped under the water so fast that it was still warming up. I let out an involuntary little shriek.

Back in my room about one minute later, I poured the dresses onto my bed and, standing before my closet mirror, frantically held them up in front of myself, one after the other. Naturally, they were all on the short side, and a couple were so slinky that I doubted the prom chaperones would've let me in wearing them. The school district had gotten strict about that. I glanced at the clock on my nightstand — 7:15 — and grabbed the next dress. It was black and long enough, but it appeared to be made of fabric, again, too sheer for district standards. My eyes began to sting as tears gathered.

Mom knocked on my door.

"How's it coming in there?" she said.

I didn't answer.

"Casey, can I come in?" She nudged the door open and, seeing me standing in front of the closet in a slip, wrinkled her brow. "Why, you're not dressed. Fletcher's — "

"I know."

"Everything OK?"

I took a deep breath and swallowed. "Just nervous."

Mom smiled the girlish smile that I usually found supremely annoying. In that moment, it was actually welcome. "Here," she said, stepping to the bed and picking up the last dress. "Let me help you."

She stood behind me and reached around so that I could see the dress in the mirror. It was very nice — longer than the others, cream-colored with the faintest shimmer. Although it was sleeveless and tied in back, halterlike, the V-neck front didn't plunge so low that I'd be showing too much skin for our school district. The dress was both modest and, in its sleekness, kind of sexy. "Oh, this is darling," Mom said. "Where'd you get it?"

"A friend loaned it to me."

"Well, she must be quite an elegant young lady."

"She is," I said and, for a second, imagined all three Sharks standing reflected in the mirror, smiling with approval. I reflexively smiled back, and Mom caught me.

"Lovely," she said. "You look lovely."

Chapter 11

Fletcher was a perfect gentleman. He pulled my chair out as we were seated for dinner at a nice inn out near the Fliverton-Brogansville line, and he stood when I got up to check my lipstick. Yes, at my mother's insistence, I'd applied a coat of glossy lipstick the color of honey. Fletcher stood again when I returned.

Our conversation got off to a slow start, mainly because we both seemed to be avoiding anything having to do with racing or Wade, which was the only obvious thing we had in common. Eventually, though, after our appetizers arrived, we settled into an easier conversational rhythm. Fletcher asked more questions about college than I felt comfortable answering, since he told me he didn't think he'd be able to go for a couple of years. The thought of him being stuck in Fliverton for the rest of his life made me sad. The thought of anyone being stuck in Fliverton made me sad.

So I got him talking about his new job. He'd been working part-time in the furniture factory on the east side of town, but one of the foremen there had recently left to start a company doing custom cabinetry, and he'd hired Fletcher as an apprentice. I came up with lots of questions about wood and how carpenters managed to get it into so many shapes. When I realized that I was eating a lot faster than Fletcher was, on account of my making him do all the talking, I began telling him about a desk belonging to my Grandma Phyllis, which had innumerable drawers of various sizes.

Fletcher said he was familiar with this type of desk. As he delved into its history, he fell behind again in the dining portion of our evening.

～

The prom was held out at the Granite County Golf & Country Club. Against their better judgment, the prom entertainment committee had hired Center of Detention, a punk band from Brogansville, and they created an undercurrent of chaos that, I sensed, would become an overcurrent of chaos before the night was through. Fletcher and I danced a little, but he seemed to enjoy it about as much as I did, which was not much, although he moved better than the average Fliverton guy. The Dolphins swam through it all, checking everyone out almost as often as they checked themselves out.

At one point, while I was freshening my lipstick in the ladies' room, three prominent Dolphins, members of the prom organizing committee named Stacey, Fiona, and Brittany—I privately knew them as Squeaky, Fishy, and Beachball—complimented me on my dress and hair, which I took to be only a half compliment, since anyone who'd ever seen me before would've known that I hadn't done anything special with my hair, just gelled it back and fastened it with a barrette. I thanked them and reciprocated, making sure to compliment their dresses as well as their choice in entertainment.

When I returned from the ladies' room, the prom was spiraling into the abyss. Some football players had taken trophy deer heads down from a special off-limits part of the club and were running around goring each other with the antlers. Center of Detention had moved into the hardcore portion of their set, so the dance floor was empty except for eight guys from the Young Republicans Club slamming into one another. Several Dolphins were taking it all badly enough to break into crying jags. The chaperones—Mr. and Ms. Weaver, U.S. History and Biology, respectively, and the new Spanish teacher, a frail-looking woman in a tweed suit—anxiously orbited the proceedings. The Spanish teacher stopped at a table where three couples were making out so vigorously that I could practically hear their teeth clacking through the guitar feedback. The teacher leaned to tap the bare shoulder of the girl nearest her.

Fletcher must've been watching me because, when I spotted him standing near the door leading to the patio, he was laughing so hard that he had one hand on his stomach, the other gripping a chair back. I started laughing, too, laughing and dodging Young Republicans who shot out from the dance floor every few steps.

When I reached Fletcher, he opened the door for me, and we stumbled out.

∾

Fletcher's Dart was about the ninth or tenth car to pull into the lot down at the fishing access. The weather had remained mild and had even cleared some. The river reflected moonlight through a smoky darkness that hung still, almost like summer. Someone had built a fire, and a cluster of guys converged around a project—a keg, no doubt—at forest's edge.

Fletcher opened my door. As I stepped onto the dirt, he gestured toward the back seat. "There's a sweatshirt in there if you get cold," he said.

"Thanks."

A few people called Fletcher's name as we approached the fire, and he returned the greeting but motioned for me to follow him out onto the dock.

Neither Fletcher nor I said anything for a while, instead just listening to the river rushing past. Finally he laughed, and I could tell, from the sound of it, that he was thinking about the prom. "What a fiasco," he said.

"Mayhem," I agreed. "Center of Detention? I mean, what was the prom committee thinking?"

We were silent again for a while, and a flock of Canada geese flew past—*Branta canadensis*—low to the water's surface. But, for once, I didn't think much about the geese. Didn't think about their migratory patterns. Didn't think about anything. I just waited for that moment when I'd feel Fletcher's arm gather me to his side.

There. Or was it a breeze glancing my shoulder?

At that very moment someone ripped a redneck wolf call into the night as a familiar engine rumbled down the access road.

I turned to see the Red Snake kicking up pebbles as Wade rocketed into the lot, fishtailing, the showoff, before pulling in behind Fletcher's Dart. A couple of guys let out additional wolf calls, in case the first one had been unclear, as Wade cut the engine and got out. Maxine

Shaw—*not* Gail Wiggans—stepped out of the passenger side.

"That pig," I muttered.

"Wade, dude," Fletcher said with a shake of his head.

I watched Wade and Maxine walk over to the keg. He waved to the people by the fire. Maxine clung to his side, casting dreamy glances all around.

I suddenly wished that I were one of those geese flying by, and I remembered everything about their migratory patterns. I wished that I were anyone, anything, but Wade LaPlante's little sister.

Wade was far enough away that I couldn't hear what he was saying, just a bunch of grunting and laughing.

"You all right, Casey?" Fletcher said. "Want to leave?"

"Fletcher!" Wade shouted before I could answer. "Get over here, guy!"

Fletcher's eyes narrowed, as if he were trying to make Wade magically disappear. He turned to me, but I looked away.

"No way am I talking to him tonight," I said.

"I'm his crew chief. I kind of have to," Fletcher said, not sounding convinced that this was true. "I'll be right back. OK? And then we can leave if you want."

I didn't say anything.

Fletcher touched my shoulder—I was positive that it was his hand this time. "You want me to get that sweatshirt?"

I took his hand and gave it a squeeze. "I'll get it," I said. "Do what you have to do. Then let's go somewhere else."

I crossed the parking lot in the opposite direction. As mad as I was at Wade, I was also experiencing something good I'd never felt down at the fishing access before: what it felt like not to be alone on a Saturday night. Still, I wished the Sharks were there. They probably wouldn't have liked the Flu High crowd, but I could see them getting along with Fletcher just fine.

"Did you see Wade's sister's dress?" a girl said as she and a group of people passed me on their way toward the fire. I must've been invisible in the darkness.

"Beautiful," another girl said. "She's actually a very pretty girl . . . for being so stuck-up."

I slowed my pace.

A couple of the others laughed, then a guy said, "Fletcher lucked out."

"Hey," a girl scolded. "You wish Wade had made *you* take her? Huh?"

Everyone laughed again.

"Fletcher's a team player, that's for sure," the first guy said. "Taking one for the team."

"A guy could do worse," the other guy said.

"Hey," the same girl scolded again.

A breeze kicked up, almost knocking me over as my knees wobbled. I took a few steps toward Fletcher's car and stopped, covered my face with my hands. Two more people passed by without seeming to notice me, as if I'd already become invisible again, as if I'd never been visible to begin with.

Wade's laugh cut through the night like a hyena calling to the rest of the pack. I turned to see him slapping Fletcher on the chest, Maxine's arms wrapped around him from behind, her head pressed into his back. Wade laughed again, and so did the people around the fire. I

155

walked directly to Wade's car, reached through the driver's-side window, and flicked my hand around until I hit the keys dangling in the ignition. In three fluid motions, I 1) opened the driver's-side door, 2) slid behind the wheel, and 3) fired up the Red Snake. I gunned the engine, threw the car into reverse, and whipped it around toward the woods. I aimed the front end at the road and pulled the lights on. I slammed the car in gear and punched the gas. Clicking on the high beams, I caught a deer bounding over the road fifty yards ahead—*Odocoileus virginianus*. "That's right!" I screamed. "Out of my way!"

❧

Uncle Harvey must've heard me coming up his road because he was standing on the front steps when I pulled into the yard. "Nice ride," he said as I got out. "Looks familiar."

"I want to race tomorrow," I said, slamming the door.

"There's no racing tomorrow. Tomorrow's Sunday."

"Demon's Run."

Uncle Harvey didn't say anything. He just let me stand there, breathing heavily. "My, don't you look fetching?" he finally said.

"I'm racing tomorrow."

Uncle Harvey sat down on the steps and scratched his ankles. "Would you mind telling me what you're doing with your brother's car?"

"I borrowed it. I want to race at Demon's Run."

"Now, just why would you want to do that?"

"It's personal."

"Oh, it's personal all right. You don't need to tell me that. It's been personal since the get-go, and here you are, in your brother's cherry Nova. Hoo!" He slapped a hand against the steps.

"I'm doing it."

Uncle Harvey rubbed his eyes for a few seconds and then leaned back on his hands. "Well, you're going to have to do it without me, kid," he said, "because I'm just plain full-out uninterested in what goes on over to Demon's Run."

"Why?"

"Never you mind why. It's a free country, and I just don't care for the way they run over there. You want to race at Demon's? Be my guest. Just don't expect me to be there."

"What are you so afraid of?"

At this Uncle Harvey set his jaw, lowered his chin to his chest, and just stared ahead.

"When my mother came up here the other day, you looked like you'd seen a ghost. What was that about?"

Uncle Harvey still said nothing.

"You afraid to show your face at Demon's —"

"I'm not afraid of anything," Uncle Harvey snapped in a gruff tone. As if he'd startled himself with his sudden change of mood, he waited a few moments before turning to me. "You want to know if I'm avoiding Demon's Run? Well, as a matter of fact I am. It's my right to go and not go wherever I want."

"But —"

"I'm not finished."

"Sorry."

He sat up and rested his elbows on his knees, clasping his hands between them. "Now, have I got reasons for not going there? I do. And they're *my* reasons. You understand?"

"They have to do with *my* family—"

"*My* reasons, Casey." He stared at me, his jaw clenched again.

I tried to stare him down, but, even as mad as I was just then, I couldn't. Even when Uncle Harvey was supremely annoyed, I couldn't help but see him as the sweetest man I'd ever met. I looked out over the yard. "What about Jim?" I said.

"What about him?"

"Think he'll bring me to Demon's Run tomorrow?"

"You can ask him yourself. He makes his own decisions."

Silence.

"Well, I am going to ask him." I looked at my uncle again. "I mean, I don't know how else to get my ride over there."

Uncle Harvey stared at me as if he were waiting for me to blink. Eventually he sighed, leaned back again, and looked into the night sky. "You're going to do it, then?"

"I have to," I said.

"Why do you have to? Let me guess. Someone tell you a race track's no place for a girl?"

"You were Big Daddy's crew chief."

Uncle Harvey made that whistling sound through his teeth and shook his head. "Let it go, Case," he said.

"I was just about to tell you the same thing."

Uncle Harvey gazed across the yard for a long time, and from where I stood, his gray silhouette could've been Big Daddy's—the jutting chin, the slightly bulging eyes. The resemblance caught me off-guard for a second, and then it angered me—angered me first because it'd startled me but mainly because Big Daddy and Uncle Harvey were not the same man. They couldn't have been more different. And some of the ways they were different had made my uncle's shop like a second home to me—maybe a first home, a real home anyway, where people paid attention to what I was saying. But Big Daddy and Uncle Harvey were different in another way that I couldn't pinpoint because Uncle Harvey refused to talk about it, even though I could tell it needled him a little more each time I went poking around for whatever it was he wouldn't tell me.

"Here's all I've got to say on the matter," Uncle Harvey said and spat. "You take what the race— "

"Take what the race brings me. I know. You've told me this before. I'm a patient driver. I run my line, I race my race."

"Are you really so patient, Casey?" he said. "Are you really racing your race? Or is that not your brother's car sitting over there?"

Maybe it was the mention of Wade's name or the whole wonderful evening rushing back to me, but I was through talking. Racing at Demon's Run wasn't up for debate.

I stood and turned so fast that I slipped on the grass in my high-heeled shoes. This just made me madder. I stormed to the Nova and yanked open the door. In the corner of my eye, I saw Uncle Harvey stand and follow me. "Promise me something," he said.

I fired the ignition.

Leaning on the open window so that I wouldn't back out, he eyed the Red Snake's front end, its gentle hump shape following smooth, arcing lines from windshield to grill. He whistled to himself. "I admire your taste in cars. I can't say much for your tactics, but when you steal someone's ride, you certainly steal something worth driving." He looked at me, and I knew that whatever secret lay buried behind those soft eyes was likely to remain there for a while. I could see too that being mad at him wasn't going to make me a better racer. I wondered if my raising some hell out on the track at Demon's Run could bring him some joy up here in his lonely little place. "Keep it between the lines," he said.

"I will."

He slapped the Nova's roof and stood back.

I backed around so that the rear was to the garage, and in the white reverse lights I saw Theo hulking in the shop. He'd taken a few knocks that afternoon, but unless I was imagining things, he looked about ready to pounce.

As I drifted down Uncle Harvey's road, freaking out at the realization, now that I was calmer, that I was driving Wade's pride and joy, my cell phone rang. My heart caught, and I nearly drove into the weeds. I tapped the brakes and checked the receiver display, relieved to discover it was Bernie, not Fletcher or Wade, on the other end.

"I was just about to call you," I said, easing to a stop at the end of the road.

"I wasn't expecting you to pick up. Tell me that tall

man you got all dressed up for is sitting next to you."

"He's not."

"What?"

"Long story."

"Good date?"

"Like I said, long story. Can you guys get here tomorrow by noon latest? It's important."

"How important?"

"I'll owe you for life."

"That's fine, Casey. But T.T. and Tam are going to want to know if you'll introduce us to Mr. Man's friends. Otherwise, that's a long way to drive."

"Oh, there are boys involved. Definitely."

"Well, then, I'll see what I can do. Call me in the morning."

∾

The whole house was up, of course, when I got back from Uncle Harvey's—and not, I was guessing, to see if I'd had a pleasant evening. Wade shot out the kitchen door before I could even turn the ignition off. I stepped out of the car and threw his keys into the front yard. He seemed stunned as I walked straight toward him. He stepped aside just before I plowed him over. "Pig," I said as I entered the garage. Mom stood behind the kitchen door, a worried look on her face.

"If you put so much as a scratch on that car," Wade said.

"What?" I spun around. "What'll you do? What can you do to me? I expect *nothing* from you, Wade. I won't *make* that mistake."

161

Mom opened the door. "Casey, please," she said. "Let's talk this over."

"I've got nothing to say."

"You took your brother's car."

"My brother is a pig-dog who treats girls like roadkill." No one said anything.

"Ask him!" I shouted. "Ask him who it is this week. Who's the lucky lady who gets to ride shotgun with Wade the Blade?"

I turned to Mom and spotted Big Daddy standing in the dining room, coffee mug in hand.

Wade slammed his door and started the engine. He backed into the road and flew off with a squeal of tires.

"Very mature, isn't he?" I muttered as I passed Mom.

"Casey," she said. "Can we talk about this?"

I said nothing and scrambled up the stairs as fast as I could without tripping over my dress. I barely got the door open before the tears started gushing.

Chapter 12

Mr. Blodgett watched with a blank expression as I rolled through the pit gate in the wrecker with Jim. I nodded and waved, but the man just kept staring. The Sharks were right behind me in Bernie's battered Toyota, and I could see Mr. Blodgett stare at them too as they passed. He checked his clipboard then watched me some more.

We found a pit about midway down the row. I wasn't even parked before I saw the other drivers pointing in my direction, some of them laughing. One crewmember waved a yellow shop rag at me—caution. I climbed out of the truck and met the Sharks at my pit.

"It's like a bad girl's Christmas," Bernie said, tightening the GO CASEY GO RACING T-shirt knot above her midriff and glancing down pit row.

Tammy fanned herself with her notebook. "It's a frickin' boyfriend store."

The moment Jim had Theo unloaded, though, the Sharks were all business. T.T. had some tire-pressure numbers in her notes from Uncle Harvey, and Jim and Tammy had been given instructions for adjusting something called the sway bar, which was supposed to improve my cornering. There wasn't a whole lot for me to do besides try to ignore the racers who alternately sneered at me and scoped out the Sharks. The guys passed by slowly, casually, chests thrust out in their firesuits like superheroes arriving to save the day. When I saw Wade and his crew coming, Fletcher by his side, I walked down to my car, pulled out the steering wheel, and sat inside, out of view. I looked in my rearview mirror as they passed. Fletcher seemed to glance in my direction from behind his sunglasses. Wade said something that made Lonnie crack up.

I started shaking lightly. I hadn't eaten anything for breakfast, and I was regretting it. "Hey, Bernie," I said, leaning out the window. "You guys have anything to eat?"

She walked up to her car and returned with half an egg-salad sandwich and an orange. I took the orange. Checking to make sure that Wade, Fletcher, and Lonnie were gone, I climbed out the window and sat on the door, my feet resting on the front seat. I leaned on the roof.

"Hey, there's Casey 'the Lady' LaPlante," Bean said over the track loudspeakers. "Seems our vixen in car six'en has come back to run those laps she didn't get a chance to finish a few weeks ago. Welcome back, Casey."

I began to slide back into the car, but Jim popped up from underneath the hood and glared at me. "Don't move a muscle," he said.

I froze.

"Wave to the crowd," he added. "Do it."

I waved, my face firing up with blood. No one in the grandstands cheered, but Bean didn't make a snappy comeback either. "Thanks, Jim," I said.

He and Tammy kept clanging away.

∽

The Sharks stood at attention as I rolled back into the pits after my practice laps. "How's it feel?" Tammy said as I handed her my helmet through the window. I popped off the steering wheel and handed it to Bernie.

"Feels great," I said as I climbed out.

And Theo did feel great. For a car that had won a street-stock feature a county away the day before, he was as quick as a kitten — but with serious claws. "I have no idea what you guys did," I added, "but this ride is definitely dialed in for cornering this track. So, where are we on track intel?"

Bernie laughed a husky laugh. "We got the goods."

I leaned against Theo and stretched my legs as the Sharks brought me up to speed on the day's field. T.T. seemed a bit quieter than usual, kind of staring off toward Jim from time to time, occasionally glancing down pit row. She left Tammy and Bernie to lay out my strategy.

Larry Greer had the ride to watch in his coffee-colored Chevy, car 44, cosponsored by BRIDGE STREET SNACK BAR and VALLEY ASSEMBLY OF GOD CHURCH. Larry had a big orange cross on his hood, which, in my opinion, didn't look good against the brown. Dale Scott was also rumored to be a threat. He'd been getting a good setup from Wade's crew, so the FUN PARK car 07 was going to be a mover. Kirby Mungeon in his FRENCHIE'S FIREWORKS number 49 little-laughing-Martian-guys truck was a ride I just shouldn't trust. I tried to take it all in, but there wasn't much room in my head for anything besides the simmering rage over my prom "date." Sharing the whole tragic tale with the Sharks back at Uncle Harvey's had helped a little, even though it brought out a few tears.

Tammy had said that Fletcher's pretending to want to take me to the prom, when he was really doing it because Wade told him to, was "a dead-cold move," which I gathered was Byam slang for mean. Sitting around waiting for the Warrior feature, I could feel plenty of surplus fury still coursing through my veins. The orange stirred the acid in my stomach, and it fit my mood perfectly.

When I heard the loudspeakers click on, every muscle in my body tensed. "All drivers to the turn-one bleachers for a drivers' meeting," Bean said. "Drivers, report to the bleachers at this time, please."

I can't honestly say I remember a single word of my second Demon's Run drivers' meeting. I sat on the bottom bench again, right in front of Mr. Blodgett, and every laugh, every snicker, every snippet of conversation seemed directed at me. I was probably being paranoid, since, if I was a joke to those guys, I was a joke they'd heard before. Still, just having to sit around for the fifteen minutes it took Mr. Blodgett to berate us reduced my self-esteem to roadkill being run over by a line of thirty cars. Every once in a while, Mr. Blodgett would look directly at me, and my pulse would start pounding so loudly in my ears that I could barely hear him.

The second he was finished with his lecture, I got up and left the bleachers. I walked quickly back to my pit, fighting the urge to run. I didn't want to look scared, and I wasn't certain that, if I started running, I wouldn't just keep on going all the way home.

About ten minutes later, Bean called the Road Warriors to the course.

Tammy flipped me the Byam grip, and I felt a tingle in my arms and legs. I glanced back at Jim, who was reading his GED booklet on the flatbed. He gave me a thumbs-up.

"Tell you what," Bernie said, gazing down pit row. "These boys are cute and all. But out there"—she pointed toward the track—"they can't wash your lingerie. I hope you know that."

Tammy handed me my helmet.

I pulled it on, but as soon as I'd secured the chinstrap, T.T.'s right hand swung up and whacked the side so hard that my ears rang. I stumbled back a step as she leaned right into my face.

"No man has the right to treat you that way," she growled.

Bernie pulled T.T. back but only so she could smack me in the butt hard enough to sting. "Git 'er done," she hissed.

I vaulted in through the window and pounded that steering wheel on like a judge demanding order in the court.

∾

The Demon's Run handicapping formula sent me out onto the racecourse eight back from the leader. Rolling around turns three and four as the pace car lined us up, I got a look at the field—eight cars ahead, nine behind, eighteen in all. Aside from what I might discover I'd actually retained from Tammy and Bernie's pre-race briefing, my strategy was simple:

- Run my line, which included rolling my right tire over an arrowhead-shaped tar blotch in turn one, another one shaped like a pistol in turn two, a wedge-shaped gash in the track in turn three, and a greasy sunburst in turn four.
- Take one car at a time.
- Avoid getting tangled in someone else's wreck.
- Try to "take what the race brings me" instead of doing what I really wanted to do, which was take Theo's front end and T-bone, chop, and ram every one of those skunk-pig-dogs.

First priority: car 44, there in front of me, Larry Greer's snackbar Godmobile.

After two laps behind the pace car, we crossed over in the backstretch. I had the inside lane, paired up with a yellow Mustang with a black number 78—a kid from Flu High I didn't know. He didn't have a sponsor, just a lot of black paint spelling things like JUST BRING IT! and THIS SPACE FOR RENT and DR. MAKEOUT'S COURTESY SHUTTLE, which was obviously a bogus sponsor. On our next lap, as I came around turn one, I saw the pace car dart to the infield, and the whole column of cars scrunched up. As DR. MAKEOUT car 78 and I rounded turn three, the leaders were rounding turn four and heading for the starting line. I could see the flagman holding the green down at his side. We were looking at a clean start.

Knowing that the flagman's attention was on the first and second cars, the instant he began to raise his flag arm, I matted the accelerator. The green flag dropped. Theo roared, and I wedged his front end in between the rear bumpers of the cars ahead of me, Larry's car 44 and a black Mustang with a baby blue number 90. Car 90's back end read, IF U CAN READ THIS . . . 2 BAD 4 U. A nanosecond later, a rumble of engines rippled through the column. I accidentally bumped 90, and he twitched to the outside. This being neither the time nor the place for apologies, I kept the accelerator floored and plunged into the space between cars 90 and 44, drawing Theo's nose up almost even with Larry's rear tires.

Knowing Larry, a former chemistry lab partner—and a pretty good one—I knew he played by the rules, which he used to his advantage by drifting across my front end. I lifted to avoid getting slapped. Fair enough: I hadn't quite reached his rear tires. I held close to his tail, though, as I ran the first lap. I slid out to my line: arrowhead, pistol. I checked my rearview mirror to find a rust red Mustang, car 11, following right in my tracks. I felt the momentum surge as Theo exited the turns. Glancing back, I saw car 11 start to fall off.

I worked Larry for another lap, coming out of the turns a bit farther up on him each time. Larry held tight to the car ahead of him, Kirby's truck. Car 11 hadn't figured out a way to take me yet, so I ran another patient lap dead to my line: arrowhead, pistol, gash, sunburst. Coming out of turn four, though, just as I accelerated and slid up on the outside of Larry's tires, I looked across the infield and saw Dale's car 07, about five cars back from the front, fish-tailing. He regained control a couple of seconds later, giving up one spot to the car on his inside, but that tiny blink of chaos created a mini chain reaction in the column of cars. I held the gas tight to the floor, kept my left front end glued to Larry's right rear. Maybe Larry tapped the brakes, maybe he lifted, or maybe the ripple effect of Dale's fishtailing distracted him. Either way, I was almost dead even with him as we went into the backstretch.

I ran my line around turns three and four—gash and sunburst—and exited with a perfectly timed punch of the accelerator. *Yesss!* I was a wheel up on Larry. With a glance in my rearview mirror, where car 11 had fallen back about a car length, I really went to work on car 44, dogging him hard, turn after turn.

Two laps later, I had a half-car lead on Larry. Coming out of turn four, I cranked the wheel toward him and then back. Larry lifted. I blew by him.

I drove right up tight to Kirby's rear end and held my speed. I might've been going a little crazy by then because I couldn't help but smile back at the little Martian guys painted on Kirby's truck. Theo's tires dug into the asphalt.

I shadowed Kirby for two laps, hovering just to the outside, following him move for move, knowing that the mental burden of his race weighed more heavily on him, being nipped at by a trailing car, than on me. I felt like I could run right up the bed of his truck and over his cab roof. At least that's how Theo was handling. I was also handling this race better than I'd handled any race so far, a rush of adrenaline and endorphins swirling through my limbs and brain, my firesuit generating a mini-meltdown of body heat. I'm surprised I didn't start hallucinating. Maybe I was hallucinating, because I felt weirdly happy— proud to have clawed my way to Kirby's bumper and delighted, in a sick way, to know that every time that freak looked in his rearview mirror, a bumper-clinging,

170

road-ripping picture of me and Theo stared back at him.

I decided to reclaim my line. Approaching turn three, I made a quick move to the inside. When Kirby tracked me, I jerked the wheel to the right and entered the corner on a perfect line in the outside groove, my right tire rolling over the arrowhead tar blotch. I hit the pistol next. Exited with speed.

My left front wheel was almost to Kirby's right rear. I could easily have tapped him. Could've done a little bump-and-run. I didn't need to, though. Kirby seemed jittery enough just to have me so close that I knew how to get him out of the way. I ran my line for another lap, and when I was just shy of even with him, I pinned him hard to the inside. Pinned him and held him there. I drifted out in the turns just enough to hit my marks but then went back to holding Kirby to the inside.

When one of the three cars ahead of Kirby, car 14, decided to bump-and-run Dale in car 07, both cars, along with car 09, which had been trying to come up on the outside, started spinning around. Their high-speed square dance spun toward the inside lane. I held Kirby still, pressed him to the inside, even when he drifted out to tap my door. I tagged him right back, screaming "You're it!" Poor kid had to brake when we caught up to the wreck. I pulled quickly to the outside groove and sailed past the mess.

Coming into the front stretch, I saw the flagman drop the yellow caution, meaning that I'd have to hold my position. Which was fine with me. I was in third place.

I took a lap with the field, a column of cars notably shorter than the one stretched before me at the start.

171

Car 14 earned a black flag—DQ, disqualification—for a flagrant bump-and-run, but Dale's car 07 suffered enough damage to need the Hook. While the track crew was hauling his midnight blue to the pits, the field ran two caution laps down the lane cutting straight across the infield, and then we ran two more back out on the track, crossing over into pairs in the backstretch on our fourth lap. When the pace car darted into the infield, I had to fight the impulse to punch the gas and ram the car ahead of me, an orange Escort with a green 33 and the words MARLIN HINES, TAXIDERMIST stenciled across the back. The Escort was running alongside an unsponsored baby blue Tempo with a white number 01. I had the inside lane on the restart with Larry's car 44 on my right again. Sliding around from turn three to turn four, I snuck a lightning-quick glance at the flagman. He held the yellow caution flag in his left hand, the green flag in his right. I had a feeling we'd get a fair start.

Coming around turn four and heading for the starting line, my legs literally shook, I was so anxious to take off. Apparently, so were cars 01 and 33. I didn't know which one accelerated first, but they led us out of turn four at top speed. We all punched the gas; I could feel the collective rumble in my bones. We held our positions and got the green.

I ran as close to car 33's tail as I could. He'd evidently been running in first place for a reason: He was clearly faster than car 01 beside him. As a result, I naturally edged up on Larry, who was stuck behind car 01 and too conservative a driver to do something crazy like jerk to the outside and try driving around car 01 three cars across. This worked to my advantage. When car 33 advanced, I advanced with him, and soon car 33 was alone in the lead and I was door-to-door with car 01. I started edging him outside, where there was plenty of room, since Larry still wasn't interested in driving the top of the bank. I kept at car 01 for a lap, nudging him out, moving closer and closer to my line. One lap later, I'd reclaimed my line.

The instant Theo's tire hit the arrowhead mark in turn one, a strange jolt of energy seemed to run through my ride, as if every mini-explosion under Theo's hood, every thrust of the pistons, had fallen into perfect rhythm. I felt as if I could've let go of the steering wheel and the tires would've dragged us around the track on a perfect line. Something completely tweaked was happening to me and my car, but I didn't fight it. For once, I didn't think about it too much. I was the car, and the car was me. We were running with these guys—and running strong.

I honestly don't remember too much of what happened next, since I kind of shut my brain off. If I had a thought, it was a desire—no, more like a hunger—for a sliver of track someone had left open like a piece of leftover pie. If someone dropped down close to me, I felt the slap of their door against mine as if they'd backhanded me across the face. But I didn't mind. In fact, as I purposely wedged Theo's front end in between the rear bumpers of the two cars ahead of me, car 01 and car 33, swaddling myself with sheet-metal chaos, adrenaline surged like a shot injected straight into my heart.

The two lead drivers must've thought I was nuts, trying to split them. It's true, there was no line to run there, but something told me—again, in my gut, not in my brain—that a dogfight was about to go down at the front of this field and that I could be more than a casual observer if I stuck close.

Car 33 sure seemed to acknowledge my presence. He drifted to the outside just slightly, as if to taunt car 01 into running closer to him, but quickly shut down the inside lane on me. I took this reaction to be a sign of, if not respect, then recognition. I was like some scavenger bird liable to snatch up anything unguarded. Inside lane, outside lane—it made no difference to the scavenger in car 06.

Still, those two drivers were running for the win, which made my pestering something other than the central conflict in this asphalt drama. In the next turn, they tapped doors. I held my line but favored the outside. Checking my mirror, I saw Larry on my tail but not that close. Tires. He must not have had the tires left. I watched car 01 fight back a little, pinning car 33 to the corner, and watched car 33 snap back, giving a tap on turn one, a stronger tap on turn three.

In another lap, my brain was functioning more normally again. *Take what the race brings you.* The words mixed with engine rumble that shook my body right up through my helmet, as if I really were a part bolted onto the chassis of my car. I stopped trying to create trouble and drove my line for a lap, watching the lead cars battle, preparing to seize an opportunity.

Coming around turn four, car 33 gave car 01 a very strong knock, strong enough to require the lead car to yank the wheel to correct his line.

174

The white flag flapped: One more lap.

I stuck tight to the drivers in the stretch and moved to my line in turn one. I watched them closely. In turn two, car 01 pressed car 33 to the inside, and car 33 gave a shove back. I ripped into the backstretch.

Coming up on turn three, I got to my mark and watched, waited, feathered the throttle as car 33 and car 01 touched doors again and ran like that, metal on metal, for a few seconds. At the shimmy of car 01's rear as he pulled back away from his opponent, I pressed the accelerator down evenly, gradually. I eased to the outside of 01 as closely as I could without touching him. Fighting Theo's tires in the turn, I held true to my line. I drove over the gash. The tires pushed. Sunburst. Accelerate. Exit.

I floored it and drifted with Theo's momentum just to the right. Car 01 and car 03 had clearly bled out cornering speed mashing against each other, and I gained car 01's rear tire and just kept gaining. I was dead even with him when the flagman leaned out with the checkered flag. I locked my arms and pushed the gas pedal so hard I was practically standing up on it. I blew across the line.

I rolled around turns one and two, and when I was coasting in the backstretch, I could make out Bean's voice over the loudspeakers. "Folks, I'm looking at the spotters' table, and . . . and . . . I don't believe it! It's Casey LaPlante by a gnat's eyelash! History in the making here at Demon's Run. It's Casey 'the Lady' LaPlante taking the Road Warrior feature today. Unbelievable."

Coming down the main straightaway, I eased way off the gas and braked across from the flagman. He handed the checkered flag to a track official, who jogged around to my window. "Good run," the guy said and handed me the flag. "Take a ride for the fans."

I tried to drive around the track by steering and shifting with one hand while holding the flag out my window with the other, but I had trouble finding second gear, and for a couple of seconds I swerved all over the place.

"Apparently, Casey, you missed the class on victory laps," Bean said. "Just try leaning the thing out the window. We get the idea. Be a shame to see you bite the wall when you're the only one on the track."

The crowd thought that was pretty funny. As I rounded turn four and headed back to return the colors to the flagman, I glanced at Beer Belly Hill and into the grandstands. People gawked at me, open-mouthed, some of them holding beer cans in mid-swig.

❧

Pulling into the pits, I was afraid I might run the Sharks over as they whirled around in a shrieking clump. Jim stood with his arms crossed, grinning what passed for a grin from him.

Getting out of the car, I was tackled by the Sharks, and through a tangle of legs and arms, I saw the rest of the crews up and down pit row staring, dumbstruck. The only person moving besides the Sharks and me was Mr. Blodgett, who was limping toward me at a brisk pace, kicking up dust in his wake. The set of his jaw suggested that he wasn't coming over to offer his congratulations. When he was about twenty feet away, he barked, "Who's the crew chief here?"

"I am," Jim said.

Mr. Blodgett jerked his head toward the tech area. "Get this car over to tech in five minutes, or you're DQ." Without another word, he turned and shuffled off.

The driver in the adjacent pit slot, Parker Hurley, laughed.

"Something funny?" T.T. said to him, peeling away from Theo.

Bernie and Tammy both grabbed her T-shirt and held her back.

"Looks like you've got yourself a teardown, Casey," Parker said. "Sure hope those springs are up to spec."

"Parker," I said, "I've been looking all over for you. Where've you been hiding, guy?"

He frowned, and his crewmembers stepped to his side.

"Next time we race," I added, "don't be such a stranger." I handed T.T. my gloves and Bernie my helmet and unzipped my firesuit.

Parker muttered something under his breath, but I ignored it.

∾

A person might've thought I was trying to smuggle drugs across the border, the way Mr. Blodgett and his tech crew made Jim and the Sharks pull Theo apart. I grew worried that we wouldn't be able to put him back together again. In the end, though, all of my engine parts measured up to regulation, and the only thing I lost was a chance to see Wade win the late-model feature. What a pity.

Back at my pit, the Sharks and I held a post-race debriefing while Jim loaded Theo onto the wrecker. It wasn't until I heard Bean say, "And we're about to see something in Victory Lane I'm not sure auto racing has ever seen before," that it dawned on me that I was going to receive a trophy while standing in Victory Lane in front of most of Fliverton *and right next to Wade.*

For a few seconds, I couldn't move. But as soon as I saw Wade swaggering down pit row toward the gate, I gave my firesuit zipper a yank up and followed him. He stepped onto the track and the crowd exploded. He waved this way and that, like a dictator greeting the masses. I'd have preferred to let him enjoy his triumphant moment alone, but I knew I was expected to step onto the track too. I took a deep breath and did what seemed natural—jogged onto the asphalt. The applause seemed to double.

"Here's your Road Warrior champion, folks," Bean said as I ran past Wade. "A familiar name but a whole new frame, Casey 'the Lady' LaPlante. Your vixen in car six'en." The cheering swelled again as I stepped into Victory Lane, where Bean—wearing a blue Demon's Run windbreaker, his lower body resembling a kettle drum dressed in brown slacks, as if to match the three strands of brown hair stretched across his bald head—took my trophy off the stool next to him and handed it to me. Wade stepped up to the other side of Bean. "And here's older brother Wade the Blade, our Thundermaker Sportsman champ," Bean added, tapping at the other trophy on the stool. "Good racing, Wade. We're going to get a word from you in a minute. But right now, I want to ask your kid sister something. Casey, about a month ago out here, you looked like you'd taken a wrong turn on your way to the library and ended up on a racetrack. But tonight, you knew right where you were going. What happened?" He moved the mike to my chin.

"Well, Bean, first things first," I said. "I've got the best crew." Three shrieks in the pits pierced the murmur of the grandstand crowd. "And to answer your question, I don't know, I've just been thinking a lot about racing since I was out here the last time. I got out here today, found a good line in practice. And, well, we've got a good car, good tires, and a good setup. We just got it done."

It wasn't exactly the Gettysburg Address, but, then, I'd never heard anything profound come out of Victory Lane.

"Well, congratulations," Bean said. "How about a big hand for Casey LaPlante, your Road Warrior champion."

The crowd cheered. Wade clapped weakly.

"Well, what do you have to say for yourself, Wade? It's starting to feel like déjà vu here in Victory Lane. Tell us how it went today." Bean reached over to Wade with the mike.

Wade gave the crowd a victory speech somehow even more vapid than my own, and I sort of zoned out. I was exhausted. After a few moments, the crowd cheered again, and I realized that the speeches were over. I turned to follow Wade to the pits, waving my trophy in the air just like he did.

Chapter 13

The post-race party back at the house, which was usually a nuisance for me, since the racket made it impossible to study in my room above the driveway, was unnerving in ways I'd never imagined it could be. Wade's crew acted all friendly to me, mainly because I'd invited the Sharks, and the Sharks encouraged, in a manner I wouldn't call subtle, a high level of friendly interaction. But every time Fletcher walked over, I found something to pull me in the other direction—another bottle of water, another handful of chips. I couldn't imagine talking to him without exploding, and I was also stunned at his stupidity in thinking that we could even *have* a conversation in front of all these people without it being excruciatingly weird.

Mom floated around with her post-race *I'm-just-so-proud-of-my-son* smile on her face. Big Daddy hung out over by the car 02 trailer, one foot up on a back tire, lecturing a couple of Wade's crewmembers he'd trapped there. Every once in a while, he gave me a look that told me he'd want to chat with me when the party was over.

I'd given the Sharks crystal-clear instructions that they were to tell *no one* about Uncle Harvey or my Corkum County Speedbowl racing experience. I told them to pretend that Jim was the only guy in the Casey LaPlante racing organization. Since he wasn't at the party—he had cars to tow—I figured the story would work. But Big

Daddy was no dummy, and his *We're-going-to-talk* looks made me think he might be putting the pieces of this puzzle together. A sip of beer. A long gaze over the yard. *Where did she* get *that ride?*

Everyone's attention was suddenly diverted to a car straining up Meadow Ridge Road. The swale of the front yard obscured the vehicle from view for a stretch of about one hundred yards before the driveway, and as we all looked, listening to the car's muffler complaining, I got the impression everyone was guessing at what the distressed vehicle would look like.

"Coates," a couple of people mumbled and returned to socializing as a road salt–ravaged Honda turned into the driveway with the telltale bark of a car suffering muffler problems.

Big Daddy stepped away from the trailer and moved toward Wade just as Mom was doing the same, the two of them converging on their son like Secret Service agents on the President. As Big Daddy said something to Wade, Mom hovered around them, wringing her hands as if she wanted to fix Wade's hair or tuck in his shirttail.

The Honda pulled onto the shoulder across from our driveway, and a heavyset guy in a green corduroy shirt, black fleece vest, and blue jeans stepped out. Before closing the door, he reached inside and retrieved a camera and notepad.

It was Vin Coates, racing reporter with the *Granite County Record*. It'd been about a year since I'd seen his bearish frame and curly blond hair crossing our driveway. The previous year he'd been driving a Toyota of a vintage and condition similar to his Honda, and he seemed to have gained a few pounds, though it was hard to tell with guys Vin's size. He chatted for a few moments with a couple of Wade's crewmembers, but not with his notebook or camera out, as if he were killing time while Mom and Big Daddy prepped Wade for the interview. Eventually, Vin looked over the crowd, caught Wade's eye, and nodded. Instead of approaching Wade, though, Vin kept looking around.

I instinctively stepped back.

The instant his eyes met mine, the crowd fell silent. Everyone turned to me. Wade, Mom, and Big Daddy didn't look pleased. Even Mom's post-race perma-smile straightened into a lipstick line.

Vin cut through the crowd and approached, his hands taking up his camera. "Casey," he said when he was about ten feet away, "how about a picture?"

I couldn't speak, not with the entire party staring.

Vin held the camera up, fiddled with the lens.

Behind him and off to the side, I saw the Sharks squeeze together, looping arms around each other, pointing to my name on their T-shirts and making goofy faces—like some lame, girl-band publicity photo. I laughed, and Vin clicked off two quick shots.

"You ran quite a race out there today," Vin said and clicked another shot. He snapped the lens cap on his camera and slung it behind his back, pulling a notebook from his vest pocket.

"Thanks."

"Didn't even know you were a driver."

"I ran that one time about a month ago."

"Oh, right." Vin chuckled. "I remember." He flipped

open the notebook and pulled his pen cap off with his teeth. "You hardly looked like a rookie today," he said.

"I had a lot of things go my way."

"Looks like you've been practicing."

"When I can."

"Tell me about your car. Where'd you get it?"

"They're not exactly rare, Warrior cars. Four cylinders. Stock, basically. Strip it clean. You know all this. Anyway, got mine off a guy outside of town. It needed some repairs, but now we've got it up to spec and running right."

"What about your crew?"

"What about them?"

"As I'm sure you know, it's almost as rare to see women back in the pits as it is to see women drivers."

"Rare but decreasingly rare, Vin," I said, trying to sound knowledgeable enough to keep him from probing my racing history. "At the national level, women are more visible in all branches of racing, from the pit crews to the drivers. You've got to figure that the short tracks around the country are seeing that increase. I mean, every racer starts somewhere."

Vin didn't say anything, just scribbled in a way that made me think that what I'd just said would be a quote in his article. It was something that T.T. had told me about. She'd read an article in *USA Today* about women in auto racing. "Who are these girls in your crew?" Vin said, still scribbling away. "I don't recognize them. The kid with the tow truck." A scowl flashed across the reporter's face.

"Him I recognize."

"The girls are from . . . they live downstate. They're old friends."

"They seem to know what they're doing."

"They pick things up pretty quickly." The moment the words left my lips, I glanced over at Bernie and Tammy, who were standing shoulder to shoulder and flirting so brazenly with Dale and Lonnie that I suddenly wished my parents had hired chaperones.

"So . . .," Vin said, looking me in the eye, "any desire to race your brother?"

I shook my head. "Not to state the obvious, Vin, but we drive in different divisions. And the equipment he uses is tens of thousands of dollars more expensive than mine—dollars that our organization doesn't have."

"Not this season anyway. But what if you went after some sponsors? You could race Wade in, you know, upcoming seasons."

"There aren't going to be any 'upcoming seasons.' If Wade has his way, he'll be on a Circuit team before too long, and I'm going to college in the fall."

Vin shifted his weight and poked at his meaty chin with his pen, as if trying to summon a particular word or phrase. "Put it this way," he said. "Can you at least imagine what it'd be like to race your brother? That'd be exciting, wouldn't it? Or would you be intimidated?"

I understood now: Vin was just fishing for a good quote. I indulged him. "Intimidated?" I said with a chuckle. I must've said the word too loudly because Wade shot me a look. "No, I wouldn't be intimidated," I added more quietly. "I know how he thinks. And I don't find that intimidating."

Vin smiled as he scratched at his notebook. I could tell that he'd collected what he'd come out here for. Mentally reviewing the brief exchange, I was satisfied I hadn't given him too much.

"Well, I guess that's it," Vin said, then flipped his notebook closed. "Thanks for your time." He turned back to the party.

Looking across the driveway, I saw Wade stand up more erectly. Vin caught his eye and nodded again, but, instead of cutting through the crowd in his direction, he started back toward the rusty Honda.

The party grew quiet as Vin shuffled to his car, packed himself inside, and drove off.

ℭ

For the first time in my life, I was the last person to leave the post-race bash, and when I stepped inside, Big Daddy and Mom sat at the dining room table, clearly waiting for me. Mom smiled a half smile, wrinkling her brow and sitting up in her chair. My father stared into his beer can. I acted as if nothing was wrong. Because, as far as I was concerned, nothing *was* wrong.

"Good party," I said to Mom as I approached the table.

"Thank you, dear," Mom said. "Casey, your father would like . . . your father and I would like a word with you."

I shrugged. "All right."

"Sit down," Big Daddy said, taking a sip of beer and setting the can aside.

Mom took the can into the kitchen. As she rinsed it and carried it to the recycling bin, Big Daddy stared at the ring on the table where the can had been.

"Casey, I want you to understand something," he began, clasping his hands on the table. "Ah, shoot," he said and leaned back.

"Did I do something wrong?"

Mom returned and sat down.

I addressed her: "What's this about? I win the Road Warrior feature and suddenly I feel like I'm about to get grounded."

"OK." Big Daddy didn't so much say the word as exhale it, his hands slapping the edge of the table. "I'll give it to you straight."

I locked eyes with him, and in that instant I knew just what he was going to say. So I said it for him: "You don't want me to race anymore."

Big Daddy wrinkled his mouth in a pained little grimace, like I'd seen him do when sorting through bills, then looked away.

I turned to Mom, who gave me the *I-know-it's-a-difficult-thing-for-you-to-understand-now-but-when-you're-older-it'll-all-make-sense* look that'd been driving me crazy since I was nine years old and Wade started racing Karts.

I turned back to Big Daddy, and already it seemed like the matter was settled. Squinting at some blank spot on the ceiling, he appeared to be calculating, running numbers—tire pressures, lap speeds, sway-bar adjustments.

186

"Is that it?" I said. "No explanation, just no racing? I'm, like, grounded from Demon's Run?"

Big Daddy nodded. "Sorry, Case. I am."

As I was about to refuse his order, I hesitated, distracted by a thought crackling across my cerebral cortex, a thought so obvious it was almost embarrassing. This was my moment, my Uncle Harvey moment. Big Daddy wanted something from me. What was he willing to give in return? Information? *Sensitive* information?

Ever since the day I drove up to Uncle Harvey's place to see about getting a racecar, I'd been anticipating the moment when Big Daddy was so overjoyed with Wade's success that he might be able to tolerate a question or two about what'd happened between him and his older brother. Mom had refused to get into that discussion up at Uncle Harvey's, and Uncle Harvey hadn't been any more willing to talk about it the previous night, but there in the dining room I suddenly seemed to have the tiniest bit of bargaining power. Leverage. I hadn't figured out how the conversation would go, and I definitely expected it would open wounds that could hurt my racing prospects. But, with Cray College on my horizon, and Fliverton soon to be a reflection in Hilda's rearview mirror, I wanted to know what I was leaving behind—not just in the place but in the people. My people.

"Why?" I asked, playing this out. "I already bought the season's license. And I won the feature today. I mean, I made all the license money back in one day."

"I know you did, I know you did," Big Daddy said, acting more relaxed now, as if certain I wouldn't disobey him. "So, it's like this. Wade is off to a very good start."

"What does that have to do with me?"

"Well, up until today, it didn't have anything to do with you."

I looked at Mom. She stared at her hands.

"So," I said, "what changed today?"

Big Daddy sighed, squinted at the table, and crossed his arms. "Case, you know you're brother's trying to get picked up by a Circuit team."

"You're kidding —"

"Casey," Mom interjected. "Your father and I support you in everything you do."

"I know," I said, trying to let a touch of the angelic Casey that I once was creep into my voice.

"Well," Mom went on, "right now, Wade needs a great deal of our support."

I looked at her and feigned a puzzled expression. "He lives here rent-free. You feed him. You look the other way as he breaks every heart in Fliver—"

Big Daddy stood up, pushing his chair back so quickly that it almost tipped over. "Look," he said, not seeming so relaxed anymore. "Here's the deal. Wade's got a shot at the Circuit, and it's this year. And one thing the Circuit teams are looking for is a driver who can not only win, but who can generate some kind of, you know, buzz. Who can get people behind him."

"Do they consider all the girls Wade's put behind him—"

Big Daddy rapped his knuckles on the table loudly enough to make Mom flinch, which sent blood flooding into my face. I turned to Mom but found her looking at her hands again.

"I know you understand exactly what I'm saying, Casey, and I know you're just being difficult because . . ." Big Daddy looked away, a gesture that seemed to mean something, I wasn't sure what.

" 'Because . . . ,' " I said. "Why am I being difficult?"

"I didn't mean anything by it."

"I think you did."

"Casey." Big Daddy leaned back on his heels, put his hands in his back pockets, acting casual all of a sudden. Acting. "I don't mean any offense. But I can imagine that Wade's success might . . . I don't know, bother you a bit."

"Bother me?"

"Yeah, well, I mean, he's a champion, Casey. He's number one. Now, you're a fine runner . . ."

"Dad, for your information, I took third in the counties. I even beat an exchange student from Africa. You want me to go get the ribbon?"

Big Daddy gazed across the kitchen in the direction of the garage. "It's Wade's time," he said in such a serious tone that I almost laughed. Almost. "No one's going to catch him. Not this season."

"Well, no one's going to catch me either," I said.

"You run a very good race, Casey. I'll grant you that. All your mother and I are asking is that you not distract attention from your brother. He needs to be the focus. We need to win the races, and we also need to get the coverage."

"The coverage? Oh, like Vin Coates tonight, out in the driveway?"

Big Daddy shook his head lightly. "No more games."

This was it. This was my opportunity.

I looked at Mom, but she was staring into the living room with the distant look in her eyes I'd seen up at Uncle Harvey's. I wanted to say something to her, to ask her where she was just then, but I knew this conversation was all about me and Big Daddy. "What do you mean, games?" I said.

Big Daddy pulled his hands from his pockets and held his arms out to his side, palms to the ceiling. "Your season's over, kiddo. Until we seal a deal with a Circuit team."

Kiddo. So, I was a kid all of a sudden? He was, like, waiting for me to hop off the merry-go-round?

He walked to the refrigerator. "You're not racing."

The slight hitch in his voice gave it away: He *really* didn't want me racing. How *much* didn't he want me racing?

Mom reached out and touched my arm, a gesture I usually took to mean that she'd like me to please be cooperative. Following her arm up to her face, though, I saw something in her expression that I hadn't seen in a long time: the faintest hint of recognition, of that connection that we were supposed to have as women—the connection that I had with the Sharks. Was that what I saw there? Was Mom *seeing* me? Seeing . . . *me?* I wondered what expression had danced across her face as I was taking the checkered flag earlier that day, if she was even watching.

"I won't do any more interviews," I said, still staring into Mom's eyes. "But I put the license money down. I earned that money, and I should be able to spend it however I want."

Big Daddy opened a beer. "Sorry, Casey."

"Oh, Wade," Mom interrupted, pulling her hand from my arm and drawing it to her temple. "She said she won't do any more interviews. Let her race."

And as quickly as she said it, she stood and walked into the kitchen, where she ran the faucet.

Big Daddy shook his head in that way that didn't say no but, rather, asked, *What did I do to deserve this?* "Fine," he grumbled and took a hearty gulp of beer.

For a few moments, no one said anything. I knew my next move was to trade my media blackout for some honest talk about Uncle Harvey, but it seemed that the time to play that card had already passed on this occasion. I also feared—no, was certain—that Big Daddy would've insisted that I stop racing in exchange. And, despite the fact that his namesake won another Thundermaker feature that day, he wasn't in the best mood, though he was a touch less cranky than he'd been when I came in from the garage. I couldn't take the risk. When I dropped the Uncle Harvey grenade, he needed to be wearing a few more coats of protective certainty about his son's professional racing future.

"Anyway, you're in the Road Warriors," he said in a tone that suggested he was rationalizing his leniency toward me—as if Dale, Larry, Kirby, and I went wheeling around the track on tricycles.

I ignored the comment and watched Mom moving around the kitchen, marveling at the notion that she also had cards to play in this crazy game. And, unless I'd misread this situation, the fact that I was still a racecar driver owed something to her having just played a big one.

Chapter 14

If my grabbing headlines was Big Daddy's concern, he must've rested easy for the next three Sundays. He definitely had nothing to worry about on my first race after winning the Road Warrior trophy. That run, on June sixth, shaped up to be a "respect race," just as Uncle Harvey had predicted. Every Road Warrior driver on the track seemed determined to see me finish dead last—if at all. And those black DQ flags must've gotten lost in the Demon's Run laundry because there were no apparent limits to how hard drivers could bump me, how annoyingly they could block me, or how obscenely they could gesture to me on the caution laps. Three specific incidents robbed me of any hope at a decent finish: 1) when Parker Hurley, driving the black-on-gold car 19 sponsored by Wee Wuns Daycare, cranked my rear bumper down onto my right rear tire, causing the metal to smoke the rubber —and sending me to the pits; 2) when Kirby Mungeon rode me into the Widowmaker so hard that I practically bounced into turn one and over the bank; and 3) after I drove through the middle of a two-car wreck, catching one of the car's rear bumper hard enough to pop Theo's hood right open. Just seeing the checkered flag waving over my ride—wherever in the lineup I finished—was a victory of sorts.

Fletcher walked past my pit that day as Jim, the Sharks,

and I were removing the duct tape that we'd used to fasten the hood down so I could finish the race, but I didn't say anything to him. Didn't even look up. Tried to look too busy. He seemed about to speak but, hearing Bean give the Thundermakers their ten-minute warning, kept moving along.

The next two races worked out better, especially the one on June 13, since, after I'd stunk up the track the previous week, the handicapping system sent me onto the racecourse in the sweet seventh position. I avoided all the accidents that day and took a respectable fourth.

Fletcher called me on my phone that afternoon, after the Thundermaker feature, but I didn't pick up.

I wasn't exactly taking the racing world by storm, but I was getting quality "seat time," as Uncle Harvey had put it. And my crew seemed to be learning a lot along the way. Just watching the Sharks climb out of Bernie's Toyota on a Sunday afternoon, I could tell they meant business. T.T. especially was getting into the short-track racing scene. She'd started bringing a stopwatch to the races and timing my practice laps to see how I ran on lines high in the turns, low in the turns, and compared to the good movers in the field. Turns out math wasn't her worst subject either.

On the third Sunday, June 20, I started toward the back of the pack and more or less stayed there—"took what the race brought me," as Uncle Harvey always advised. And what the race brought me was nothing special. No wrecks. No dramatic, come-from-behind victory. No trophy.

Nevertheless, my mediocre racing ability had impressed

someone. As I handed Tammy my helmet and Bernie my steering wheel and climbed out of Theo that third Sunday, I spotted two girls—maybe ten or eleven years old—waving at me over by the pit gate. The girls had pens and race programs in their hands. I took a few swigs of water from the bottle T. T. tossed me and walked over. Some junior high school kids were performing bicycle tricks out on the track, but back in the pits, I still felt like all eyes were on me. I strode as calmly as I could over to the gate and did something I never, not in a million years, imagined I'd do: signed autographs. The whole exchange seemed surreal, and as I watched the girls walk away, I felt dizzy. I also failed to notice Fletcher approaching.

"Hey," he said, startling me.

I pretended I didn't recognize him and started walking back to the wrecker.

"Can we talk?" he said, following.

I said nothing as I watched Jim and the Sharks load Theo onto the flatbed.

"I want to know what I did wrong," Fletcher said.

I caught the Sharks watching me, their expressions hidden behind sunglasses. "You didn't do anything wrong," I said. "You just did what you were told."

"What's that supposed to mean?"

"You didn't have to ask me to the prom," I said.

"I wanted to," Fletcher said. "Really."

Bean's microphone clicked on: "And not to take away from the incredible feats of these kids on their bicycles, but at this time I'll give the Thundermaker ten-minute warning. Ten minutes, Thundermaker Sportsmen, until your feature. To your pits at this time, please."

194

"Coffee break's over, Fletcher," I said.

"Casey, I wanted to ask you to the prom. That's why I asked you."

"Whatever. I'm over it. You better get going. Looks like Wade may have some further instructions for you."

Fletcher gave me a puzzled look. "Further instructions?"

From down in Wade's pit, Lonnie waved to Fletcher and gestured to his wristwatch.

Fletcher held up one finger—the universal sign for *Give me one more minute.* He stared at me. "I don't get this."

"No," I said. "You don't."

Fletcher shook his head.

I didn't say anything else. I just watched Jim haul my ride away, watched the Sharks watching me, hanging close in case I needed them, and listened to Fletcher walk away.

~

Instead of going straight home, I decided to stay and watch the Thundermakers. I'm not sure what compelled me, but I guess I'd begun to feel more a part of the whole Demon's Run scene in recent weeks, so I walked out through the gate and in front of the grandstands, my firesuit on but unzipped nearly to the waist like I'd seen some of the other racers wear them after a race. More or less complete strangers waved to me and gave me the thumbs-up. I made it about two sections of bleachers along the main straightaway before Bean spotted me. The loudspeakers clicked on:

"Looks like Casey LaPlante, we'll call her your Road

Warrior Princess, has come out to greet her subjects. How about a wave for the little people, Casey?"

A few people laughed at Bean's comment, astoundingly enough. I'd already learned that, out there at Demon's Run, it was pointless to try and hide from Bean, so I faked a smile and waved in the general direction of the announcer's booth. Then I turned and headed back to the pits.

I sat in the pit bleachers along with a few dozen crewmembers from Thundermaker teams and watched the big boys run their feature. I had to admit, the roar of those eight-cylinder engines got a person's attention, and the way the Thundermakers instantly accelerated and decelerated as the pace car took them around the track at top speed gave the impression of jungle cats, maybe cheetahs, tearing into the earth on the hunt. The more closely I watched the cars prowling the oval, I figured they were probably accelerating and braking, accelerating and braking. Otherwise, there'd be no way they could speed up and slow down as quickly as they did. I was tempted to ask one of the crewmembers if I was correct in that assumption, but I was struck by just how serious everyone looked there in our little stand of bleachers.

Two laps later, the Thundermakers crossed over in the backstretch and got ready to run. Wade, the unchallenged leader so far in the season, started at the very back of the field, in a position Bean called "shotgun," for some reason. It'd been a couple of years since I'd seen Wade race, and even then, I hadn't paid much attention to him. On that particular June day, though, I went to school on his driving technique. He was good. No, not good—gifted.

To be brutally honest, I'd have preferred not to give my brother credit for anything at that point in our lives, but to see him on the racecourse stirred a strange sense of family pride. I'd have sworn that every single car out there, from the car right in front of Wade at the back of the pack to the car in the pole position, drove as if aware of Wade's presence. When the green flag dropped, he toasted the first four cars in front of him like they'd been stuck in first gear.

Two laps in, and I could see him running his line in the turns. All around the track, he kept his front end right up close to the car in front of him, just to the point of bumping. He claimed whatever asphalt he wanted with each yank of the wheel, slipping like mercury through traffic, the other drivers backing away from the poison.

I watched him, mesmerized, as he untangled the field and tossed his competitors aside. As he held second place in the last five laps, I could almost sense him grinding down the lead car, Johnny Savard's WILLOW RIVER INN car 11. Wade waited until the white-flag lap to make his move, as though he'd been toying with Savard. The fans rose to their feet.

As Wade sailed underneath the checkered flag, a solid car length on Savard, I found myself on my feet too. I couldn't help it. While I hadn't been paying close enough attention to Wade's racing career to have watched his progress, I was genuinely impressed by his skill. And it dawned on me in an instant how he got to be so good: by focusing on nothing else but racing.

I climbed down from the bleachers and headed back out to the grandstands to catch a lift home with Mom. Passing through the concession area, I heard my name uttered in a woman's voice. I didn't look, but a few steps farther, I heard someone else, this time a guy, say my name. "She's my new favorite," someone else, a young girl, said. "She kicks butt."

I won't deny that hearing a compliment brought a smile to my face, but having just seen Wade do his thing, I knew I was still a complete rookie. Or maybe he really was ready for the Circuit.

Chapter 15

The big news at the post-race party that afternoon was that Big Daddy finally got a call from a Circuit team scout who'd heard about Wade and wanted to see him race. In fact, that phone conversation was the only thing anyone talked about. It got so boring that the Sharks couldn't stand it. They left after an hour or so, and I headed upstairs to my room.

I booted up my computer and hit the Cray College website. I clicked through pages, imagining myself in each scenario: peering through a state-of-the-art telescope; strolling through fallen leaves with a look of philosophical contemplation on my face, hands clasped in the muffler pocket of my Cray College sweatshirt. The fantasy images seemed so real, more real than they'd ever seemed, that I opened my desk drawer and retrieved my acceptance letter just to be sure. I pulled the letter out and laid it on my desk, using my pencil cup and cell phone as paperweights. Here and there a smudge marred the fine paper, which was understandable, since I'd handled the document more than Jefferson must have handled the Declaration of Independence. *Congratulations* . . . I was in. I was really in.

I was going. Leaving. And not turning back.

But did anyone really care? Sure, people knew me a little differently than they had before I started racing, but instead of being "Wade LaPlante's little sister," wasn't I just "Wade LaPlante's little sister who drives in the lowly Road Warrior division"? I'd made Big Daddy nervous for a few days. That was fun. The first night Vin Coates came up, I'd stolen Wade's media spotlight for a few minutes, something I'd never even thought possible. Still, as I sat in my room and listened to the party going on down in the driveway, laughs and indecipherable conversation mixing in a murmur of voices, I was nagged by the feeling that whatever I'd been chasing the first time I took Theo out onto the Demon's Run racecourse wasn't something I could catch out there. I definitely caught something, namely a nasty case of short-track racing fever, but not even my two shiny trophies glimmering among a dozen cross-country ribbons and that nice "coach's award" plaque Coach Meserole gave me at the fall awards banquet seemed to add up to much. I didn't need any more trophies or ribbons. I needed answers.

One by one, Wade's crewmembers took off in their muscle cars, the barking mufflers fading down the hill of Meadow Ridge Road and winding up again as the guys blasted off. When my window was a slate-gray shade of dusk, and the driveway was silent, I walked downstairs.

Big Daddy and Mom sat at the dining room table, Big Daddy with a can of beer and a folder full of papers in front of him, Mom with a glass of iced tea and a catalog. She smiled as I sat down next to her.

"Good news, huh?" I said.

Big Daddy smiled but didn't look up. "Very good," he said and took a swig of beer.

"The Pembroke team is sending two people to the

200

Firecracker 50," Mom said. "They sounded very interested in bringing Wade onboard."

"Onboard, as in, down . . . wherever they're—"

"North Carolina," Big Daddy said, finally looking at me over the tops of the pages.

"He'd move there?"

"That's the idea." Big Daddy kept reading.

"It's an amazing opportunity," Mom said.

"He'll be a Tarheel."

"Sorry?" Mom said.

"I said he'll be a Tarheel. That's what people are called in North Carolina. I don't know what it is, exactly."

"Oh." Mom let out a little laugh. "That's right."

Big Daddy set his beer can down, and I could tell from the sound of it clanging on the table that it was empty. I got up to get him another one. On my way back to the table, I popped the top. He looked at me and smiled in a way that I hadn't seen in the longest time: a *That's-a-good-girl* smile. "Thanks, Case," he said as I set the can down.

"You're welcome." I leaned against the counter and watched him take a drink, trying to pick up any final clues about his mood. He let out a satisfied "Ah!"

"The Otters," I said.

Mom gave me a curious look, and Big Daddy kept reading.

"That's the Cray College mascot. They're the Otters."

"The Tarheels and the Otters then," Mom said with another girlish laugh.

Big Daddy turned back to me, smiled, raised his beer can in a toast. "Go, Otters," he said.

I watched Big Daddy read for a few more moments, struck, as I had been out at Uncle Harvey's, by how much he resembled his older brother. But they really did live in separate worlds now—my father with his dutiful wife, his established business, our modest but comfortable home, his daughter on her way to the college of her choice, and his son poised to make the Circuit dreams come true that had eluded him. How did the two brothers end up on such different planets? The question nagged at me, but, still, something told me that to pollute this blissful moment with questions about Uncle Harvey would bring that other world into this one, where it was not merely unwelcome but forbidden. Forbidden. No one had told me it was forbidden to discuss Uncle Harvey there, but I knew it was. Just plain was.

Yet I also knew that I would ask the questions on my mind—just not that night. I decided to let my father enjoy a moment he'd been dreaming about since he was Wade's age. Maybe it'd prove to be what he'd needed all along to reconnect with that other world, that other life that really was part of his world—his family—whether he accepted that or not.

"I'm going to run some errands," I said and headed for the garage door.

"Not too late, OK, Casey?" Mom said.

"Not too late," I replied.

Chapter 16

Graduation day was a bit of a letdown. Anticlimactic. Not that I'd been expecting fireworks. The humidity inside the Flu High gym didn't help matters. After Marla Dietz's speech, on the theme of seeing individual differences as potential assets to society, which made sense as a topic for her, given that she was known for being different —perfect, in other words—my mind began to wander. At one point, during a speech by Dr. Hollingsworth, our principal, I almost fell asleep. But when Hollingsworth started announcing a round of scholarships, I got elbowed on both sides by Brad Lambert and Ruby Loh. When I looked up, Hollingsworth was beaming at me from the stage, holding a scroll with a blue ribbon. I went up and received the award.

It wasn't until I returned to my seat and unfurled the paper that I discovered the local Rotary Club had given me a small scholarship for no apparent reason. As I listened more attentively to the rest of the ceremony, I learned that several local organizations were giving scholarships, each going to a student who had done well academically while also doing something else pretty well —athletics, community service, that sort of thing. I certainly didn't mind having the extra cash, but part of me also wondered if I were getting this scholarship because everybody knew that I was going to Cray College and that it was going to put a financial strain on Big Daddy—and, by extension, on Wade LaPlante Motorsports. Maybe this was the Rotary Club's way of helping Wade out, even though he'd barely graduated Flu High.

❧

Early the next day, Sunday morning—race day—I looked in the shop for Uncle Harvey but didn't find him. I checked inside his house, but he wasn't there either. I sat on the front stoop and took note of how well his flowers were doing. A few moments later, I got up and walked to the shop as Jim rolled up in the wrecker. That's when I saw Uncle Harvey coming out of the tin shed with its back to the pasture, the one with the motorcycle frame leaning against it. He was wiping his hands on a rag and wore a look of intense concentration as he crossed the yard, dodging smashed car bodies and his boat. When he finally saw me watching him, he seemed startled. "There you are," he said, as if he'd been looking for me and not the other way around.

"Everything all right?" I said.

"Fine, fine." He gestured for me to step into the garage, where Jim was setting two cups of coffee and a bottle of orange juice on the workbench. "Your rig's in good shape." He gestured with a thumb toward the wrecks scattered around the yard. "I hauled out some new springs. You should like your setup all right. I want to watch the weather, though. This haze is burning off awfully fast. You might have to make a last-minute decision about your tire pressure, but your crew should be able to handle that by now."

"I imagine so." I watched Uncle Harvey step up to the workbench and take one of the coffees.

"The juice is for you, Casey," Jim said.

"Thanks, guy."

I kept watching Uncle Harvey as he blew on his coffee, his eyes narrowed, his brow wrinkled. Again, I noticed the resemblance to Big Daddy. I resisted the urge to ask him to come watch me race, because I already knew what his answer would be.

Chapter 17

At Demon's Run, I ran my practice laps and then more or less stood back as my crew worked. It was as if they'd been doing this for years. I told them what I knew: Car felt a little tight, but, otherwise, he settled well in the corners. They conferred about the tires, measured them with the stagger gauge, and inflated and deflated them with the portable air pump. When they were satisfied that they had the tire pressures right, they began sharing the intelligence they'd gathered on the other racers.

"Word is, Dale Scott's got the fast car today," T.T. reported.

"Kirby Mungeon is talking about taking you to the wall again," Tammy added.

"He doesn't scare me. Where am I starting?"

"Third," Bernie said. "Kirby's at five."

"He'll never catch me."

"Allen Jervis is in the fourth position, and he's been complaining about his steering all morning," Tammy said. "You're going to have Kirby on your butt for all twenty-five laps, Casey."

"Guess I better get a car between us."

"That means getting out in front of Dale Scott," T.T. said with a grim nod. "He's starting in second. Good luck. Larry Greer, car 44, is on the pole."

"Fair enough," I said.

Bernie handed me my helmet. "Beatable, Larry. Doesn't like the bump-and-run."

"Neither do I," I reminded her. Seeing Fletcher, Lonnie, and Wade walking down pit row, I turned my back to them and stared at the track.

ᔑ

Out on the racecourse, I tried to block out Bean's tedious nattering about "the vixen in car six'en" as I followed the pace car around. I focused on the flagman, watching him like a redtailed hawk from a telephone pole. He rested the flag on his right shoulder. The pace car cut to the infield, the field compressed, and the flagman shuffled his feet. I slipped up to Larry's rear bumper and backed off, drifted out toward Allen Jervis on my right, and backed off. Around turn four, seeing the flagman favoring the green, I matted the gas along with the leaders and got ready to rip a hole in the race.

The only hole I ended up ripping in anything was in the palm of my right-hand racing glove, probably from twisting the steering wheel in frustration as I ran a clean but absolutely uneventful twenty-five-lap sprint. With my eyes darting back and forth from the rearview mirror, where Kirby's FRENCHIE'S FIREWORKS 49 truck clung to my tail, to Dale's right rear wheel, I struggled to pick up a position. I drove a good line and felt my tires settle Theo in the corners like he was running on rails. But I couldn't gain a foot on Dale, and I never lost Kirby by more than half a car length. And I never got out of third place by the time I was zipping underneath the checkered flag.

The crowd hardly cheered at all, although there were a few boos as Kirby finally gave me the tap on the rear bumper he'd been threatening. Behind my back. A bump from behind. What bravery. Even Bean seemed speechless in the face of such a boring run.

"Good race, Larry," he said, and I could've sworn I heard him yawn into the mike. "Larry Greer is your Road Warrior winner, folks, with Dale 'the Dude' Scott in second and our vixen in car six'en, Casey 'the Lady' LaPlante, taking third. Thundermakers, please report to your pits. And, race fans, get ready for a special treat—the Granite County Antique Car Club is here to take us back to the golden age of the automobile with a few classic laps around the high-banked oval."

❧

I took my pit crew, minus Jim, who had to get back to work, out for a third-place celebration at the Coffee Pot Café, which I knew would be empty until dinnertime, since everyone in town was still up at Demon's Run, watching the *real* race, the Thundermaker Sportsman division. I tried to seem happy about my finish and let the Sharks know that they were the best friends I'd ever had, even though I still feared for Jim's life when I heard them talking about him as a romantic prospect. I also tried to hide the pain in my gut from how I'd left things with Fletcher. Tried. I knew it was futile to try and hide anything from the Sharks. I waited for the moment when Bernie, who was sitting next to me, bumped me with her shoulder and said, "Let's hear it, Casey. You need to get this *out*."

"I'm all right," I said. "I'll get over it." I almost added *when I'm gone*, but the thought of being away from the Sharks made me sad every time I thought of it.

I noticed Mr. Hart, the café owner, eyeing me through the window connecting the kitchen and the dining room. I could only see his eyes, but the way they squinted made it seem like he was smiling.

I smiled at him just in case.

"Congratulations, Casey," he said.

"Thanks," I said, hoping that he didn't come out of the kitchen to talk about my college plans because that would *force* me to think about leaving the Sharks behind.

He turned up the volume of the radio back in the kitchen, and I heard Bean's voice:

". . . *amazing story, folks. She comes out of nowhere, Casey 'the Lady' LaPlante, a solid third-place finish here today, and as I reported just before the break, we have learned that she's your Demon's Run Fans' Pick for the Firecracker 50 Extravaganza. It seems she's already left the track, but, Casey, wherever you are, get yourself a Thundermaker ride, and you can make Demon's Run history being not only the first female racer, but the first sister-and-brother competitors we've ever heard of. Don Blodgett, Demon's Run director of racing, do I have that right? Is this a first?"*

"Well, it's definitely a first for Demon's Run. I can assure you of that."

"And how much do you think that factored in the fans' choice here, the novelty of maybe seeing Casey and Wade run against each other?"

"Oh, I think that had a lot to do with it. I mean, she's a good driver, there's no question, but Thundermakers are a different breed. And, well, if she can even get the equipment to race —"

"Can she? Can she get a Thundermaker car? Anyone going to lend her his ride?"

"It'd have to be someone who didn't qualify to run based on today's results. So that limits the prospects right there. And, Bean, generally speaking, the sponsors don't love the idea of having another driver in their car."

"I also hear a lot of people, I'm talking about the drivers, they don't like the attention she's getting and would just as soon not see her run."

"Well, the fans apparently feel differently about that."

"Yes, the fans have spoken. We need to break for a commercial, but there it is—Casey LaPlante is the Road Warrior Fans' Pick for the Firecracker 50. And that's going to be right here at Demon's Run Raceway next Sunday, Independence Day, the Fourth of Juuuly. Come on up. Bring the whole family. And we'll be right back with our Thundermaker wrap-up after these messages."

Mr. Hart turned the volume down and stood there smiling for a few moments, hands on his hips. "How about that?" he finally said.

I didn't know what to say, so I just said, "It sure is some thing."

"It's worth a few slices of pie at least," Mr. Hart said. "On the house." He returned to the kitchen.

"So, what does this mean?" Bernie said.

"It doesn't mean anything."

"It means you can run in that Thundermaker race," T.T. said, always a stickler for details.

"If I had a Thundermaker car, that is. Which I don't. Which are about a zillion bucks."

"Another driver can lend you one," T.T. said. "That's what the announcer guy said."

"He also pointed out, quite astutely, that I'm not so popular among the other drivers. And, anyway, who's going to lend his car to a girl? These guys can't stand get-ting *passed* by a girl."

No one said anything, as if we were all considering my options. "I've got my trophy—two, in fact—and I'm happy with third place for today," I said, which was a lie. "Maybe next week I'll win again."

"Road Warriors?" Tammy said.

I nodded.

The Sharks sighed in unison, which made us all laugh. I was happy to see them laughing, although it hurt to think that my days of laughing with them were running out.

Chapter 18

The usual post-race party was clogging the driveway, so I parked Hilda on the side of the road and walked up to the house. I crossed the yard where Wade had left tire marks about a month and a half earlier and tried to sneak in the front door without being noticed. Just my luck, Big Daddy and Vin Coates, the *Granite County Record* reporter, were blocking my path. They were arguing about something, but they quieted down when they saw me.

"Hey, Casey," Vin said as I passed him and walked up the front steps. "Good race today. Congratulations."

"Vin," Big Daddy said in what sounded like a warning.

"Thanks, Vin," I said and walked inside.

I grabbed an apple out of the refrigerator and headed for my room only to meet up with Big Daddy again as he came in the front door. I didn't like the look on his face, and it didn't seem to be bringing him much joy either. "Casey," he said. "We need to have a little chat."

Any time Big Daddy used those words, *little chat*, I knew that he meant a *big* chat, although he almost never had big chats with me. He often had them with Wade, usually about how my brother should maintain a better rapport with his racing sponsors, how he should do more public relations outreach, visit the schools, the hospital, build up his image in the eyes of the Circuit scouts. If Big Daddy wanted to have a big chat with me, it must've been about Wade. "Aren't you going to congratulate me?" I said. "I was the Fans' Pick."

Big Daddy crossed his arms and looked past me into the kitchen. "Congratulations."

"Thanks." I walked to the foot of the stairs and rested my torso on the banister. I decided to spare him any more stress so that he could get back to the party: "Don't worry. I'm not racing against Wade."

Big Daddy exhaled as if he'd been holding his breath. "That's right, you're not. Not only are you not driving, but you're not to talk to your Uncle Harvey again."

I froze.

"I should've known something was up. Vin Coates says he followed your crew chief, the punk—"

"Jim's not a punk."

"Followed his tow truck out to your uncle's garage."

"You can't stop me from going there."

"Oh yes I can."

"No you can't."

"Well, I sure can stop you from going to Cray College, now, can't I?"

The words were like a boot to the stomach. I dropped onto the stairs, looking up to see that pained grimace of Big Daddy's blurring behind tears pooling steadily in my eyes.

"Look, Casey," Big Daddy said, trying to sound more reasonable. "That Pembroke Circuit team is sending two people up on Sunday. We can't show them some kind of three-ring circus."

"I love Uncle Harvey," I said. "He's a good man."

"He's a snake," Big Daddy said, seething.

"What did he ever do to — "

"That's between your uncle and me."

The first tears spilled onto my cheeks. I wondered where Mom was, what she could do to help me. I thought about telling Big Daddy that she'd known for a while that I'd been training with Uncle Harvey. In that moment, I couldn't figure out whether ratting my mother out would help or hurt matters. All I knew was that I felt sick.

"You're not to see him, to race in the Warriors on Sunday, or to talk to Vin or any other reporters. Understand?"

I tried to answer him but couldn't get any words out.

"We're too close to blow this now."

Again, I started to speak but failed to form words. I listened to Big Daddy walk into the kitchen and out through the garage door. I wiped my eyes, stood, and headed for my car.

☙

Uncle Harvey seemed to have been waiting for me on the front steps of the cottage. He didn't even wave as I pulled into the yard. He scooted over on the steps so I could sit.

"Keep it up, Casey," he said, "and you could be Rookie of the Year."

"I'm finished."

Uncle Harvey nodded, as if he'd been expecting that too. "Guy from the newspaper came out. He tell your dad?"

"Yes."

"So it goes, then."

"What happened, Uncle Harvey?" I said and almost started bawling again. "What is *wrong* with him?"

Uncle Harvey sighed. "It's a long story—well, not that long, but it happened a long time ago."

"I need to hear it."

"Yeah, you'll probably end up hearing it sooner or later anyway. That reporter seemed to know a fair bit of it. Just promise me one thing." Uncle Harvey looked me in the eye. He appeared tired, haggard even.

"What?"

"Promise me you'll let this whole matter rest right here. People move on, as they should. And when you can't change things, then, well, the best thing to do is leave them behind."

"What did my father do?"

"Are you saying you'll keep this promise?"

I gazed toward the shop and didn't speak. Anyone else, and I might have said yes, but I didn't want to lie to Uncle Harvey. I just didn't feel like I could promise anything to anyone, not as angry as I was about the pileup of secrets, lies, and ultimatums my life suddenly amounted to.

Uncle Harvey sighed. "Well, thanks for being honest anyway." He leaned forward, clasping his hands beneath his chin. "The story actually begins with your mother," he said.

Uncle Harvey's story didn't take long, but each word stung like a hornet. He'd been Big Daddy's crew chief, just like everyone knew. What I didn't know was that, for as long as Uncle Harvey could remember, he'd also had a desperate crush on Carol Beech, a local girl he remembered from high school, a girl with dreams of seeing the world. My mother. The season when Wade LaPlante started winning a lot of races, Uncle Harvey said, he almost mustered the confidence to ask her out. But my father beat him to it, even though, by that point, Wade LaPlante could've dated any girl in Granite County—did, in fact, "go with more than his fair share," as my uncle put it. Wade and Carol apparently made a match, and after the final race that season—the Granite Bowl 75—they made it official. My father stood in Victory Lane to receive his trophies for winning both the Bowl and the track championship, and when the announcer asked him to share a few words with the fans, the champ took the microphone and proposed to my mother. In front of the hometown crowd, she said yes.

Uncle Harvey was devastated, he said, but he blamed only himself for hesitating. He and Big Daddy even talked it out, since it'd been no secret to anyone in town that Harvey had been pining for Carol. The brothers agreed to keep the racing team together. If they could get over this bump in the road, then maybe Wade LaPlante Motorsports would prove to have the stuff to make the big time. The Circuit.

Wade Junior was born midway into the following racing season and, with him, a new name for Wade Senior—Big Daddy. Fatherhood seemed to light a new competitive fire under Big Daddy, and by the time the Firecracker 50 had rolled around, some Circuit scouts had called to say they'd be coming up to see him run. On the day the scouts came to Demon's Run, however, Big Daddy ran the worst race of his career—a showing as poor as his rookie days in the Road Warrior division, fans were saying. "He was all over the track," Uncle Harvey said, "bumping-and-running, biting wall, and generally making a nuisance of himself. Any other driver would've been DQ'ed and on an extended vacation from the raceway." But the track officials bent every rule there was to keep Big Daddy in the race so the Circuit scouts could see him run.

And run he did, right down into the turn-three ditch on about lap thirty in the fifty-lap race. He didn't even finish.

The scouts lost interest, the whole town was devastated, and people immediately started looking for someone to blame. With Big Daddy's help, they all pointed their fingers at Uncle Harvey. "They said it was sabotage," Uncle Harvey said. "They said I was still jealous about losing your mom, which was true enough. But, still . . ." Uncle Harvey stared across the yard in the direction of town and sighed. "Your father came up with about a dozen complaints about the car that'd never been issues before. The springs, tire pressure, sway bar, even his safety harness was too tight. There was nothing right with his car, which told me that there was something definitely wrong with him."

"Did you ask him?"

"Ask him what?"

"Ask him if anything was wrong with him?"

Uncle Harvey shook his head. "Didn't need to. I knew."

"Well, what was it?"

Uncle Harvey stared at me as if pondering something. Then he looked down. "I'm afraid I can't tell you," he said. "That's a part of the story I'm not bringing back."

"But—"

"Let's just leave it like this: It was easier for your father to go along with his failure being my fault than his. That was the simplest explanation. And, in all honesty, I can't say now that his decision wasn't the right one. People were certainly willing to believe him." Uncle Harvey laughed to himself—bitterly, it seemed. "As if my whole career as a crew chief didn't hang on your father's success. But did anyone consider that?" He scratched at green paint on his fingernails.

"So, you were barred from Demon's Run?" I said.

"Not barred, but I was definitely unwelcome."

"And you didn't fight it? You just gave up?"

Uncle Harvey looked at me and chuckled, but I didn't get what was so funny. "Aren't you the one who told me, not ten minutes ago, that you're quitting?" he said.

"I have to. My father said he won't pay for my college if I race again."

Uncle Harvey made the whistling sound with his teeth. "Well, then, he's got you. He wins again." He looked across the yard. "Fact is, the whole ordeal made me realize something. I could see that people around here had put your father so high up on a pedestal, were so desperate to see him make it, that they just couldn't accept that he'd let them down. They'd made him into an idol. They believed in him."

"They're doing the same thing to Wade."

Uncle Harvey nodded. "Don't get me wrong, I love short-track racing." He looked at me as if knowing what I was about to say.

"Me too."

He smiled but quickly frowned again. "But if people were going to lose all sense of . . . of . . . of *proportion*

218

over this thing, well, then, I'd just as soon walk away."

I knew so well what that felt like that I didn't need to say anything. I took a look around the yard, recalling my first run up here, the day Jim almost ran me over, and then my first laps around the pasture in Theo. My eye fell on the shed set way back. I noticed the grass surrounding it was flattened. Focusing a little harder, I also saw what looked like flattened grass in the shape of tire tracks connecting the shed and the shop.

I stood and started walking over there.

"There's no point, Casey," Uncle Harvey said. "It's too late."

I threw open the shed door to find a gleaming Thundermaker car painted forest green with gold trim, gold letters spelling GO CASEY GO across the hood and front panels, and a number: 06.

My limbs tingled as if I were seeing an image from a dream, like I'd felt the day I opened my Cray College acceptance letter.

Uncle Harvey came up behind me.

"You built this for me?" I said.

Uncle Harvey sighed. "I probably shouldn't have, but once I got the idea in my head, I couldn't stop. They call that color British Racing Green. Not sure why."

I didn't know what to say. I wanted to cry.

"It's not such a big deal. I mean, take a look around my yard. Spare parts I got."

"Can I drive it?" I said.

Uncle Harvey walked into the shed, reached through the driver's-side window, and yanked out the steering wheel. "Strap in," he said, "and tell me if you think those

Thundermaker boys are half as special as they think they are."

I took a spin around the pasture and felt the engine rumbling through the marrow of my bones. I cursed Big Daddy, and then cursed the whole Demon's Run crowd for making me Fans' Pick. I liked the way this car handled, yes I did, and I fit snugly behind the wheel, as if my hands were destined to grip it.

Chapter 19

The post-race party had long since ended by the time I got home. In fact, I'd pushed my luck a little bit by staying at Uncle Harvey's till about eleven o'clock. That wasn't so late for me to be out on a summer night, but, then, I rarely went anywhere at any time of year, so I figured my parents would wonder where I'd been. At least I knew my mother would wonder. As far as Big Daddy was concerned, unless I wanted to go to State instead of Cray College, which I didn't, I was no longer an obstacle to the destiny of Wade LaPlante Motorsports. He and Wade were sitting at the dining room table, looking at spreadsheets, when I came in through the door connecting the garage and the kitchen. Neither looked up at me, but I could see Wade's jaw muscles working as I passed him on my way upstairs.

I wasn't in my room for more than a minute or so before Mom knocked on my door. I sat at my desk, picked up a magazine, and said, "Come in."

"Hey, Casey," she said. "How are you doing?"

"Fine. You?"

"I'm fine. Any big plans for the week?"

I stared at my blank computer screen for a moment, gathered my thoughts, and gave my mother one last chance to show me that she was on my side, that she agreed that Big Daddy's ultimatum was a pretty lousy way to treat me, that she understood Uncle Harvey was a living, breathing person who deserved more respect than she or anyone had given him. "I don't know what to do," I said. "On the one hand, it seems like I should get in my racecar and run some practice laps somewhere. I mean, I was the Fans' Pick, after all."

"Well, Casey," Mom said delicately, "as I know your father asked you—"

"He didn't *ask* me anything."

"He'd prefer—"

"Demanded."

"Casey, *please!*" Mom snapped. She rested a hand on her forehead for a few moments, like I'd given her a headache. "Wade has been working extremely hard for this opportunity to race for the scouts."

"I understand. I do. I just . . ." I stared at the ceiling, as if reading the answer among the glow-in-the-dark stars I'd stuck up there when I was ten.

"What is it?"

"I just wish he'd come about this golden opportunity more honestly."

Mom sat on my bed but said nothing.

I faced her. "Why did you come in here?"

Mom ran her hands along the knees of her pants as though warming her palms. "I just wanted to see how you're doing."

"This isn't about Uncle Harvey?"

Mom looked into the corner, as if more pleasant words might be over there, waiting for an opportunity to enter the conversation. "What about Uncle Harvey?"

"Oh, just that I think it's awful the way he's been

treated by people around here. By you and Big Daddy. Like he doesn't exist."

Mom pressed her hands more firmly onto her pants and rubbed.

"You know," I continued, "I could almost forgive the ultimatum Big Daddy gave me, despite the fact that it's a lame way to treat a kid who's worked so hard to get into a school like Cray College, if he were just big enough to apologize to Uncle—"

"Casey, that matter does *not* concern you," she said, rocketing to her feet.

"Why not? He's my uncle and I love him. But when did family ever matter to anyone here at Wade LaPlante Motorsports?"

Mom loomed over me for a second, then crossed to the door. She grabbed the doorknob but didn't turn it. "Do you have *any* idea what this means to your father?" she said in an unsteady voice. "Do you have *any* idea what he's sacrificed for this? Do you *know* how hard he works so that you and Wade can—"

"I just think that—"

"Well, maybe you don't know everything, Casey. Maybe there are things that you just don't know."

She glared, a curtain of black hair hanging over one eye, her chest rising and falling.

"What happened to Big Daddy that day," I said, "that day the Circuit scouts came? He had some kind of melt-down."

Mom's glare softened, as if punctured by a memory flashing in her mind. Her hand loosened on the doorknob and, a few seconds later, slid to her side. She leaned on the door and placed a hand on her forehead again. "Your uncle told you about that day?" she said.

"Yes. He said it was a disaster. He said he took the blame for it. Sounded like it wasn't his fault, though."

Mom looked at me for a long time, almost a minute, it seemed, staring blankly for part of it, seeming to drift into a memory for another part. "I cared a great deal for your uncle," she said quietly, as though sharing a secret.

"You loved him."

Mom's eyes widened, as if I'd sworn at her, but then settled back into a sad, distant look. "Yes."

"But you married his brother."

"I loved your father, too."

"You loved them both?"

Mom closed her eyes and sighed. "I was young," she said, eyes still closed. "Things were starting to really take off for your father." She opened her eyes. "I was swept up in it, you might say, drawn into his dream."

I didn't know how to respond. I knew that, in the time when my parents were growing up, relationships developed differently than they did for me and my peers. Still, this whole being "swept up in it" made their courtship sound like something out of an old movie. Then again, life in Fliverton often felt like an old movie. Not exactly the most cutting-edge town on the map.

"So, what do you think set him off that day at the track, when the Circuit scouts came?" I said.

Mom crossed her arms and looked past me, out my bedroom window, the curtain billowing in the night breeze across my desk.

224

I privately noted that my mother had just admitted, in acknowledging that Big Daddy had been upset "that day," that his lousy racing performance might not have been Uncle Harvey's fault. The blood rose in my face, coaxing beads of sweat along my temples. "No clues at all?" I said, trying to conceal my snippiness. For the first time in my life, I was actually getting something close to answers from Mom about what had gone on in my own family all my life.

"He and I had a conversation the morning of the race," she said. "A good conversation."

"You and Uncle Harvey."

She nodded. "Before the rest of the team arrived. I guess I wanted to apologize."

"For what?"

Mom shook her head in a strange way that seemed not to convey disagreement or anything negative, just a sense of bewilderment at how life unfolds. "For not letting him know how I felt . . . before it was too late."

"Too late?"

Mom looked at me and smiled, then laughed to herself, as if amused to have shared any of this with me, as if the notion that I might understand were laughable. "I'd agreed to marry your father in front of all those people—people who worshipped him. And I loved him, I really did, but . . ."

"But . . . ?"

"I know it sounds silly to you, being so independent, but my feelings were complicated, and I was uncomfortable with that. People considered me lucky to be with your father, and I listened to them. I was ready for something new, something bigger than the life I lived here. Like I said, your father had a dream, a big dream, and I guess I couldn't resist it." She crossed her arms as if feeling a chill. "And I don't regret it. I love your father." She looked at me. "And he and I love you very much."

The sound of Wade's voice carried through my open window as he complained to one of his crewmembers about some automotive matter. Mom's face darkened, her gaze fixed on the window. "It's hard to find any privacy around here, isn't it?" she said.

We both listened as Wade then told a crude joke, which drew someone's grating laugh. It sounded like Lonnie.

"You think Big Daddy overheard you and Uncle Harvey that day?"

Mom nodded, eyes still fixed on the window. "I know he did." She shook her head. "It was reckless, talking so openly about it."

"It doesn't sound reckless," I said. "What's reckless is that Uncle Harvey had to take all the blame. It's not just reckless. It's mean—"

"Casey," Mom interrupted and reached for the doorknob again, her crisp, formal, motherly tone now returned. "We want the best for you, your father and I. Try to understand."

"That's the end of the discussion?"

"There's nothing more to discuss. Please do as your father says. I can't even tell you how important this is to him. And when it's all over, we'll all sit down for a long chat." She stared at me, and when, after a few moments,

I hadn't said anything, she opened the door and left.

Listening to her footsteps retreating down the stairs, I believed her. I believed that she and Big Daddy did want the best for me. But if that came at someone else's expense —someone I loved—how could that possibly be *the best*?

Chapter 20

The week that followed was bizarre. As angry as I was at my parents, especially Big Daddy, at times I wished that he'd broadcast to the whole town his command that I not race again. Then maybe Vin Coates wouldn't have sent me e-mail after e-mail asking whether I was running in the Firecracker 50. Wade's crewmembers could've withheld the cold looks they gave me as I passed them in our driveway, where they worked more or less around the clock on car 02. Fletcher's expression was a little harder to read, but I was able to avoid eye contact with him most of the time. If Big Daddy had shared with others the news that he'd sent me permanently to the pits, then people in town might've stopped giving me smiles and thumbs-up as I walked along Main Street, minding my own business. One day that week, as I walked through town on my way home from a morning run, I had to stop four times to chat with people—my seventh-grade art teacher, Ms. Rhiele, some random friends of my parents, and even two Dolphins, Squeaky and Beachball. At one point, while I was tying my shoe in front of the Coffee Pot Café, two girls in a passing car shrieked, "Go, Casey, Go!"

So I took longer and longer jogs across the summer fields, trying to erase racing from my mind and replace it with thoughts of Cray College. It didn't work. No matter how much I feared the prospect of not being able to go to

Cray if Big Daddy refused to pay for it, I was having trouble accepting the idea that my racing days were over. My short-track fever hadn't broken. Not even a little.

Though it didn't make much sense, given my father's threat, I was still spending time hammering around Uncle Harvey's pasture in the Thundermaker car 06. I mean, my uncle had built me the car, so I figured the least I could do was drive it. Besides, I knew that Big Daddy and Wade were too caught up in preparing to run for the scouts to keep track of where I went and what I did. And, no offense to Theo, but the way that eight-cylinder Thundermaker engine rumbled in my bones made driving the Road Warrior car seem like a major step backward. Like spending a week at college and then getting sent back to high school. I just had to drive that Thundermaker ride.

As I wound around the pasture, I carefully studied the snappy yank of the tires at the gentlest touch of the steering wheel. I learned to judge how close I was from the trees lining the meadow from my way-sunken-down seat. I flew across the field as fast as I could, braking in the turns, setting the car for another straightaway. Brake, accelerate, brake, accelerate. Once in a while Uncle Harvey came out, usually with a sandwich for me and something to drink, and asked me what I was doing. I told him I was just messing around. Then I'd spend the next couple of hours running practice laps in Theo just to assure Uncle Harvey that I wasn't thinking crazy racing thoughts. In truth, I was consumed by them.

Toward the end of that week, on Friday, as I was flying around the pasture in the Thundermaker, I noticed Jim watching from the path cutting through to Uncle Harvey's yard. I ran a good, hard lap, showing off a little, and pulled over beside him.

I popped the steering wheel and climbed out the window. "Now *this* is a racecar," I said and slapped the roof.

Jim walked over and, standing next to the hood, ran his eyes along the length of the car. "Your uncle does nice work. I think I've seen bits and pieces of this rig somewhere else." He flipped his chin at me. "You going to race it?"

I leaned against the car. "Haven't decided."

"Harvey says you're not."

"So you already know. Why'd you ask me?"

"You just said you haven't decided."

I crossed my arms. "Well, that's because I haven't."

Jim leaned against the car next to me. Neither of us said anything for a few moments. Finally he turned to me, his eyes narrowed as if in concentration. "Can I ask you a personal question?" he said.

I laughed, remembering how I'd tried to pry into his background a few weeks earlier. "Sure," I said.

"Don't take this the wrong way."

"I'll try not to."

"Well . . ." He scratched at his shoulder and crossed his arms. "What is it you've got against this place?"

"Fliverton?"

He nodded.

"Be easier to tell you what I *don't* have against it."

"I don't think you mean that. I mean, how could you?"

I gazed across the meadow toward Uncle Harvey's cottage and thought of how I'd felt the night he and I crossed paths down at the fishing access. I was already drifting away from Fliverton, and no one noticed or cared. Then I'd gone and made all that noise—the sound of Theo's unstoppable engine—and became somebody. But who? A Demon's Run racecar driver, complete with my own nickname. I was a licensed member of the very community I desperately wanted to escape. But how long had that even lasted before I became unwelcome, an intruder—at least to my very own family? Wasn't that, in essence, how Big Daddy saw me? As an obstacle, a pothole, a wreck to drive around on the path toward his racing destiny? If someone had to be driven off the road to clear the way, even if that someone was his brother or daughter, then that's what he'd do.

I looked toward the sound of Uncle Harvey working on a car in the garage on the other side of the trees, tucked away in the little box Big Daddy and everyone else had stuck him in. "Trust me, Jim," I said, "I'm nobody around here." I might just as well have said, *My uncle and I are nobodies around here.*

Jim shook his head. "I hear them talking about you. On the streets, in the grocery store—"

"That's ridiculous." Blood rushed into my face as I considered how invisible I'd once been, never mind my cross-country ribbons and my academic achievements, and how popular I suddenly was by virtue of being able to make four left turns faster than a bunch of guys. There really was something ridiculous about it—ridiculous and unfair.

"I'm not saying it makes any sense," Jim said, "but it's true. I've heard it with my own ears. You've got people talking here. You had your name in the paper every day so far this week. Sounds like that reporter, Coates, is getting

231

downright irritated that he can't nail down if you're running on Sunday or not."

"Must be a slow news week."

"And didn't you sign autographs for those girls?"

I shrugged.

"I'll tell you something," Jim said in a tone I'd never heard him use before. He didn't seem angry, but he wasn't pleased. Considering that, in the span of a few minutes standing around in a pasture, we'd exchanged more words than in all the conversations we'd had up to that point combined, I turned to give him my full attention. "I know what it's like to be invisible," he said. "Poor. Homeless. A delinquent. Now, you don't want to know my life story—"

"Sure I do."

"Well I don't want to tell it to you. But I do want you to understand that there are a lot worse places than Fliverton and even Byam. I've seen them. I've lived in a few, got chased out of a few, and I consider myself lucky to be standing right where I am today."

I didn't know how to respond. I felt like telling Jim that we all wanted different things out of life and that I was entitled to my opinion about whether Fliverton's obsession with racing made it a crazy or sane place to be. But I knew that, looked at through his eyes and experience, my problems with my hometown were just petty complaints. Still, that didn't diminish the anger that'd built up inside me while we'd been talking: anger at the fact that to be somebody in Fliverton was to be a *racing* somebody, anger at myself for knowing this before I started racing but still thinking that proving myself on everyone else's terms was going to change something—in me or in them. I'd driven all that way for what? To be told what to do. To be put in my place. To be told, yet again, who I am. "I'm glad you're feeling at home here," I finally said, as much to calm the bitter storm swirling in my gut as to recognize Jim's perspective on the matter. Still, I couldn't help adding, "But you don't know what it's like to be me."

Jim shrugged. "No one ever does, right?"

"Why are we having this conversation?" I grumbled. "You want to know if I need a tow on the Fourth of July."

Jim's expression darkened. "I don't work for you," he said.

"Then why are you doing this? Why do you even care?"

Jim jammed his hands in his pockets and looked away. "I'm not sure. I guess I'm trying to learn something."

"Learn what?"

"Learn how to get on in a place."

"Well," I said with a laugh that came out sounding snottier than I'd intended, "don't look at me."

Jim looked directly at me—and it wasn't one of his sunnier looks, not that he'd ever displayed many of those. "I was thinking about your uncle." He flipped his chin toward the path to the yard. "There's a guy who survives on what he knows, what he can do." Jim slapped the Thundermaker's front panel. "I admire him." He wore the faintest smile as he said this, as if he were trying to conceal it. Something had definitely changed in him since the day we met. "But I've got to tell you," he said, his expression growing serious again. "Harvey gets agitated whenever you're out here in this car."

"Why? He built it for me."

"Sure, but now you can't race it because of your dad. You told Harvey you're not racing, but I'm not sure he believes you. He's not stupid, you know."

"That he is not."

"And if he thinks racing this car is a bad idea, well, I'd take that under consideration."

"I will," I said, trying not to sound snippy, like I sometimes did when people offered me advice I didn't ask for.

Jim gave me those narrowed eyes again, and then—classic Jim Biggins—he just walked away.

❦

I passed through the garage and opened the kitchen door, spotting Big Daddy and Wade in their usual place, at the dining room table surrounded by spreadsheets. I sat down with them, right across from Wade with Big Daddy on my left, and said nothing. Big Daddy frowned at me, and Wade squinted with more open annoyance. "What's up?" I said.

Wade snorted. "We're working."

"Oh." I reached for the wicker basket of napkins in the center of the table and began working on some grease under my fingernails.

Wade snorted again.

"Need a tissue?" I said.

I could feel Big Daddy's eyes on me, but he didn't say anything.

"You guys ready for the big race?" I said. "It's less than forty-eight hours away—"

"Casey, your brother and I are right in the middle of

something," Big Daddy said, still sounding fairly calm about my interruption.

"I got an e-mail from the cross-country coach at Cray," I said, which wasn't a complete lie, since I'd received a general welcome e-mail from the athletic department about a week earlier.

"Who?" Wade said.

Big Daddy sighed. "That's great, Casey."

Mom walked into the kitchen from the garage, and Big Daddy looked at her. I kept watching my father. A pleading expression flashed in his eyes, as if he were desperate to be rescued. From me. His daughter. I looked at Wade, and he was making the very same face.

"Casey," Mom said, obviously getting the hint, "I found a few things I thought you could use in your dorm room. Come have a look."

"Maybe in a little while," I said, turning back to Big Daddy.

He was already immersed in his spreadsheets again.

I really was already gone.

I went upstairs and called Jim. I told him that I was sorry if I'd seemed cranky earlier in the day, and I let him know that I was taking the next day, Saturday, off from racing in Byam. "I need a break," I said. "I've had racing on the brain."

"That can't be good," he said.

Then I called Bernie and told her my plan.

Chapter 21

Sunday morning, I hit my alarm clock the moment it went off. I dressed and then crept downstairs. I eased open the door leading from the kitchen to the garage and nearly screamed at the sight of Wade sitting behind the wheel of car 02. He watched me pass the car, but when I was out of the garage, he slid out his window and followed me. "You're going to do it, aren't you?" he said from a few steps behind. "You're going to race."

"People are sleeping," I said.

"Why are you doing this? Why do you have to do this?"

"I don't *have* to do anything. I make my own decisions. That's the whole point."

Wade stopped walking.

I got into my car and looked at him standing there, arms at his sides, shoulders slumped. He looked sad, pathetic even, and I wondered where all his action-hero cockiness had gone. He walked over to the passenger side and knocked on the window.

I rolled it down.

He reached in, unlocked the door, and climbed into the passenger seat.

"What are you doing?" I said.

"No, what are *you* doing? Are you racing?"

"I was thinking about it."

"Don't. At least not in the Thundermakers. I heard you got a ride."

"Where'd you—"

"Doesn't matter."

"One of your butt-kissing crewmembers spied on me."

"Just don't, Casey."

"Why?"

"Please. The scouts aren't coming to see brother-sister racing circus nonsense. This is my day. This is all I've got."

"You want my sympathy? After the way you treat people? And besides, no day belongs to anyone."

Wade looked ahead, as if he were a driver's ed instructor bracing for a first lesson. "You don't understand," he said. "You think it's easy?"

"What, treating girls like shop rags you just toss in the wastebasket?"

"I'm back with Samantha."

"What?"

Wade nodded.

"How'd you manage that? She actually seems to have a brain."

"I apologized like I've never apologized before. I *begged.*"

"I'd have loved to see that."

"You want to know why I'm back with Samantha?"

I couldn't imagine why my brother would make one decision or another on any matter that didn't have four tires attached to it. "Let me guess. Those 'fun' team T-shirts Mom bought didn't look good enough on Gail or Maxine, and Samantha bumped her head on something."

"She wants me to stay," he said in a small voice.

"What?"

"Here in Fliverton."

"But if you get on a Circuit team— "

"I know."

"You can't stay."

"I know, I know." Wade snorted. "Believe me, I know. Since the day I strapped in for my first Kart race, everyone's been talking about the day I leave—*dreaming* about it." Wade just kept staring ahead. "Point is, if Samantha had her way, I'd stay."

"You don't want to go to North Carolina?" I said.

Wade shrugged. "I guess I do. I mean, of course I do. It's what I've been working toward. But, I don't know, it's like I never had a chance to work toward anything else."

"I thought you liked racing."

"I do." Wade turned toward the garage, where car 02 sat awaiting its glorious destiny. "I just . . . I don't know. It's just weird, that's all, growing up hearing everybody talk about how they can't wait until you're gone."

"Well, but Wade, that's not exactly what they're saying. People want you to succeed."

"I know, I know. And Samantha and I have been talking."

"Talking about what?"

"You know. Like, if I do get on the Pembroke team, maybe she'd go down there with me. And if I don't, we'll maybe move in together here." He looked at me. "Point is, people are going to miss you, Casey. Nobody besides Samantha really cares about me."

"You know that's not true."

Wade arched his eyebrows. "Big Daddy?"

I didn't know what to say. Part of me wanted to disagree with him, but another part wanted to think he was right, to think that Wade—selfish, immature, cocky, man-child Wade—maybe saw something that I'd missed. It was a strange idea to grasp, and I wasn't sure I trusted it.

"I wouldn't exactly call Big Daddy *my* biggest fan. He said he wouldn't pay for Cray College if I raced."

"So don't race," Wade said. "This is my day."

A car turning up Meadow Ridge Road caught my attention. I watched the rig crest the swale: Fletcher's Dart. The thought suddenly came to me that maybe Wade was just psyching me out. As the Dart dipped again, my stomach clenched. "I make my own decisions," I said. "Now I've got to go."

Wade watched me. "You know I'd miss you if you go," he said. "I would," he said. "Take the only thing I've got, and take it away with you to fancy college land."

I fired Hilda's ignition.

Wade got out and slammed the door.

A light turned on in my parents' bedroom.

∽

I drove Hilda to the fishing access and pulled up next to Bernie's Toyota. I opened the passenger door for T.T., who got in. I led Bernie and Tammy to Uncle Harvey's road, where I had Bernie pull over about one hundred feet from his driveway. I told her to turn the car around to face back in the direction from which we'd just come. Better for a quick getaway. I put Hilda in neutral and got out so that T.T. could get behind the wheel.

I walked up Uncle Harvey's driveway and crossed the yard. I opened the shed door as quietly as I could, climbed into car 06, and took a deep breath. In three lightning-quick motions, I fired up the ignition, put the car in gear, and drove across the yard. I didn't even look in my rearview mirror.

On the road, I slipped in between Bernie's car and Hilda so that they were leading and tailing me. I began my journey to Demon's Run sandwiched between the cars, low to the pavement, stealthy and out of sight.

Chapter 22

I was the first car in through the pit gate, so I took a pit at the end of Thundermaker Row. I killed the engine, climbed out the window, and Byam-gripped my crazy crew.

We wandered to the snack bar together and got some breakfast. Vin Coates, sitting at a picnic table and drinking a cup of coffee, nearly spat his doughnut out when he saw me. Looking toward my pit, he must've figured out that I'd found a Thundermaker ride after all—and that he'd been missing the story in the *Granite County Record* all week.

I sat on the hood of car 06 and reviewed what I'd learned in the past couple of months about racecar driving. I visualized the track, the turns, my front end drifting somewhere out there just beyond my vision. I ignored the other drivers who filed into the pit slots around me and, instead, reminded myself that I had no idea what it was going to be like racing the Thundermaker drivers. As the sun burned off the morning haze, I tried to think of names for my ride. The Green Ghost. The Green Snake, which made more sense than the Red Snake. The Green Girl, which sounded too girly. The Green Party. I couldn't think of anything clever, so I settled on Green.

The Road Warriors ran their practice laps, and then Bean called the Thundermakers to the course. I'd eaten a decent breakfast, but I still felt lightheaded as I rolled onto the track and began circling with the twenty-five other cars. I was shaking too, as much from the rumble of my engine as from nervousness. I focused as intently as I could on finding my line, trying to suppress any thought or impulse that didn't have to do with keeping my speed up.

Every other lap or so, a driver pulled alongside and gave me a dark look, but mainly I expected that drivers would try to stay away from me, since, as Bean had reminded the crowd as we were lining up for practice, "the last few street-stock Fans' Picks have made better roadblocks than racers out there, the exception being, of course, Wade 'the Blade' LaPlante three seasons ago." Because my decision to race in the Firecracker had been a secret, my rig hadn't been set up with the close mechanical attention that I'd grown used to. Still, Green responded like a whip to every jerk in my wrist at the wheel, the tires seeming to grab at the asphalt and tug it close.

I ran my practice laps and nailed down a line: In turn one, I'd roll my right tire over the star-shaped crack. In turn two, I'd roll my right tire over a tar blotch shaped like the state of Florida. In turn three, my left tire would split two parallel skid marks. And in turn four, I'd aim for another tar blotch, this one shaped more like New Hampshire. This would be my best route for control and cornering force, my ticket to good exit speed. Drive the line. Drive the line. Drive the line.

I pushed the speed a little, feeling the tires hold.

I drove two laps behind Johnny Savard, in his WILLOW RIVER INN car 11, maintaining his speed. Coming out of turn four, I accelerated and tried to take a lap as fast as I could up high, then another down low, knowing T. T. was behind the pit gate with her stopwatch and notebook. I wondered if I was going to be able to run anywhere near fast enough. Or would I bookend my racing career, and kill my college dreams, in another publicly humiliating wreck of sheet metal and rubber? I passed Wade in car 02 midway around but didn't look at him.

I tried another lap at full speed and passed him again. This time, I gave him a quick glance.

He stared straight, shaking his head.

The pit gate swung open. Practice over.

∽

The drivers' meeting was the most torturous one I'd endured. I sat on the front bench but as close to the end as possible to escape as soon as Mr. Blodgett was through. The main topic of his diatribe was the Thundermaker drivers' tendency to throw themselves immediately into a race without taking a lap to let the field settle. "If I've told you once, I've told you a thousand times," he said, whapping his leg with his clipboard, "I've never seen a race won in the first turn of a race—or the second! Give it a lap. One lousy lap."

The one thing different about this Demon's Run drivers' meeting was that I didn't feel like anyone was laughing at me anymore. I was sure no one expected I'd be able to compete with the Thundermakers, but a general sense of hostility swirled around the bleachers regarding the fact that I'd decided to race at all. If drivers didn't think I was acting selfishly by soaking up some of Wade's limelight on the day of his Circuit tryout—and I'm sure many of them did—then they were probably annoyed at the prospect of taking time to dust me out there on the track before getting on with their race.

∾

Walking back to the pits, I spotted Jim's wrecker pulled up to my slot with Theo on the flatbed. As I climbed out of Green and pulled off my helmet, I saw a familiar silhouette in the passenger seat of the tow truck cab.

I walked over to the passenger window, nodding to Jim, who sat on the tailgate. Uncle Harvey slumped over to his left and looked blearily ahead, as if waiting for a traffic light to change.

"I couldn't tell you," I said. "I was afraid you'd try to stop me."

"I am going to try to stop you," Uncle Harvey said.

"Why?"

He turned to me.

Bean gave the ten-minute warning for the Road Warrior feature.

"This is not your race to run anymore, Casey," Uncle Harvey said. "You proved your point long ago, not that you should've had to. You can race. Now get your Warrior ride down—"

"It is so my race to run," I said, struck by how, every time I'd jumped over one obstacle—my failed Demon's Run debut, the Corkum County enduro, trophies at both tracks—I'd merely encountered another one. Wade and Fletcher's cruel joke. Big Daddy's ultimatum. And now Uncle Harvey telling me to back off.

I looked around, taking in the carnival atmosphere of a race day: the fried-dough stand; families milling about, waving to one another, exchanging Sunday-morning pleasantries; rowdy, beer-drinking spectators on Beer Belly Hill getting a head start on the day's blitzing; an announcer who, in another venue, could actually be a barker trying to lure people into a freak show.

I spotted a group of girls—little girls and older girls, some girls my age—watching me from behind the pit gate. A few of the little ones waved.

I waved back and felt that surreal aura wrap itself around me, like it had when I'd signed those two girls' autographs. I remembered the feel of Green's tires grabbing at the track, the vibration of the Thundermaker engine dancing along my bones. They were strange sensations, but they also seemed somehow . . . inevitable. As if every muddy trail I'd ever run with the cross-country team, every geometry test I'd ever aced, every afternoon I'd tutored the lawyers' kids, every Saturday night I'd spent home alone studying, every reckless race up Meadow Ridge Road I'd ever won against Wade, and every kind of race I'd run since then had been leading up to this one.

I stared through the windshield from Uncle Harvey's perspective and looked to the horizon, treetops stretching like low-hanging clouds to the river. *Why does the place I'm so sick of have to be so beautiful?* I wondered.

"You can't win a race in just one lap," Uncle Harvey said, "but you sure can lose one."

He'd given me advice before, but that morning his words struck me differently. They seemed almost like a riddle. I saw they could mean two things: race and don't race. It all depended on what race I thought I was running, the one out on the quarter-mile oval with the high-banked turns or the longer, even more perilous race that lay beyond. Way beyond. It was a test—something I used to be pretty good at taking. What was the answer?

"Did you set the tire pressures on Green this morning?"

"That what you call the rig?"

"Did you?"

Uncle Harvey scratched at some green paint on his pant leg. "Old habits die hard. And I know you well enough now to know you're following your own course. I respect that."

I reached into the cab and hugged him. I gripped him even more tightly as Bean called the Road Warriors to the course for their feature. I held on until the engines passing down pit row to the track gate had all rumbled by. I kept holding another minute until I was sure the gate was closed. I let go and stood back.

"Keep turning left," Uncle Harvey said. "Take what the race brings you. And be careful."

I sat on Green's hood and tried my best to listen to the Sharks' rundown on the day's competitors, but I knew there wasn't much point in strategizing. I'd have to keep things simple. Just staying focused would be challenge enough. I noticed Fletcher walking down pit row, and my stomach grumbled—equal parts orange juice and anger. I told my crew that I was ready, that I just needed a few moments alone to get myself together.

"Liar," Bernie said and gave me the Byam grip. She, T.T., and Tammy walked over to the wrecker tailgate, where Jim sat, hands on his knees, not reading his GED book for a change. He'd pulled on his GO CASEY GO RACING T-shirt. He looked downright nervous as T.T. plunked down and kind of leaned up next to him.

"Sorry to bug you," Fletcher said.

I said nothing.

"Listen, Casey, I figured out what happened. I traced it back to Lonnie."

I stared at the track, where the Road Warriors were running their feature. "Lonnie?"

"Yeah, I don't know why he said that," Fletcher went on, "that thing about Wade ordering me to ask you to the prom." Fletcher paused as the Warriors roared around the near corner. "It wasn't true. It was just something Lonnie made up and said to someone, like a joke. Someone else heard it and, well, you know how these things go."

I *did* know how those things went, but what could I say about it? Now that I'd been so cold to this guy who was sweet enough to walk over to my pit, where he definitely shouldn't have been, fraternizing with the enemy. I turned to him. "Lonnie been working on the fuel tank?" I asked. "Lot of fumes around the fuel tank."

Fletcher smiled and kicked a hunk of asphalt across the pavement. "Sorry about the mix-up. No hard feelings, I hope."

"I'm sorry, too," I said, though *sorry* hardly seemed a fitting word to describe the collision of misunderstandings and grudges heaped behind us.

"Good luck today." He started jogging away.

I watched him and smiled, even though I knew that the Sharks were watching me and that they'd soon give me a ton of crap for acting like a schoolgirl with a mad crush. Fact of the matter was, only the schoolgirl part was false.

"And Dale Scott in the number seven car is your Road Warrior champion," Bean announced. "Congratulations on a fine run, Dale. And he'll take the checkered flag for a victory lap. Next up, down on the main straightaway, our traditional Demon's Run Independence Day apple-pie-eating contest, followed by the day's special Thundermaker Sportsman—make that Sports*person*—feature, the Firecracker 50. And it's going to be a family affair here for the first time in track history, folks, as Fans' Pick Casey 'the Lady' LaPlante tries to fend off brother Wade, your Thundermaker defending track champion. We're just about a dozen apple pies away from fifty laps of Demon's Run racing history in the making."

∾

I rolled Green onto the track, and the cars moved into position for the start. As Bean had announced, and as Demon's Run tradition dictated, the Road Warrior Fans' Pick started in the pole position—first car in line, inside lane. Not that it mattered where I started. With the exception of Wade LaPlante Jr., the Road Warrior racer up for the Firecracker slipped to the back of the pack after a few laps and stayed there. Until then, the Fans' Pick was more nuisance than threat. Also per Firecracker tradition, Wade's car 02, the season's track leader, started in the very last position, the "shotgun."

I ran my line around the track a couple of times behind the pace car, reacquainting myself with the marks I'd try to hit, the various tar blotches, cracks, and skid marks.

I pulled in behind the pace car and took deep breaths, trying not to impulsively jam on the accelerator and rear-end the guy. I glanced once into the packed stands, noticing ten girls holding ten white posters with black letters spelling G-O C-A-S-E-Y G-O-! When, after two laps at various speeds, the pace car cranked to the left and cut into the infield, my heart nearly pounded a hole in my fire-suit.

The only advantage I had at the start was that, being in the pole position, if I didn't cross the starting line in first place, then we'd have a false start. Starting on my outside was a black car with yellow number 22 and SLATTERY, BAIRD & PECK ATTORNEYS and scales of justice painted across his hood and front panel. As we rounded turn four and headed for the main straightaway, he gunned his engine, as if trying to get me to pick up the speed. The whole field behind us roared.

I instinctively accelerated. The race wasn't really on yet, but once I'd started matting the gas, I couldn't stop. Two car lengths into the straightaway, I pushed the pedal hard to the floor. Car 22 gunned along with me, holding his nose just inches from mine. The flagman dropped the green. Clean start.

Heading into the first turn, car 22 gave me some wiggle room on the right, so I drifted to the outside as far as he'd let me, and we took the first corners dead even. I braked, hit the marks on my line, and accelerated out of the turn. In the back stretch I still held my position.

I raced car 22 for another two laps like this, nudging him out, working my line in the outside groove. Crossing from turn one to turn two on lap four, I hit my star-shaped crack and glanced across the infield. Wade's car 02 had picked up two positions. I hit Florida and exited. Car 22 held tight.

In the next turn, I hit the skid mark and New Hampshire, but this time I accelerated a half second earlier. I felt Green grab the track and sling us into the stretch. Car 22 dropped in behind me. I'd successfully fought him off.

I drove my line like it was the only thought my brain could hold. I drew and redrew an imaginary white arc against the blacktop in the turns. Connected the dots. Drove.

Aiming for New Hampshire in turn four, I felt a shove from behind. I looked back to see car 08, white with red numbers—and a big cartoon hound dog smiling under the words DIAMOND DUKE'S SPORTS BAR—working his front end to my inside. I couldn't fight the movement of Green pushing to the outside at the collision, and I rolled over the New Hampshire mark with my left tire instead of my right. Car 08 held his snout to my inside, keeping me from returning to my line. Classic bump-and-run. I couldn't tell if his front tires were up to my rear tires, but I wasn't giving him the benefit of the doubt. I cranked the wheel left and shut the door on him.

He was pesky enough, car 08, to take a knock on his front end as I slid back to the inside track. I lost momentum and was immediately running even with the scales of justice car 22 again.

I ran with car 22 for another lap, watching my inside coming into the turns, making sure I kept the inside track closed. I seemed like I had a better line than car 22. His ride was tight, too: As he tried to accelerate in the corners, his tires pushed up the bank, not wanting to turn. I regained half a car length. Another lap, though, and we were dead even again. The guy must've had the horses under his hood that day, but I was pretty sure I had the tires. I ran with him, sticking to my line like the world dropped off into an abyss on either side. The next time car 22's wheels slid a touch and I got the half-car-length back, I glanced across the infield. Wade was now only five cars from the lead.

From me.

Car 08 came back for another shot at the inside lane, but I closed him down before he tried sticking his nose where it didn't belong. I lost a wheel on car 22 in the process, but I got it back on the next turn. I drove like this —shifting back and forth from my line to protecting the inside—for another few laps before car 08 fell back a car length. He'd pinched his ride and wasted his tires biting his way around the inside—good geometry, bad physics. I fought car 22 for another lap and glanced in my rearview mirror. Car 08 was even farther back, with another car trying to take him on the outside. In the next straightaway, I watched car 08 lose his place—to car 02. Wade "the Blade" LaPlante.

As if just taking a nanosecond to process the reality of Wade being two cars back were a distraction, I lost a flicker of speed somewhere, and Wade was on my tail in one full lap. Apparently, he was track champion for a reason. Car 22 was fighting valiantly for the far outside, and while this line was clearly not the most efficient, his car seemed strong enough to keep pace. I drove my line as tightly as I could, knowing that there was just a smidgen of room on the inside for Wade to stick his front end. If I slipped too far to the inside, car 22 would take me on the outside. But if I didn't leave my line by a couple of feet to close out Wade, he'd snag the inside track on me. If either of the drivers bumped me, the other was guaranteed to take the lead.

I'd lost track of how many laps I'd driven, and I didn't dare waste a second's glance at the lap clock, but I could tell, from the push in Green's front tires, that I was deep into this race. I regained my focus. Star, Florida, skid mark, New Hampshire. Accelerate. Star, Florida, skid mark, New Hampshire. Accelerate.

In between skid mark and New Hampshire on my next lap, car 22's rear wheels slid again, this time more violently than before. I instinctively punched the gas to stay ahead if he started to spin. The sudden acceleration threw my own front tires into a microskid. My corner exit speed dragged by a mile or two per hour, and that was enough for Wade to move up on the inside.

Car 22 drifted back half a car length, but I knew how his story would end. His car was too tight and hadn't loosened up. While he and I'd been running even since the green flag dropped, his line way outside basically meant he was about to miss the entire race. The race—the whole race—was down with Wade and me in the meat of the track.

The flagman leaned out over the track, flashing ten

fingers—ten laps to go. This was it, the last chapter in a story that had dragged on much longer than I'd expected —and certainly longer than anyone in my family had hoped. The beginning and middle chapters were written. I'd held the lead, I had the best line, but my tires were fading. How would the story end? As far as I understood this crazy sport, the answer hinged on one clue: Wade's tires.

Because I'd made my decision.

My older brother had chosen the inside track, snatched it up, in fact, with impressive skill. And that's where I intended to keep him. It was the only strategy that gave me any advantage. I could move outside if I wanted, but on the inside Wade could drift outside only as far as I'd let him—unless he wanted to bump me. In front of Circuit scouts? After dusting eleven cars to reach me? No way.

Wade's front wheels were still short of my rears. He'd passed every car in the field except mine. That must've been some superb driving to watch. As I ripped down the stretch close to the stands, out of the corner of my eye I saw the spectators on their feet.

Wade and I rolled around turns stuck together like two magnets. He seemed as committed to beating me on the inside as I was to pinning him there. But I had to ask myself: *Are there tires that can pass eleven cars in a fifty-lap sprint and gut out the last few laps on the inside lane?*

Unlikely.

Wade's strategy suddenly hit me like a slap to the side of my helmet. I jerked my wheel to the right and looked in my mirror. Wade slipped in right behind me: I'd beaten him to it, stopped him from taking the outside groove. So he hadn't been planning to run this out on the inside after all.

I plunged into turn one and hit my marks.

Drifting farther outside as we came out of the turn, Wade had lost half a car length driving the longer line. Now he needed engine *and* tires to beat me. He couldn't do it. I knew he couldn't do it. When, in the next turn, he dropped back to the inside, I concluded that he was getting desperate, grasping for geometry to rescue him when that was only half of the equation. I clung to my line in the outside groove, and as he crept up on the inside, I moved closer to him. Pinned him. He stayed put. I made sure of it.

Coming out of turn four, I saw the flagman waving the white flag: last lap.

Wade was glued to my left rear tire, as close as two cars could be without touching. I could've tapped the brakes and he'd have rammed me. Bump-and-run. The scouts might've thought he'd done it on purpose. *But what would I gain from that?*

Star crack. Florida. Accelerate.

Flying down the backstretch, the sweat streaming down my face, I felt a hollow space open up in my chest. Wade shook in my rearview mirror. Or maybe that was me shaking—shaking as the Widowmaker wall to my right faded away and disappeared, dissolving into an old stone fence fronting a neat, green lawn. The turn one–turn two bank became a grassy hill, with people sitting, reading, studying, learning. The pit gate was the on-ramp to the highway that would lead me away forever. Was that sweat in my eyes, or were those tears?

Wade got his right front tire up to my number in the backstretch, but I knew it wasn't far enough. As we rounded turn three—skid mark—I saw the flagman leaning out over the track, checkered flag held aloft. The Beer Belly Hill crowd was jumping up and down like they were watching a concert.

Turn four—New Hampshire. Accelerate.

In the main straightaway, Wade drifted up inches on the inside. I could see him pulling up to my window, and I could almost feel car 02's vibrations tingling along my arms. I'd become fused with his car and mine. Lightheaded and on fire, I experienced the illusion of silence amid the deafening noise enveloping us. A peaceful silence. Not like a racetrack. More like a tranquil college campus in autumn.

I lifted the gas pedal just slightly.

Just slightly . . . lifted.

And watched car 02 glide past.

I trailed Wade under the flag and coasted into the turn. Star crack. Florida. Just for old time's sake.

Other drivers rolled up to me and gave me the thumbs-up. The sight of them startled me, as if I'd forgotten they were even out there. I nodded and shook the sweat from my eyes.

The pit gate opened, and the cars started to file off the course. Across the infield I saw the flagman hand the checkered flag to someone who ran it down to Wade's window. The crowd roared as Wade began his victory lap. When he got to the turn in front of the pit gate, though, he stopped. If he didn't move, he'd block my way. He waved for me to pull alongside. When I did, he tossed the flag in through my passenger-side window and then pulled off the racecourse.

"How about that show of sportsmanship, folks," Bean said as I began a lap around the track. "A truly historic Firecracker 50 for you."

I ignored Bean, focusing on the way the wind caught the flag as I held it out my window, the black and white against a cloudless blue sky. The breeze carried the scent of fried dough and exhaust—not the most environmentally friendly concoction, but a comforting smell nonetheless. Lost in my thoughts and delirious from the heat inside my car, I forgot to stop at the finish line and return the colors to the flagman after my lap. So I had to complete another one.

This gave Bean a golden opportunity to make a crack about how I should just pull over and ask for directions if I didn't know the way to the pits. The crowd thought that was funny. I could actually hear them laughing over the rumble of Green's engine. Or maybe that was me.

ॐ

I pulled into the pits and braced myself for whatever would come next. Of course, the Sharks tackled me the moment I was out of my car. Uncle Harvey gave me a big hug. Even Jim gave me a hug. Beyond Jim, I saw Big Daddy approaching from down pit row, and he looked furious. "I apologize in advance for what you may be about to witness," Uncle Harvey said. "If I live through this, Casey, I could sell this ride and help you out with school. I bet I could get good money for it, you know, now that it's been road-tested."

Big Daddy was about fifty feet away when Bean's voice crackled over the loudspeakers: "Wade, you did it, boy."

"Yeah, I did, but I'll tell you what, it wasn't easy."

"Little sister gave you a run for your money."

"Little nothing. She's as big as they come when she's settled in the outside groove."

Big Daddy slowed down and stopped two pit slots away.

Uncle Harvey approached him.

The two just stood there, saying nothing.

"So, here's your trophy, Wade," Bean said. "The Firecracker 50. You're our champion. Nice work."

Finally, Uncle Harvey extended a hand. Big Daddy shook it. Then they stared at the ground, identically awkward expressions on their faces.

"Thanks, Bean," Wade said over the speakers. "And I want to thank my sponsors, Valley Savings & Trust and Granite Autoland. I also want to thank my crew and the other drivers for pushing me so hard. But this trophy isn't for me."

The crowd quieted down a little.

Big Daddy and Uncle Harvey turned toward the track.

"You know," Wade continued, "everyone thinks it takes courage to drive a racecar, and maybe it does, a little. But I'll tell you something. What you really need to succeed is people who support you and are always there for you, pulling for you no matter what. Even if you make mistakes. And to me, that's what family is all about. This one's for my family."

Wade held the trophy in the air, and the crowd rose to their feet again.

I looked at Big Daddy and Uncle Harvey, who stared blankly toward the track.

I spotted Fletcher standing in Wade's pit looking at me and shaking his head, as if he were amazed by it all.

I shook my head back at him because it really was amazing. It was amazing how much more there was to racecar driving than just driving around and around in circles.